TINKERS CREEK

TONY BULL

PROLOGUE

His orders were clear enough: shoot the farmer dead. If the hired hand wants to make trouble, okay, kill him too, but don't touch the woman.

He'd seen the woman once before, outside the store in town, a big, tow-headed female, dressed in man's clothes, heaving sacks of supplies onto her buckboard as easy as any man could. This was one woman he wouldn't want to touch. Later, in the saloon, he'd jokingly referred to her and had learned that she always came for supplies Tuesdays.

It was Tuesday today.

He watched now as she maneuvered the buckboard out of the yard, across the bridge over the creek and down the trail to town. He'd give her time to get well away.

His carbine traversed the yard, following the route the farmer would take when he came back out of the barn. He'd get him when he came in line with the big cottonwood in the center.

The hired man led a saddled horse from the stable, mounted up and rode slowly away to the east.

Time passed.

He eased himself into a more comfortable position behind the rocks. It was getting hot, but he'd chosen his spot well, shielded from sight by the rocks and from the sun by the shade of two small scrub oaks.

A small boy ran out of the house and crossed the yard into the barn. Nothing had been said about a kid. Well, it made no difference.

The boy reappeared, leading the farmer by the hand back

towards the house.

As the farmer came in line with the big cottonwood, the sound of a single shot rang out over the valley.

CHAPTER ONE

Judd Petersen reined up at the crest of the hill, relaxing in the saddle and shifting his weight. Tall, lean, and wide of shoulder, he sat loose and straight, accustomed to long hours in the saddle.

Quiet in manner, with curly blond hair, he had an easy smile which made the women look twice. But his sun-browned face was solemn as he looked down over the town below.

Twin Springs had started out as a settlement around an old army outpost situated at the base of the hill from where Judd was gazing now with interested eyes; it had grown some since he'd last seen it. Where there had been gaps in Main Street there were now substantial new two-story buildings, and new blocks that appeared to be mainly residential had been put up running south, with large back lots and small orchards nestling behind picket fences. Beyond that the land had been enclosed into large cultivated fields. To the north, where the Fort Collins trail began, there had been more building work, including a small saw-mill.

This was his home town that he hadn't been near in ten years.

He nodded slowly, a crooked half-smile giving him a rueful look. He'd had some fancy notions about himself in those days. All that, though, had been rubbed into the dust of ten years hard living, first down south in New Mexico and Texas, and latterly in Kansas where he'd more or less settled to being a Deputy U. S. Marshal - until the letter telling him of Sten's death had arrived.

***

Having memorized the layout of the town, Judd angled the big buckskin down the slope, aiming to cross the flat behind the town and pass through the wagon camp that had grown up in back of the livery stable.

His plan of action was to ride in quietly, find out what had actually happened to Sten, and do what was necessary to settle his affairs. The place held few pleasant memories for him and he had no desire to stay around any longer than it took.

He swung down out front of the livery stable and tied his horse by the trough at the old water pump built over one of the springs for which the town was named. He spent a few moments beating the dust out of his clothes with his hat, and while the horse had a good long drink, he had a look around. Main Street had never been welcoming, it was either cold and muddy, or dusty and too hot like today. The old feeling of not belonging came back to him.

First thing he noticed was that a new front had been put up joining the stable to the saddle-and-harness shop. A large sign declared that Sam Cowan's Livery supplied everything for horses.

"There goes my first contact," he thought. "Wonder what happened to Joe Healey?"

Right across from him, on the east side, the barber shop and bath house still had the name Reynolds over, and next to it Sorrell, the mortician, had a smart new front. Further on a two-story stone building stood where he remembered the Drovers saloon and the sheriff's office and jail had been. He'd never been in either of them.

A stocky young man of about Judd's age came out of the stable entrance, wiping his hands on a leather apron. He had a swarthy skin, thick jet-black hair and a prominent hooked nose between deepset eyes.

Judd nodded, "Howdy, amigo. Put my horse up for a few hours?"

The man came forward, showing large white teeth. "Certainly, sir."

"He needs a good rub down and a feed, and have a look at his shoes, will you, we've traveled a goodly distance over some rough territory."

"Certainly sir," the man said again. "Fine looking animal."

"Two questions," said Judd, "Where can I get a good meal, and where's the lawman's office?"

"Three answers to question one," replied the swarthy man. "The hotel for the best quality and the highest prices. That's farther on down on this side. Then there's the Drovers, for cattlemen, over there in that stone building, or Bradman's, turn right at the end, for the farmers. Question two - next to the Drovers."

Judd smiled and flipped a half-dollar, "Thanks, amigo."

The swarthy man caught it and flipped it back. "We charge

9

a dollar a day, sir."

"Okay," said Judd, "Payable in advance?"

"If you wouldn't mind, sir. And there may be a charge for the shoeing when you collect your horse."

Judd was intrigued by the man's manner of speech. He looked like a Mexican Indian and spoke like a New England storekeeper.

"Been here long?" he asked as he handed over the dollar.

"Four years." The man looked him up and down, his eyes resting for a moment on Judd's two guns, low-slung and tied down. "If I may say so, you might not be very welcome at Bradman's. The farmers tend to resent strangers."

"Okay, sure."

Judd hitched up his gunbelts, slipped the thongs from his guns and stepped up on the boardwalk. He wore a black, flat-crowned, flat-brimmed hat, buckskin vest, dark gray shirt, and black trousers, and he was aware that he was being subjected to careful inspection by the men along the walk, some of them seated at the benches against the walls. Watching him pass by, their eyes lingered on his two guns.

As he came opposite the big stone building, he saw that it was made in two main sections, divided at ground level by a wide passageway stretching from front to rear. Over the center of the passageway a large clock showed a few minutes after two. On its left was The Drovers Bar and Restaurant, and on the right a row of offices: Sheriff, Lawyer, and Land Agent.

There was a notice on the sheriff's door.

Judd went across and read: "Back mid-afternoon. Any messages next door --->." An arrow pointed to the Lawyer's office.

He turned and went along to the Drovers. Bat-wing doors

opened off the boardwalk. He went in and paused briefly to let his eyes adjust to the change from bright sunlight.

Inside, the saloon was big, clean and comfortable, with several small tables and hardback chairs. Near the door two tables had been pushed together and half a dozen rough looking men were sitting around playing cards. A carved mahogany bar with mirror glass behind it stretched almost the whole width of the room. To the right of the bar, and opposite the entrance doors was an open doorway with a sign "Restaurant" above it.

At the far end of the bar, three men dressed in range clothes were leaning on the counter, talking to the bartender.

Judd went to the corner of the bar by the doorway, took off his hat and ran his fingers through his hair. The men at the counter looked up and stared as he stood waiting. The bartender, a big, heavy man, said something in a low voice and they laughed aloud and turned back into a huddle.

Judd waited a few moments more, feeling a heat building inside him.

"Can a body get a drink here?" he asked, slowly and deliberately.

"Wait a minute!" snapped the barman over his shoulder.

Judd made a show of pulling out his pocket watch. "Okay," he said, "I guess I can wait one minute for a beer." He put the watch on the counter.

All four men looked round at him. Two of them came away from the counter and moved slowly towards him. One was a big, heavyset red-head. He had a glass of beer in his hand and looked as though he'd had plenty. The other was a young dandy, dressed all in black except for a pearl handled pistol in a tooled leather holster slung low and thonged to his left side.

"Howdy," said the dandy with a smile. Judd noted that the smile did not extend to his cold, gray eyes. "I'm Billy Bates. I

11

ain't seen you around here before."

"No," said Judd, mildly.

"Where are you from?"

"If it's west of Kentucky I may have been there," said Judd.

"So what are you doing here?"

"I've got some business to attend to."

"What kind of business?"

"My *own* business," Judd said, patiently.

"Here in town?"

"Mebbe."

"What's your name?"

"Folks call me Judd. Seems as good a name as any."

"You got a given name?"

Judd gave the dandy a steady, considering look. "Mister Bates," he said in a gentle voice, "You sure do ask a lot of questions."

The young man's eyes glinted and the fingers of his left hand drummed lightly against the butt of his gun. The card players were watching, and the big red-head glared hard at Judd.

"You ain't very friendly," he said. "You're asking for trouble!"

Judd ignored him and stepped out from the end of the bar so Bates could see his guns.

"Hey!" said big Red, "I'm talking to you!"

The big man was spoiling for a fight and Judd knew this was one time it was better to face trouble than avoid it. He turned slowly and looked at him.

"I never learned anything from a drunk," he said.

He'd spoken so casually that for a moment his words failed to register.

"What did you say?"

"You're too drunk to talk sense."

When the meaning got to him, Red smiled. He moved very slowly to put his beer glass on the counter and, still smiling, took two quick steps towards Judd, reaching to grasp the front of his shirt. Judd sidestepped, gripped Red's wrist with his left hand jerking him forward and down, and swivelled on his left foot, to bring his right fist down with all his strength onto the back of the redhead's neck. The big man fell as if pole-axed and remained face down on the floor.

It happened so quickly that Bates had not had time to move.

"Now, Mr. Bates," said Judd, as if there had been no interruption, "I see you're left-handed. I can use either hand. You want to see who can draw his left gun quickest?"

The youngster licked his lips. Suddenly he was not so cocksure.

Out of the corner of his eye Judd noticed one of the card players, a thin, gingery haired man, get up quickly and go out the door.

"How about it?" said Judd, "Let's stand side by side as if we're going for your friend the barkeep, and let him be the judge. How about it, Mr. Barkeep?"

"Okay, you made your point," said the bartender. "I'll get your beer."

"Thank you." said Judd, "Well, Mister Bates, let's hope we never do have to find out who's fastest. Now, introduce me to your friends, will you?"

Bates indicated the man on the floor, who was beginning to stir. "This here's Carl Voller and that's Micky Mason."

"Okay, so now we all know each other. Now, Mr. Barkeep, I want a beer and a meal, and I came in here because I didn't feel pretty enough for the hotel and I was recommended not to go to the other saloon. So what do I have to do to get fed?"

"Here's your beer, go on through. I'll send someone out."

Judd paid for his beer with a silver dollar, and while he waited for his change he watched Mason helping Voller to a seat at a table. A couple of small-time crooks, he decided, who wouldn't know an honest day's work if it was offered to them. Bates was different. Bates could be dangerous, because although he clearly fancied himself tough and had a reputation to build, he was careful enough to back off when there wasn't much at stake. Judd hoped there wouldn't be any occasion for them to meet again before his business in town was done.

As he went through to the restaurant a family was leaving by a door that opened out into the passageway. There was nobody else in the room. Stools stood by a small counter, and a half-dozen empty tables each had a clean white cloth and four straight-back chairs around. He took a place at a table in the corner where he could see all the doors.

A woman came out of the kitchen and told him they could do steak, hash brown potatoes and stewed tomatoes, followed by pie and coffee if he wanted it. He wanted it.

The food was good, and the service was quick and attentive, and when he'd finished his meal, he read over once more the letter telling him of his uncle's death.

"It had been written a couple of weeks before," addressed Judd Petersen - Lawman - Kansas, "by someone who signed herself Fran Healey (Cassie's sister)".

She explained that she'd been working for Sten Petersen for four years, and then one afternoon she'd come back from her weekly trip to the store and found him shot in the back in his own yard. The hired man was missing and hadn't been seen since, but nothing had been stolen and there appeared to be no motive for the killing. The bank had taken over the running of the homestead for the duration and she'd been told to move out. As far as she knew nothing was being done to find Sten's killer. She knew Judd was Sten's next of kin, and she'd heard he was a lawman somewhere in Kansas, and since no one else seemed willing, she felt it her bounden duty to let him know the state of affairs. She was greatly sorry to be breaking such bad news.

Judd sensed a bitterness in the phrasing of the letter, almost as if Sten had been her kin instead of his, and he tried again to summon up a memory of the girl, but all he could come up with was a dim idea of a hefty, freckle-faced kid in bib-overalls and yellow pigtails.

He remembered Cassie, though. She had been the final reason why he'd gone away. His lips pulled again into that lopsided smile as he recalled the intensity of his wounded pride at the way she had dismissed him.

For about a year he'd been making a point of calling to see her whenever he went to town and he'd come to think of her as his girl. Then, one day he'd ridden in and found Butch Watkins putting his arm around her waist. She was making a show of objecting, so Judd intervened, whereupon Watkins had used his five years and thirty pounds weight advantage over the raw eighteen-year old to beat him almost senseless.

Eventually Cassie had called a halt to the one-sided affair, saying, "Aw, leave him be, Butch, he's only a poor damn sodbuster!"

And that had done it, made up his mind at last to get out of the rut the Petersens had been digging in the ten years since they had trekked west from Kentucky.

He'd never been fond of his uncle; the man had always seemed cold and forbidding, and when Judd's parents had died within months of each other, Sten's hard, inflexible discipline had driven a wedge between himself and the boy, so that Judd had felt little desire to contact him in all the years he'd been away. But now he felt guilty, knowing that he should have kept in touch, and now it was too late.

He folded the letter and put it away, paid the woman for his meal and went out the side door. Across the street the thin, gingery card-player he'd seen leaving the saloon was talking with a smartly dressed man. They turned and stared in his direction.

CHAPTER TWO

Back at the sheriff's office the note had gone, so he knocked on the door. A voice shouted "It's open!" and he went in. He heard water splashing in a back room, and presently a strongly-built man of about fifty appeared, stripped to the waist and toweling himself vigorously.

"Howdy. I'm Sheriff Kramer. What can I do for you?"

"Howdy Sheriff. I'm enquiring about Sten Petersen," he said.

"Are you now? And just who might you be?"

"His nephew, Judd Petersen."

"The devil you are!" Sheriff Kramer stood stock still, staring wide-eyed at him. "Waal now, if that don't beat ever thing! Mister Petersen, you sure cut it plenty fine! Wait a minute, though," he changed his tone, "I take it you know your uncle died?"

"Yes, that's why I'm here. I came to see what needs to be done to settle his affairs. What d'you mean, cut it fine?"

"Waal, Mister Petersen, those Petersen holdings is going up for sale tomorrow at noon!"

"Is that a fact? Well now, I reckon that sale better be called off then. Right away."

"Uh huh. I take it you can prove who you are?"

"Yes, I guess I can, but there must still be folks around who'll remember me from ten years back."

"Yeah, I recall you was spoken of at the time, but nobody knew where you was at, so Lawyer Higgins put out a notice. But how come you only just showed up? I mean, Sten Petersen's been buried over a month."

"I only heard about it three days ago, and I came as quick as I could. I never saw any notice, either."

"How did you come to hear about it, then?"

"I got a letter."

"Yeah? Who from?"

Judd was becoming impatient with the Sheriff. "Does it matter?

"Sure it matters. See, I'm kinda new here, only bin here a few months, and I find folks kinda closed up about a lot of things. Like your uncle's death, now. Somebody shot him in the back, did you know that? One shot from a Winchester."

"One shot, huh? And have you found out why? I mean, he always kept himself private, never got close enough to anyone to make enemies. Or friends."

"If'n I knew the why, I reckon I'd be along the way to knowing the who. It never made sense. He wasn't robbed nor nothin. I got out there soon's that wild Healey woman came in an told me. Rode straight back out there with her. Had a real good look around. No strange tracks closern a hundert yards of him, but I found where the shot was fired from. Seems he was just shot down for no reason."

"You mentioned a woman name of Healey," said Judd. "Would that be Fran Healey?"

"Yeah. You know her?"

"No, but it was her that wrote me."

"How come, if you don't know her?"

"Well, I ain't seen her in ten years and she was a kid then."

"How'd she know how to find you, then?"

"Yeah, now we're getting right down to it, ain't we, Sheriff? Seems to me that if a so-called wild woman could find me, an educated lawyer and a sheriff - who's paid to find people - should be able to, but you didn't and I sure mean to find out why!"

"What's that supposed to mean?" He paused as he tucked in his shirt-tails, and glared at Judd.

"It means what it says. You tell me my uncle's been buried over a month. Well, I want to know what you've been doing to find his killer, and I sure as hell want to know why you and that lawyer weren't able to find me in all that time, 'cos I ain't been in hiding!"

"Where have you bin then? You ain't bin anywheres around here, that's for sure."

"Why didn't you ask the Healey woman? She knew how to find me."

"It's plain you don't know her, or you wouldn't ask. She's plumb loco if you ask me, bin squattin on that homestead, refusin to leave, and claimin your uncle left it to her!"

"Well, maybe he did." said Judd.

"What's with you, Petersen? You seem all-fired anxious to pick a fight with me, and I don't cotton it."

"I'll only fight you if I have to, Kramer, but the way I figure it you haven't been doing the job you're paid to do, and that ain't right!"

"Why, listen here, you goddam …!"

"No, you listen! I ride in here to settle my uncle's affairs, and I find his estate is up for sale, only just over one month after he died, and no real effort's been made to trace his rightful heirs and successors. That's against the law and you damn well ought to know it!"

"Against the law? Who says?"

"Just what kind of a sheriff are you? Hell, it's plain enough to me already that this Higgins ain't all a lawyer should be. Are you in cahoots with him, or what?"

"I ain't in cahoots with no-one, goddammit! And how come you know so all-fired much about the law?"

"It's my job," Judd said quietly, "I'm a Deputy U.S. Marshall, operating out of Ford County, Kansas."

"Hell's Bells! Well, why didn't you say so straight off?"

"Why should I? I'm not here on Federal business."

"Okay, okay," The sheriff looked suitably chastened, "I guess it don't look too good from where you're standin. But it ain't my only concern. I know it sounds like I'm makin excuses, and okay, I allow I've bin more than happy to let the Petersen business take its own course, but I got my hands full to overflowin here." He paused. "But lookee here, we better get along to the Land Office and put a stop to that sale."

"Will you do that then? I'm going to have a word with that lawyer!"

The sheriff turned as he reached the door and gave Judd a searching look. "Think it might be better to cool off a little first, Marshall?"

"No, I reckon I'm in just the right mood to tackle that shyster. And I'd rather be just plain Mister, okay?"

"Yeah, sure. And, ah, " he paused and cleared his throat, "I'm real sorry bout this." He opened the door and went out in a hurry.

Judd was left in two minds about sheriff Kramer, and before going next door to see the lawyer he took the opportunity to look around the office.

A large, tidy desk with a padded swivel chair behind it

faced the door. In the far corner was a rifle rack and between it and the pot-bellied stove stood a solid-looking safe. Along one wall was a row of wooden chairs, and another was hung with Wanted flyers. He moved to have a closer look but there were none he recognized. He opened the door at the rear which opened into a short, wide corridor with a barred door, double-locked, at the end. Behind it was a row of six cells, all empty. Off the corridor on one side was a washroom and on the other a room with two bunk beds.

Judd had seen the inside of a good many law offices in the course of his duties, and this one looked as clean, neat and efficient as the best of them, and although Kramer had been less than competent in his handling of the Petersen case, he had readily accepted the fact, and even had the decency to apologize. On balance Judd decided to give him the benefit of the doubt.

He was just closing the rear door, when a voice behind him said, "You! Stand still and put both hands high above your head."

Judd raised his hands slowly. "Sheriff's in the Land Office," he said.

He felt the barrel of a pistol pushed firmly in his back as his guns were taken.

"Okay, turn around!"

He turned and saw a younger, taller, slimmer version of the swarthy stableman pointing a pistol at him. He was wearing a Deputy's badge.

"Who are you, and what are you doing in here?" the Deputy demanded.

"Name's Petersen, and I'm just leaving," said Judd.

"What were you doing back there?"

"Just looking," said Judd, "Sheriff Kramer knows I'm

here."

"Are you saying the sheriff left you alone in here?"

"It's okay," said Judd, "I'm a Deputy U.S. Marshall, off duty. I've come home to settle my uncle's affairs."

"Petersen! Ah, yes, I see!" exclaimed the Deputy. "You've left it rather late though, haven't you?"

"Sheriff and I have already been through all that." Judd slowly lowered his hands. "I'll have my guns back."

"Hold on a minute! How do I know you're who you say you are?"

"I got a badge in my vest pocket," said Judd, taking it out and offering it to the deputy.

The deputy glanced at it and lowered his gun. "Okay, sorry Marshall. But we can't be too careful these days. Some hard men have arrived in the area recently. Gunfighters probably."

"Yeah, sure, and just call me Mister, huh? I'm not here on Federal Business."

"Oh, that's a shame," said the Deputy, "We could do with some help. I'm Ben Cowan, by the way."

He offered his hand and Judd took it briefly. "You look and talk as if you're kin of the stableman."

"Yes, I am," he said. "Actually I have three brothers. Dan and Isaac run the livery stable and wagon camp, and Michael has the haulage, that is to say the drayage business. Our sister Ruth, helps Father with the Saddlery, etcetera. And to save you the trouble of asking, we came here directly from London, England, four years ago. Father made a bit of money in the gold fields, you see, and persuaded the family to come and make a new life out here."

Judd smiled, taking a liking to the talkative young Deputy. "Well, you sure seem to have a good set-up. But how come you taken up as a Deputy?"

"Shortly after Tom Kramer came, he asked me if I'd like to try it. He made a point of saying he needed someone like me especially."

"Oh? Why was that?"

"Oh, that's easy, I'm neutral, you see, neither homesteader nor cattleman."

Judd nodded, "Figures."

A picture was beginning to build up in his mind. First the warning from the stableman to avoid the farmers" eating house, then Kramer's complaint about having his hands full, and now the Deputy's comment about the need for neutrality.

Judd had seen situations like this before. Farmers moved in on land they had purchased from the government and plowed it up. Established cattlemen, who up till then had free use of the grass and water, resented the incomers. The reasonable, law-abiding among them would either come to some agreement with the farmers about access to grass and water, or move out, on to the free-range lands farther west. All too often, though, one or more of the ranchers would try to force the farmers out, hiring gunmen to harass them, cutting off their supplies, destroying their crops, poisoning their wells, and burning their buildings.

It looked to him as if that was in the offing around Twin Springs.

There had never been any love lost between the cattle ranchers and the homesteaders. Cattlemen and townspeople alike looked down on the settlers, and that had been another reason why he'd been restless as a youngster; he couldn't think of himself as just a dirt farmer. In fact he still couldn't.

"Sheriff was telling me he's got his hands full around here, Ben."

"Yes. There's been a lot of complaints about rustling recently. All the big cattlemen have been affected, and they are getting edgy because we haven't been able to catch anybody."

"Rustling, huh? Well, where there's cattle there's like to be other critters help themselves to free beef." He paused. "But if all the cattlemen are losing stock it sounds like an organized set-up."

"It certainly seems to be. The cattlemen are accusing the new settlers, because the rustling began just after they moved in. So, of course, when the settlers started being attacked at night, they suspected the cattlemen. But there isn't any proof in either case."

"Would that be the settlers south of the town?"

"No, they've been there some time. It's those on the government land along Tinkers Creek, south of your family's place."

Judd was puzzled. "How's that again? When I left all that land was taken up."

"Ah, well, when we came here four years ago, the farmers had all moved out - all except the Palmers, and Mr. Petersen, of course."

"Why did they move out, do you know?"

"Well, it seems most of them never got over the depression of "73", said the Deputy. "And there was talk of ill-feeling amongst them, as well as hostility from the cattlemen."

"So the land was just left?"

"Well, not exactly," the Deputy made a wry face, "Star B ran cattle on it, which made life difficult for the Palmers. Did you know them?"

"Yeah," said Judd, "I remember them."

"Well, they tried to protect their land by putting up fences, but time and again gaps appeared and cattle would get through. So then they left too, last Autumn. I mean Fall. I was sorry to see them go," he grinned self-consciously, "Gwen and I had started walking out together. Everyone thought they had gone for good, but at Easter they came back again, with another twenty-odd families, and since then they've been setting up a completely new settlement."

"All legal is it? I mean, have they got title to those lands?"

"Yes," said Ben, "We know that because Shepherd, the Land Agent, said he enquired in the County Offices."

It struck Judd as odd that the local Land Agent would have to make enquiries about transactions concerning local land. He also set to wondering how Sten's land had been affected by the changes, and he decided the sooner he rode out to the Petersen homestead the better.

"Well, Ben, when you came in here I was all set to rattle lawyer Higgins's teeth for him, but I'm going to leave that little chore for another day. What you've been telling me about the changes round here has made me mighty curious to see the old homestead again, and I figure to get me a few supplies and head on out that way."

"In that case I suggest you avoid the new settlers if you can."

"I was figuring to use the Tinkers Creek Trail," said Judd.

"Well, Palmer's men have built a fence from the creek all the way across to the other side of the valley. There is a gate across the trail but there are some extremely rough men among them who are unlikely to let a stranger through."

"Okay, thanks for the warning. I'll take the Fort Collins trail then, and cut across the hills back of the Double Diamond range. Reckon I should just about make it by nightfall."

The sheriff came in just as Judd was leaving. "The sale's off, Mister Petersen. Lawyer Higgins was there as well and he sure is mighty sore."

Judd nodded. "From what Ben here has been telling me, it

seems there's a lot going on that ought to be looked into. That lawyer's like to be mixed up in it, too. How it ties up with my uncle's affairs I don't know yet, but before I start asking around I'm going out to check on the homestead."

"Ben tell you bout the fences?"

"Yeah," said Judd, "I'm figuring to go round the back way, through the hills back of the Double Diamond."

"Are you now? Waal, mebbe you can help me some, if you're willing. DD's bin hard hit by rustlers lately, usually thirty, forty head at a time. The tracks lead off into the rocky ground in the foothills but after about six miles or so we lose them. I ain't had a chance to scout around further out, and I'd appreciate if you'd keep a lookout for places where cattle could be holed up. But watch your step. Watkins and his men are liable to be a mite suspicious of any rider out thataways."

"Yeah, okay, I'll keep my eyes open."

"I'm obliged to you. Oh, and I didn't say anything about you being a lawman and all. Figured there's no reason you'd want it known."

"Nice meeting you fellers," said Judd, "Be seeing you."

CHAPTER THREE

In his private sitting room over the bank Leo Marburg lit a fresh cigar and tipped back in his leather armchair. He stared thoughtfully out the window toward the sheriff's office.

He'd come a long way in the past year, and not just in miles traveled. Thinking back to the day he left New York, he grudgingly admitted to himself that he'd been scared. It had been a near thing, a very near thing indeed. But he'd got away with it and they would never find him now because he'd been too smart. He always was too smart for them.

Meeting Con Higgins in the hotel at Cheyenne had been a stroke of luck. This small, neatly dressed man had asked to share his table in the crowded dining room the evening he'd arrived. After some preliminary small-talk Higgins had introduced himself as a lawyer come to town to do business on behalf of his local Cattlemen's Association. In response, he told Higgins he was a businessman with banking experience, which was true as far as it went, that his name was Leo Marburg, which was not true at all, and he'd come west looking for opportunities to invest his capital. Capital he certainly did have, in the form of banknotes in two large suitcases, the security of which had been a constant worry to him all the way from New York. But he didn't tell Con that.

Realizing that Con had taken him for a greenhorn, Marburg

had been content to listen while the lawyer spent the rest of the evening selling the idea of investing in Twin Springs. He did not, of course, need much convincing. The way Con described the town it sounded just the right kind of out-of-the-way place, somewhere to hole up for a year or two and quietly increase his capital. As he listened to the lawyer he became aware that here was a kindred spirit who could be a very useful partner, so he played along with him and eventually agreed to accompany him on his return the next day, to see the potential for himself.

Before leaving Cheyenne he'd taken five thousand dollars out of one of the suitcases and opened a bank account in his new name, giving his address as Higgins's law office in Twin Springs. He was not required to identify himself in any other way, the amount of the deposit being more than sufficient reference. It was also enough to impress the lawyer, which is what he'd intended.

He'd let Con Higgins help him settle into the town, saying he would be happy to be guided by him in the matter of investments, and would pay him a commission to act as his agent on all successful deals, provided that he as purchaser could remain incognito.

As a result, nobody but Higgins was aware of Marburg's financial resources, and even Higgins did not know where the money came from.

In due course the contents of the two suitcases had been reduced by financing the new building for the Drovers and adjacent offices, acquiring the hotel and the Tomahawk ranch of the Mannion Brothers by redeeming their mortgages, and purchasing the building which housed the bank, where he now had a comfortable apartment. In this last instance it suited him to let it be known that he'd bought the building in order to give him an acceptably modest position in town.

These investments were providing a steady income, which was increasing the balance of his account in the Cheyenne bank. But it was not money for its own sake that he wanted. What he really wanted was the power that wealth could bring.

The money he'd brought to Twin Springs had given him influence over Higgins from the start and he soon had the lawyer under his control. Early on he instructed him in the importance of knowing what was going on around the country, and Higgins had discretely developed several sources of information. Among the most useful was Peretz, the big barman in the Drovers. Higgins had hinted generally that he wanted to hear about new arrivals in the town, and indeed about any occurrence that was out of the ordinary. Thus it was that Peretz had dispatched Sandy with word of the encounter in the Drovers.

Higgins was a thinking man, quick to put two and two together, and he recognized the name Judd as that of Sten Petersen's next of kin. With a sense of alarm he went immediately with Sandy to wait outside the Drovers to see for himself. When Judd came out the side door and went to the Sheriff's office his fears were reinforced. He told Sandy to report Judd's movements to Peretz, and then brought the bad news to the apartment over the bank.

"I'm sure it must be him," he'd said. "I was afraid this might happen. Just as everything was coming together! It's too bad! What are we to do?"

"If it is Petersen's nephew - and we don't know that for sure - Kramer will tell him about the sale tomorrow. Go wait in the Land Office, see what happens."

"He'll call the sale off, that's what will happen!"

"Just go, Con, and we'll see."

Higgins had done what he was told. A few minutes later

29

Marburg saw Sheriff Kramer come out and go into the Land Office. So, it looked as if Con was right, the man was Petersen's nephew.

It was unfortunate that he'd appeared at this time, but it was of no real consequence; he would be out of the way within hours. Then the sale could go ahead and the woman moved out, a little later than intended but still in good time. He smiled as he congratulated himself on the way his plans were working out.

The basic idea he owed to Con Higgins, or if he was really honest with himself, to his careful training of Con Higgins. Con had come to him at the beginning of the year with a story about correspondence between Clem Palmer and Shepherd, the Land Agent.

"This guy Palmer," he'd said, "Moved out of his homestead on the government land along Tinkers Creek a few months ago. He was the last of the homesteaders out there, except Petersen up at the far end. They couldn't take all the rough treatment the cattlemen were handing out. Well, now it seems he is coming back. He says he is forming a cooperative and is acquiring the papers for all the abandoned homesteads up that way. He wants Shepherd to let him know if there are any quarter sections along the creek available for purchase."

"Interesting. Wonder why he is coming back so soon?"

"Exactly."

"I'm not sure I recollect how the land lies up that way, Con. Let's take a walk to the Land Office and have us a look at the map."

Seeing the location of the homestead lands in the context of the territory as a whole had given him the germ of an idea. Later he told Higgins to ask Shepherd to make certain inquiries in Washington, and the scheme had developed from there. Shepherd had to be taken into it, of course, and then they had to get an agreement with Palmer, but apart from the failure to buy out Petersen, all had gone smoothly so far.

He drew on his cigar as he watched Kramer go back to his office. Shortly afterwards the Petersen fellow left and set off down the street. Then Higgins came out the Land Office and hurried straight across to the bank. Marburg frowned in irritation. It was a little too obvious. He would have to remind Con to be more discrete. With a sigh, he stood up, ground the butt of his cigar in a marble ashtray, and waited.

Higgins was flustered. "It was Petersen's nephew and he has called off the sale. The Sheriff said he was plenty mad and warned me to keep out of his way!"

Marburg grunted. "You should worry about that! He's only one man and won't amount to much. But he can't be allowed to start poking around, so you'll have to get rid of him."

"That may not be so easy. He's a very salty customer by the sound of him."

"Con, how much are you paying those fellows Bates brought in?"

"Well, we agreed on fifty dollars a month, didn't we?"

"Yes, each! And Bates is living free in my hotel. It's about time they did something to earn their keep. See to it."

Higgins looked sick. As far as he was concerned it was one thing in the privacy of his office to give advice on where the law could be bent or even broken; it was quite another to be directly involved by telling criminals to break it. He was in too deep now, though. He would have to see it through. Not for the first time lately he wondered how he'd allowed himself to be dragged in so far.

He hurried back to his office and sent his clerk with a message for Bates.

31

CHAPTER FOUR

Judd walked down to the livery stable to collect his horse, and met another of the Cowan brothers.

"Just been talking to Ben," he said, "You Dan or Isaac?"

"Isaac. You'd be Mister Judd. I heard about you."

Judd smiled, "What do I owe you, Isaac?"

"One dollar twenty, and you owe that horse a little more care. I changed his shoes, but his hind feet needed a lot of attention." Isaac lifted up a hind leg and pointed into the hoof. "See that? I took a stone the size of my thumbnail out of there. It had been there some time. Another few miles and you would have had a very lame horse. I put some salve on it but it's probably going to be quite sore, so I should take it easy for a while."

"Yeah, sure. And thanks. Lucky I ran into you I guess."

Judd led the buckskin up to the cattlemen's store, where he replenished his traveling pack, then mounted and set out at a steady walk until he was well clear of the town. Satisfied that the horse was not lame, he then settled down to a quicker pace.

His route took him in a wide arc, east and then across the north of the rocky ground the sheriff had mentioned. He kept a good look out but he saw no traces which would indicate stolen cattle. Nor did he see any sign of Watkins and his men.

The sun was low over the snow-capped peaks in the west, shining straight into his face as he came down the steep, pine-clad slope into the northern end of the high valley that led down to the Petersen holdings. To the east the lower slopes were covered by aspens with occasional dark fingers of spruce running down. The floor of the valley was a sea of grass, with occasional islands of woodland. It was more or less level, varying from half a mile to a mile wide and about ten miles long, running north to south. To the west the land was more rugged, steep foothills slashed by canyons rising up into the mountains. As he descended he was struck by the beauty of the park-like view before him, as if seeing it for the first time.

At this time of the year the grass would normally have been close to stirrup-high if the farmers hadn't made hay, so he was surprised to see that much of it had been trampled and grazed. Clearly a good-sized herd had recently located here. This puzzled him, since the only way cattle could get into this end of the valley was through the Petersen holdings.

He crossed the valley at an angle to where a branch of Tinkers Creek flowed out of a wide, shallow canyon on the western edge. Following it south, he found a small pool fringed with willows below some rapids, and while his horse was drinking, he refilled his canteen and then splashed cold, refreshing water over his head and neck.

He leaned back against the base of a tree, enjoying the shade after the heat of the day. On the other side of the pool he saw a trout leap and he could hear yellow warblers calling among the trees. Then a strange noise, out of place in the isolated spot, made him sit up and listen for a long minute.

He'd just decided he'd imagined it when he heard it again, a low moan coming from a willow thicket at the edge of the pool across to his right. He scanned the opposite bank carefully, but could see no sign of movement. Cautiously, he stood up, drawing his right hand gun, and holding it loose but ready at his thigh.

"Okay, come on out," he called, and waited. There was no reply.

Keeping his eyes on the thicket, he moved back to his horse a few yards downstream, mounted, then called again, more forcefully.

There was still no response.

Gun at the ready, Judd walked his horse slowly across a shallow part of the stream, up the bank and along towards where the sound had come from. He paused. There was neither sound nor movement. He slid from the saddle and edged warily forward, looking for sign.

Almost at once he found marks where something had dragged along the edge of the water and he followed them as far as he could into the dense mass of bushes. Even so he might not have seen her had it not been for the splash of bright red on her jacket. Half-submerged at the water's edge was a young Indian squaw.

He holstered his pistol and crawled towards the girl. Her pulse was strong, but she was badly hurt. The bright red was blood from a long gash across the top of her shoulder to her neck. The side of her face was bruised and swollen, and one leg was twisted awkwardly, broken just below the knee.

Carefully supporting the leg, Judd pulled her out and carried her back to where he'd left his horse. He laid her down and wrapped a blanket around her. Mercifully she remained insensible while he cleaned up her injuries and set the broken leg. Then he cut some sturdy branches for splints, binding them tight with rawhide from the girl's own clothing.

Satisfied, he set about building a fire and brewing a pan of coffee.

As he put his arm under her shoulders to raise her up, her eyes flickered open, focused on him, then widened in terror.

Knowing what happened to squaws when found by some white men, Judd understood all too well. "Okay, little lady," he said gently.

She drew back staring at him.

In his travels Judd had acquired some knowledge of the sign language common to many of the Plains Indians. He also had a smattering of the Sioux language, and using a combination of the two he pointed out that she was badly hurt and needed help.

He held the cup of coffee towards her and after a moment she reached out for it cautiously.

"How far to your camp?" he asked.

She remained silent, sipping the coffee, still staring wide-eyed.

"I'll take you to your family," he said, indicating his horse.

"My brothers kill white men!" she said fiercely.

"You're badly hurt," he said, "You can't stay here."

She glanced down at her leg, apparently considering. When she looked up again there was a sly expression on her face. "West from here, as far as the sun moves one hand-width in the sky, is a cave. I will make fire there and my brothers will find me."

"Good," he said, "If you're ready, I'll take you there."

When she'd emptied the cup he lifted her up and placed her gently on the horse. She swayed and almost fell, weak from her injuries. She soon recovered, however, sitting up straight and proud, and it occurred to him that she had not once complained of pain.

"North, beyond where the stream bends, there is a track,"

she said.

Judd led the horse upstream along the west bank and followed the creek into the canyon. "How were you hurt?" he asked.

She glared down at him, hatred in her eyes.

"White men!" she spat the words out. "I was walking. My pony was lame. Two came on horses. They shot at me and laughed. I got on my pony and they chased me. They shot my pony, and one caught me and tried to tear my clothes. I fought him and cut him with my knife and got away into the rocks where the horses could not go. They ran after me and I had to jump into a gully. It was too high and I fell a long way."

"How did you get here?"

"I do not remember," she said.

"These men," said Judd, "What were they like? Big, small? Young, old?"

"One who shot my pony, was short, fat, no hair on his scalp, broken teeth. The other taller, younger, with much dark hair on his face. He had a white horse. My brothers will know them!"

"What are you doing in this area anyway?" said Judd. "I thought all you folks had agreed to stay in the reservation lands?"

"That is not our land. This is our land, this is where our fathers lived and hunted. We will stay here."

"The government won't like that," said Judd.

"It is your government, not ours. We do not want the white man's ways."

Judd was aware that there were still a few small bands of Indians refusing to go along with the majority and live in the Reservations. They were known as renegades and were often the cause of trouble, especially in the more remote areas.

"How many of you are there?" he said.

She stared straight ahead and made no answer. Clearly she'd said enough.

A mile later she pointed out a track leading up the canyon wall.

"We follow this track all the way up, and then over into the next valley. Afterwards we climb high."

The first part was just a steady climb out of the canyon and along the side of the ridge for about three miles. The track twisted and turned through trees. Quaking aspens, their leaves dark green above, gray-green below, shimmering in the breeze, gave way to spruce and lodgepole pine towards the top of the ridge.

Judd was familiar with the land on this side, but all he could recall of the terrain to the west was that it was high, rough and barren. Sure enough when they left the track and came out of the trees on the far side of the ridge, the landscape was nothing but parched scrub, rocks and shale, leading via a shallow depression to a much higher ridge a couple of miles away.

The girl pointed to a high, rocky spur directly opposite.

"We go there," she said.

They picked their way with difficulty, and by the time they came to the base of the spur the sun was setting over the top of the mountains. Judd made out a large cave near the top of the north face. He pointed and she nodded.

"There is a path, but the last part is not safe for the horse."

"How will you get there?" he asked.

"I will get there," she replied.

Judd looked around. A short distance away there was a gnarled, old thorn tree. He cut a long forked stave out of it, trimmed it, and putting it under his armpit, he demonstrated using a crutch. Then he cut a foot length off it to allow for the difference in height and passed it up to her. Just for a moment he thought she might be thinking of hitting him with it, but she just nodded solemnly.

A rough path wound up the side of the spur. Judd led the horse as far as it could go, then tethered it to a rock and lifted the girl down.

She leant on the crutch, "It will be night soon. You go now."

He looked up. The cave was not far above but the path zigzagged so steeply that he could not see how she could get up there on her own. "I'll help you to the cave," he said.

"No," she insisted. "I am rested now. My brothers will come soon. You must go. I will tell my brothers not all white men are bad. What are you called?"

"Petersen," he said.

"Petersen," she repeated. "I have heard that name. I am called Snow Flower. Go in peace, Petersen."

Judd touched his hat to her. "You sure are a tough little lady, ma'am."

He turned and led the horse back down to the foot of the spur. By the time he'd ridden out to where he could see the cave she was standing in the entrance, looking out. He waved and she raised her free arm in reply, then turned back into the cave.

The light was now fading fast and Judd realized he would not find his way back to the track through the trees, so he headed south-east towards a deep notch in the high escarpment to the south, hoping it might lead to a way back towards the creek.

When he reached the pass there was a way down but it led in the opposite direction, into a canyon running west, straight at the fading light from the setting sun. Far down the canyon light reflected on running water, and he let his horse pick its own way towards it. He followed the stream for about half an hour and came out into a flat grassy area surrounded by pine trees - a good place to camp.

He unsaddled, rubbed the horse down with handfulls of dry grass, and hobbled it so that it could graze free but not wander far. Then he made a small fire near the base of a large pine, cooked and ate a meal, and turned in for the night.

CHAPTER FIVE

Judd was awakened at first light by the lowing of a cow. He raised himself cautiously and looked around, mindful of Sheriff Kramer's suggestion about looking out for rustled cattle. His first concern was for his horse, but it was quietly grazing a few yards away. He saw that he was in a park-like area, with about fifty head of cattle scattered around. One cow not far off, had just calved; he guessed it was the one which had woken him.

After making sure he was alone, he checked the brands on the animals nearest to him. They were all either Star-B, or M on W, the Double Diamond brand.

He went back to the entrance of the canyon, climbed up to a high ledge in the north wall, and looked around to get his bearings.

The park was roughly circular, about half a mile across. Behind and to his left, bright light from the rising sun outlined the top of the high escarpment in silhouette. Looking up the line of the canyon, he could make out part of the high V-shaped notch of the pass. To the west and southwest the land rose steeply, and he picked out a tall, narrow peak directly in line with the canyon and the pass.

Having noted these points of reference and covered all traces of his visit, he rode around the southern edge of the park. There he found where the cattle had been driven in, and after following their tracks downhill for half a mile or so he came upon another set of tracks branching off to the east.

Sure enough these led to another park, where between two and three hundred head of cattle were grazing, brands mainly K-Bar and Double Diamond, with a few other brands he didn't recognize. This convinced him that he really had stumbled on the rustlers" hideaway. Again he took note of his position, then rode back along the cattle tracks until he came to an outcrop of rock and shale where he could branch off without leaving sign.

He headed east at a steady pace through rough hilly country, making careful note of his route, and by the time he came at last to familiar territory, the sun was well up. It promised to be another fine, warm day.

He'd been following a game trail which was leading him down into a narrow tree-lined valley, when he recognized in the distance the outline of the ridge above Tinkers Creek, south of where he'd found the Indian girl. He reckoned he had at least another hour's ride to the homestead, so when the track came to a small pool at the bottom of the valley, he swung down and trailed the buckskins reins - breakfast and coffee were well overdue.

There were plenty of dry sticks nearby and he quickly built a small fire, just enough to boil water for his coffee. He sat on a small rock near the edge of the stream, chewing on a few strips of jerky while the water was heating, and tried to make sense out of what he knew so far. Three events were connected. First the shooting of Sten. Then the intervention of the Bank to take over the homestead. This was puzzling because the Petersens had never had debts and furthermore, Sten had been hard-working and frugal, and the rich soil of the homestead would always give such a man a good living. Finally, the place had unlawfully been put up for sale, so there must have been

41

collusion between the Bank and the lawyer, with possibly the land agent involved also.

As well as this there was trouble between the cattlemen and the farmers, with rustling being a significant factor, but he could think of no way that Sten could be involved in stealing cows.

Well, maybe things would be a mite clearer when he got to the homestead.

It was mid-morning when he came over the ridge. He angled down towards the great rock wall that divided the upper grasslands from the homesteads. In places the going was very rough. Branches and brush snapped at the big horse as he shouldered his way around fallen timber and craggy rocks and a couple of times he lost his footing on the scree and slid down several feet before regaining his balance. At one point the slope below became so steep that Judd had to head him up a hundred feet or so to where the going was safer. Here he came upon a narrow trail, obviously well-used, running parallel to the top of the ridge high above. He dismounted to get a close look at the tracks in the dust, and saw among the deer and other small animal prints, recent hoofprints of unshod horses. Indians came this way.

Before remounting he checked his horse's feet; it had had a hard day so far, but had stood up well to all the slipping and sliding.

Several hundred yards later the trail breasted a large outcrop and he could look down towards the homestead lands to the south. He could just make out the Petersen house and out-buildings, next to the creek about two miles away as the crow flies. Unexpectedly, a lump rose in his throat at this first view of his old home and he paused, letting the memories come back.

In the spring of 1861, when he was eight years old, his parents, Olaf and Anne Petersen, had trekked west seeking good land where they could farm in peace. They had been displaced from their Kentucky farm by the War between the States. Sten, Olaf's younger brother, had come with them.

They came eventually to a large fertile basin, running south and west, with hills curving in at each end. At the northern end they found a green valley with high ridges towering on either side, walling it in, and they settled there at a place where Tinkers Creek came out of a narrow rocky gorge through an old layer of rock which lay across the entire valley like a wall. A quarter of a mile south of the wall the creek formed a horseshoe loop, and there they built their cabin, on a high bench surrounded on three sides by water. Those early days had been the happiest.

He shook his head, urging his horse onward and smiling his lop-sided smile as he chided himself for getting sentimental.

Just beyond the outcrop the trail forked. The tracks of Indian horses continued straight ahead, but Judd followed the fainter line heading down in the direction of the creek. Soon it was winding back and forth down the steep side of a narrow canyon, and when he was about halfway to the bottom, Judd caught sight of a dark shape huddled among the rocks near the base of the opposite wall. He kept an eye on those rocks as he continued down, but nothing moved.

He crossed the floor of the canyon, tethered the horse, and climbed up fifteen feet or so through the rocks until he reached the huddled shape. It was a man's body and it had lain there several weeks. Wild creatures had mutilated it so that Judd couldn't see how the man had died, but it looked as if he'd fallen directly on to the rocks from the canyon's rim, two hundred feet above.

Judging by the remnants of his clothes the man had been a farmer. Maybe he had a family. Somebody would be missing him anyway, so Judd set himself the unpleasant task of searching the pockets. There was a bunch of keys, a knife, a small amount of money, a finely carved model of a horse, and a folded piece of paper with Joe 14th and drawings of horses on it. He made a bundle in the man's kerchief, scrambled back down and remounted.

The trail continued along the floor of the canyon, curving eastward, and finally came out onto a small, flat area some fifty feet above the creek. He looked out over the valley. The evidence of cattle grazing, which he'd noticed further up the valley the previous day, was clear to see here too. He was about level with the top of the great rock wall and a quarter of a mile north of it, but the only way down was by a narrow and perilously steep slope. Even then it looked as though the creek was swimming deep for as far along as he could see. He looked for likely places to get ashore downstream on the opposite bank, then swung down from the saddle and led the buckskin towards the top of the slope.

Not for the first time Judd was grateful for the animal's trust in him as it followed carefully but steadily. At the bottom he took out his Winchester and tied it along the horse's back, then he wrapped his twin Walch, 12-shot Navy pistols in their oilskin bags and tied them by the drawstrings around his neck, under his shirt. The water surged and swirled past, two feet below the bank. The horse stood, head up, looking out over the water, ears pricked. Judd patted its neck, and made a few soothing sounds, then took the reins in his left hand and stepped in.

The water was so cold it made him gasp. The current pulled at him and the reins became taut. He called and the horse plunged in, striking out powerfully, so that Judd had to swim hard to avoid being hit by thrashing hoofs. The current took them quickly downstream, but the big buckskin soon came to shallower water where it waded across, pulling Judd to the shore. While the horse had a good shake Judd checked his guns and re-holstered them.

He mounted up and followed the creek down to the great rock wall, where it descended rapidly through a gorge a hundred yards long. This gorge was the only safe route between the grassland and the lower valley, and the only access to it was through Petersen land. In summer the farmers had always got together to clear a track for wagons to bring out the hay for winter fodder, but he could see that no wagon track had been made for some time. A good many cattle had been driven through in the recent past though, and when he came out of the gorge Judd saw the effect on the fields: the once good soil had been reduced to churned-up dust.

He rode around the horse-shoe loop to the bridge over the creek. A makeshift barrier blocked the way, presumably to keep cattle out. He dismounted and cleared a space, then walked the horse through and up into the yard. The place appeared to be in good order, but although he called several times there was no answer, so he led the gelding into the empty corral and stripped him. He hung the saddle and the rest of the equipment to dry out, and went over to the stable to prepare a stall. There were six stalls, and four had horses in them. He stopped to examine the nearest one and something hard pushed against his spine.

A voice said, "Raise your hands and turn around, real slow."

CHAPTER SIX

Judd did as he was told, and saw a tall, well-built young woman dressed in man's clothes, with a determined expression on her face and a shotgun in her hands.

"Guess you're Fran Healey, ma'am," he said.

"Right." she said, looking back at him steadily.

"I'm Judd Petersen."

"Prove it," she replied, still looking straight back at him.

He slowly lowered one hand to his shirt pocket and pulled out her letter, soggy wet from its soaking in the creek. "Bin swimming, ma'am" he said as he made to pass it to her.

"Both hands up!" The big woman motioned with the shotgun. "Back off. Outside."

He walked slowly backwards, watching her carefully. She seemed calm enough, but he had no doubt she would use the gun if provoked.

"Okay, drop the paper," she said. "Now, take your guns out, finger and thumb, one by one."

He did so.

"Back over by the tree and sit."

A big cottonwood in the center of the yard had a plank seat fixed beneath it. He sat down and lowered his hands.

A quick glance at the letter reassured her and she put up the gun.

"It's good to see you," she said. "Guess you've filled out some, I didn't know you."

"You've changed a mite too, ma'am. I never would have known you, and that's a fact!"

"You took your time getting here," she said.

"Only got the letter four days ago."

She nodded. "You know they're selling this place today?"

"Sale's off," he said, "I saw the sheriff in town yesterday."

She visibly relaxed. "That's the first good news I've had this year. Come on in. I'll find you some dry clothes and fix a bite to eat while you get cleaned up."

"I'll tend to my horse first, ma'am. He's had a rough time lately."

"I'll be in the kitchen," she said.

Judd rubbed down the horse and fed and watered him in the corral, leaving him to dry off for a while in the sun. He collected up his traveling gear and the dead man's belongings and went in.

Fran had laid out a set of Sten's clothes on the kitchen table. "We have a lot to settle," she said. "We'll have a talk, soon as you're cleaned up. There's a bath-house." She pointed through a door at the end of the kitchen. "Sten put it up for me. There's hot water and I've put towels out."

Judd took the clothes and went through. The center of the room was taken up by a large bathtub. Next to it was a small stove with a big kettle of water warming, and on the other side he recognized the old yard pump, cleaned up and painted black. Towels and soap were set out on a stool. He pumped cold water into the tub, topped it up with the warm, undressed, sat down in the tub and soaped himself all over. The soap was highly scented, and he grinned at the idea as he shaved three days stubble off his chin.

His first impression of Fran Healey was that she was strong and capable; wild, or plumb loco as Sheriff Kramer had called her, she sure was not. He wondered why she'd stayed on at the homestead. Maybe she did have a claim on the place. If so, she wasn't the kind of body who'd give it up without a fight.

His uncle's shirt and pants were a tolerable fit - at six foot tall, Sten had been a couple of inches shorter than Judd, but about the same width around shoulders and hips. Judd left his boots to dry by the stove, threw his wet clothes into the tub and scrubbed them with the scented soap.

He heard Fran talking to someone, and eased the door open. A small child with wild yellow curls came running over and stopped, gazing up at him wide-eyed.

"Howdy," said Judd, "Who are you then?"

"Joe Petersen," the boy replied.

Judd looked over at Fran.

She handed him a cup of coffee. "Your cousin," she said, smiling, "And no, Sten and I weren't lawfully married. He wouldn't marry me while his wife was still alive."

Judd blinked. "I never knew he had a wife!"

"She went off with a soldier in the war," she said, "That's the reason he decided to come out here with your parents when they left Kentucky."

"Well, I'll be . . . How'd he know she was still alive?"

"When I told him Joe was coming, he wrote a letter to a lawyer in Louisville, and the lawyer traced her. I didn't really mind. Sten was a good husband to me in all but the law. But let's sit. We can talk while we eat."

They sat at the table. Young Joe couldn't take his eyes off Judd.

"Sheriff told me you said Sten left this place to you, ma'am," Judd said. "Guess that must be right, then, huh?"

48

"He left everything he owned to me. All legal. I've got his will. But your parents" original quarter section, and that includes this house and the buildings, he turned over to you years ago."

"So you just own the other quarter section, then?"

"No, there's more than that. Sten bought up the two homesteads to the south when they moved out, and we put a claim in my name on the quarter section to the north, along the creek. I've got all the title deeds, yours as well, here in the strongbox."

"Now, whoa there ma'am! There's something mighty peculiar here. If you've got the papers showing title to all this land, how come it was going up for sale without your say-so?"

"Well, it's a long story. For a start, they never believed Sten left me the land. Sten reckoned Higgins, the lawyer in town, is crooked, so he arranged all his affairs through the lawyer in Louisville. I wrote him, asking what to do, same time as I wrote to you, but I haven't heard. I daren't leave this place empty - you must have seen what their cattle have done - and no-one comes way out here, so for all I know a letter may be waiting for me somewhere."

"Yeah, but even if they didn't know who Sten left his land to, they couldn't sell my land legally without confirming I was dead too." He paused, thinking about it. "Have you any idea why anyone would be so keen to get this land?"

"Well, your land controls the way to the grass up the valley, but I wouldn't think it was worth breaking the law just to get to it, would you?"

"No. Must be something we don't know."

"Whatever it is, you better watch your back - they killed Sten for it, and probably Jack Marnier too,"

"That the hired man?"

"Yes, he disappeared the day Sten was shot. I think they got him too. He was a good man. He wouldn't have just run off."

Judd had a sudden thought. "On my way here I found a body." He got up from the table. "Got his things here."

He untied the man's kerchief and laid the contents on the table.

Little Joe grabbed at the carved wooden horse. "Jack!" he said, and smiled up at his mother.

"Oh, poor Jack," said Fran. Tears welled up in her eyes. "He was carving that for Joe's birthday. That's his kerchief alright. And these are the spare keys - he must have taken them off Sten and then gone after the killer."

Fran sat silently toying with the keys for a moment.

Then Judd said, "Begging your pardon, ma'am, but in your letter you said the Bank had taken over the running here. There don't seem to have been much running done, though."

"They sent a feller out to tell me to move off." she said. "Clem Palmer brought him. The feller got uppity so I showed him how a shotgun works, and he was the one moved off!" She smiled at the memory. "Clem says I ought to join in with his Cooperative, as he calls it. I guess he means well, but I don't know. He sent a couple fellers to help me bury Sten. Next to your Ma and Pa." She gave a sigh, then smiled self-consciously, as if to apologize.

"So the Bank hasn't actually taken over the place?" said Judd.

"No. I've been left to myself. The sheriff came out the day Sten was shot, poked around for a while, and then left. Then the feller from the Bank was here and the next day Butch Watkins - you remember him, Double Diamond? - he came over across the east pasture with a couple of cowhands."

"What did he want?"

"He wanted to know what had happened. He told me I should send for you and stay here till you came. He waited while I wrote the letters and said he'd take them to town. Then they rode up through the gorge and in the afternoon, a herd of cattle, thousand head or more, was driven through to the grass. Took our cattle with them. They drove them back through here a couple of days ago. Only other folks I've seen is Clem Palmer when he brought that feller from the Bank, and the sheriff when he came out last week and told me about the sale."

"What about your family, they not around anymore?"

"Cassie's married to Butch Watkins. Haven't seen her since before Joe was born. Sten and Butch never got on, and Cassie don't take kindly to kids whose ma and pa ain't wed!" She smiled a wry smile.

Judd nodded. "Figures," he said. "And what about your pa?"

"Pa's dead. That's how I come to be here." She paused, eyes cast down. "Pa went to help a farmer that was being set on by a couple of DD riders in the livery. Sten came in and he sided Pa. The DD men drew their pistols and fired. Pa and the farmer were both hit but Sten got both the gunmen with his scatter gun. I saw it all happen. Sten sent me for the doc, and carried Pa into the house. The farmer was past help. Doc did what he could, but Pa died next day. Sten stayed on for the burying, and then he arranged for the sale of the business, because he reckoned Butch Watkins would try to get my share of it through Cassie. Lawyer Higgins took care of the legal side, and Sten always said he cheated us. I don't know. I was all confused at the time."

She was silent for a moment. "Anyways, Sten offered me a job here looking after the horses and livestock till I could get fixed up proper, and I just stayed. I guess I got real fond of him. You know, he was a hard man outside, but inside he was gentle, and kind, and caring. He just didn't like to let on."

"Reckon you knew him better than anyone ever did, ma'am," said Judd, quietly. "But how've you been getting along on your own?"

"Well, I'd fetched in a couple of weeks" supplies, so with Sten and Jack both gone there's been enough for Joe and me. And we've got the chickens and goats back of the yard, and there's fish in the creek. Gonna have to restock pretty soon though."

"But no work been done on the land," said Judd.

"No, nothing, and no cattle now. We had about eighty head all told, mostly young stock. But the sheep and hogs are still okay, least they were yesterday."

"So, what are you figuring to do, ma'am?"

"I guess that depends on you - and stop calling me ma'am, will you. Fran is what I'm used to."

"Okay, sure. But why does it depend on me?"

"Well, we have to come to some agreement about your land. I've got four hundred and eighty acres south of the Wall, but the upper grassland is cut off by your quarter section. And you've got all the main buildings. I haven't got the money to buy you out, so as I said, it depends on you."

"You'd want to stay though?"

"Oh yes, I surely would, but if you want to sell, I'd put my land up with yours and sell it all as one lot."

"Well, ma'am - ah, sorry, Fran, - I have to tell you I rode over from Kansas expecting to make a straightforward deal to sell this place off for what it would fetch, and then go on back to Marshalling."

She gave a long sigh. "I guessed that would be the way of

it," she said. "And I'll go along with it. It's a pity though. Sten set high hopes by this place."

"Now hold on there, 'cos it ain't so straightforward as I'd expected. For one thing I got kinfolk to consider now." Little Joe was standing by his chair. Judd looked down at him and ruffled his hair. "And for another I reckon I should find out why Sten died. There's something mighty strange going on, and I mean to look into it before I make up my mind."

"What are you figuring to do?" she asked.

"First off I want to take stock of things here. Is there a map or something showing the boundaries?"

"Yes. Sten made a map of the whole spread, showing fence lines and markers. I'll go get it."

She went through to the main living room. Joe came and showed Judd the wooden horse Jack Marnier had carved for him, then ran after his mother.

Judd stood up and went to the window overlooking the yard. A movement high up on the western ridge caught his eye. He marked the place in his mind's eye and fetched his field glasses from his traveling bag. He was scanning along the ridge when Fran came back with the map.

"What is it?" she asked.

"A saddled horse. Seems to be tethered. Near the end of that big clump of pines. Aha! I see his rider now! Higher up in the rocks to the right." He passed her the glasses.

"I see him," She said. "He can look right down on this place, see every move we make."

"You seen anyone up there before?"

"Indians, time to time."

"That feller will have seen my horse in the corral, so he'll know you've got company. Keep the glasses on him while I go outside, let me know what he does."

Judd went out onto the porch and looked up towards the rocks where the watcher was hiding.

Fran called to him.

"He's got glasses too, Judd. he's looking at you, I think."

"Watch him," said Judd. He waved both hands at the watcher, and pointed vigorously across the valley to the east. "What's he doing now?"

"He's standing up. He's pointing his glasses towards the other side of the valley," she said. "Wait a bit, now he's looking back at you again. He's gone behind a big rock. Hey! He's got a rifle! He's lining up on you, get back in here! Quick!"

Judd stepped back inside, not too soon. A shot rang out from the rocks above, echoing around the valley, as a bullet thudded into the floor of the porch.

"Well, guess we know the score now. Did Sten still have his long gun?"

"Yes," she said, "But if you're figuring to dust that critter up there I'll fetch my Henry rifle."

She gave the glasses back to him, and looking back up at the gunman's position he calculated that the straight line distance would be close to five hundred yards. Aiming that high would be tricky, but he'd give it a try.

Fran returned with the rifle.

"I've been keeping it ready loaded," she said. But instead of handing it to him, as he expected, she rested it against the wall.

"Give a hand will you," she said, taking one end of the heavy kitchen table.

Together they moved it to the open window. She up-ended a small stool and placed it on the table, then reached for the rifle. Judd watched, not quite sure what she intended. Then, to his surprise, she knelt, and using the stool as a support, lined up the Henry on the spy's position.

"This thing'll be a mite noisy indoors I reckon," she said, in a matter-of-fact voice. "Joe, you go in the parlor now, and hide."

The little boy ran into the next room.

"That's a game we played since he learned to walk," she said. "Now, will you take the glasses, and tell me where the first shot goes?"

"Yes, ma'am!" said Judd, highly amused. He grinned at her. "Sheriff told me you was a plumb loco, wild woman. I can see how he got that idea!"

"What I mebbe lose in feminine charm, Mister, I make up for in other ways. You ready now?"

"Yeah. he's still there by that big rock."

"I see him," she said.

"If you can see him, you got better eyes than anyone I ever met!"

"I've got him dead to rights. You just watch and tell me how close I get!"

She took a deep breath, and as she slowly let it out she squeezed the trigger.

A second later Judd yelled. "Jee-zus, woman, you hit him! He's down! Where in tarnation d'you learn to shoot like that?"

"That's the first time I ever aimed to hit someone," she said. "Did I kill him, d'you think?"

Judd kept the glasses on the rocks where the man had fallen.

"Can't see any movement. If he's hurt he'll go for his horse, that's for sure. If not he may figure to return the compliment. Better keep well back."

They waited a long time. Judd scanned the area between the rocks and the tethered horse but there was no sign of movement.

"Feels kinda funny, shooting at a man," Fran said. "Kinda fierce and sad at the same time. But I meant to hit him. Inside, I was saying: Here's one of them for you, Sten!"

"That really was some shooting, Fran. Do you always hit what you aim at?"

"I don't often miss with my rifle. Sten made me practice, two hours every day till I could outshoot him. He said it cost him thirty dollars in shells to make a sharpshooter out of me."

"Well, he sure got his money's worth!"

"I had to learn to shoot," she said. "I didn't want to, but he said troubled times were a-coming, and we have to be prepared to defend what we've got. He taught me pistol shooting, too. Bought me my own gun, a Walch Navy, twelve-shot, .36, like those two you've got thonged down."

"Well, you really are something else, ma'am, and that's a fact!"

"You see, he tried to get more hands, but nobody would hire on with him. I reckon they were scared off. So he only had Jack and me."

"Yeah," said Judd. "I guess I should have kept in touch."

"Oh, I didn't mean it like that!" she said.

"I know that, ma'am, but I was thinking a while back there, things could have been different if I'd come by once in a while."

Judd was still scanning the ridge, but there was no sign of the gunman. It occurred to him that whoever it was that wanted the place had been happy to leave Fran Healey alone until the sale went through. They didn't figure on her being any real trouble. But now, he'd shown up and stopped the sale, and they hadn't wasted any time sending someone after him. He was sure he hadn't been followed to the homestead, so his arrival must have been anticipated.

As if following the same line of reasoning, Fran asked, "Who'd know you'd be here?"

"I told the sheriff and his deputy I was coming, but Higgins and the land agent could have figured it out for themselves."

There was still no movement on the side of the ridge and the man's horse was dozing, hipshot, completely at ease in the shade of the pines.

"I reckon I better get up there and see," he said. "And there's a good view of the whole spread from up there. Let me see that map."

She passed it to him and pointed out the boundary markers for each of the four quarter sections south of the wall.

"This here is the south boundary," she said, "The new folks that came back with the Palmers are fencing that off with barb wire, right across from the creek to the rocks on the east side. They're leaving us a gate across the trail into town. This here is where Sten reckoned the east boundary would be. It's all rock and shale from there on over. The west boundary runs along the side of the creek, but there's markers where the creek wanders about. On the upper part, north of the Wall, there's no markers. We reckoned to graze the whole valley. After all, nobody can get to it except through us."

Judd looked at her, realization dawning that here was the possibility of a good-sized ranch. The upper valley was at least ten square miles, most of it potentially good grass, and with its own water from the creek.

"You're talking about raising cattle?"

"Yes, but not like the cattlemen hereabouts."

"Hmm. Fran, we got to have a proper talk about this. But right now I won't be easy in my mind till I know what's happened to that hombre up there. I'll take the map and the glasses, and while I'm up there I'll spy out the land."

"That'll be quite a climb," she said.

Judd grinned. "I was eight years old when I first went up that ridge. I had myself a hidyhole in the rocks."

"Well, I'll keep my eyes peeled and the Henry ready."

"Now, it looks likely I'm going to have to bring that feller down, dead or alive," said Judd. "And in any case I'm not leaving that horse tied up there, and the only way I know of to get a horse down from there is on the other side. What I'm saying is it could be some time before I get back. Will you put my horse in a stall for me? And, ah, I left my clothes soaking in your bathtub…?"

"Okay," she smiled, "And if you're figuring on staying around a while, I'll fix up a bed in the back room. Your old room, huh?"

"Oh, well, ma'am, I'd just as soon bunk down in the barn . . ."

"A man's surely entitled to a bed in his own house. You get going now. I'll stand by with the rifle till I see it's okay.

CHAPTER SEVEN

The ground west of the house sloped back up to the valley wall for a hundred yards or so and then rose, almost sheer in places, for two hundred feet. After that it was a steady climbing walk all the way to the top of the ridge.

Although the first part of the ascent was not difficult climbing, Judd found it hard work in the full heat of the sun, and he was glad to take a breather when he came over the rim. From there on he kept well to the left of the gunman's position, and made his way steadily up past the big clump of pines, so that he could come upon him from above. When he'd gone high enough, he took out his field glasses and scanned the ground below. He soon found the gunman, flat on his back among the rocks, shot through the head. It was the man Mason that he'd seen in the Drovers.

He dragged the body down to the tethered horse and hoisted it across the saddle, lashing it tight with the man's own rope. Then he went back for the rifle. Looking down at Fran standing in the doorway, he was even more impressed by the awesome accuracy of her shooting. He waved the rifle back and forth to confirm he was alright.

He walked the horse back up to the top of the ridge, following the tracks it had made on the way down. There he paused to look down over the Petersen spread.

The valley was a mile wide at this point. South and west of the farm buildings a few acres of woodland, mostly scrub oak with some cottonwood, grew along the bottom of the ridge, following the line of the creek.

Judd took up the field glasses again and looked south, along the trail to Twin Springs. A mile away he could make out the posts of the barbed wire fence put up by the new settlers. That identified the southern boundary.

Taking out Sten's map he compared it with actual points on the ground. The homestead this side of the fence had been settled by a hard-working Polish family. They'd had two little girls, he remembered, and wondered what had become of them. Over to the east he recognized Sten's original cabin set in his quarter section at the edge of a group of trees and he smiled as he remembered the day it was completed. Sten could not wait to move in, so they had all pitched in and helped him set up home, and Ma had broken in his new stove by cooking them all the best meal they'd had in weeks.

The quarter section to the south of Sten's had been homesteaded by a young couple who had planted fruit trees, mostly apples, as he recalled. He could make out rows of trees which he guessed must be the remains of their orchards.

So, at one mile square, there was indeed a lot more to it than he'd expected. Together with all the grassland beyond the rock wall, it sure needed considering.

When he'd memorized the entire layout he led the horse along the top of the ridge, retracing its hoofmarks until they joined what he guessed was the continuation of the narrow game trail he'd followed earlier in the day. Again there were clear signs of recent use by unshod ponies.

The trail headed southwest, angling down the far side of

the ridge. After about an hour of rough walking he came to a traverse trail that climbed to the east across the lower end of the ridge, back in the direction of the creek. He reckoned he must be about a mile due west of the crossing at Clem Palmer's place, so he turned on to this trail, and sure enough, when he came over the next high point he saw a cluster of buildings ahead. He also saw that a high barbed wire fence barred his way down to the creek.

Scanning south along the fence to where it turned at right-angles to the east and then down to and across the creek about half a mile downstream of the ford, he could see no obvious gate or way through. His view north was cut off by a spur but he felt sure there would be no gap that way either. Palmer's intention was clear: visitors were not welcome whichever way they came.

There was no other easy crossing of Tinkers Creek that he knew of, and he had no desire for another swim, so he walked the horse down to a little hillock close to the wire where he would be in plain view, and fired off three spaced shots from the dead man's rifle.

A man came from behind one of the buildings, shading his eyes from the sun as he looked up towards him. Judd waved the rifle in the air, and the man waved back in acknowledgement before backing out of sight. Judd waited.

Two horsemen came out of the farmyard, walked their horses down the track and across the ford, and approached to within fifty yards of Judd's position. They were both young men and carried rifles across their saddles.

"Waddya want?" one of them yelled.

Judd walked the horse down to the wire. "Tell Clem Palmer it's Judd Petersen," he shouted back. "Got a dead gunman here for Sheriff Kramer in Twin Springs."

The two men conferred for a moment, then one of them came up to Judd while the other covered him with his rifle.

"Who'd ya say ya was?" he said.

"Judd Petersen. Sten Petersen was my uncle."

"The feller that got hisself shot up the valley?"

"Yes. Clem Palmer will know me," said Judd.

"Who's the dead un?"

"Name of Micky Mason. He tried to kill me."

"Waddya doing over there?"

Judd's patience was beginning to wear. "It's a long story," he said. "He was up on the ridge above the homestead. I had to climb up and get to him. There's no way down for a horse on our side. I followed a game trail. It led me here. These boots weren't made for hill-country walking and I was hoping to borrow a horse or buggy from Clem Palmer. I didn't know about the wire."

The man appeared to be satisfied.

"Okay," he said, "jus' walk on up along a ways. There's a place where the wire opens."

As soon as Judd was through the wire the two men closed in on either side to escort him down to the creek and across the ford to the farmhouse. Neither of them spoke until they came into the yard. Then the one who had questioned him indicated a post by the barn.

"Tie up there and wait. You stay with him, Jim."

The man dismounted and went into the farmhouse. After a minute or two he came out with Clem Palmer. Judd recognized the tall, ungainly man immediately, although his once thick brown hair was now sparse and streaked with gray.

"Yeah," said Palmer, "That's Olaf Petersen's boy alright." There was little warmth in his greeting, however, as he looked

62

Judd over, taking in the two guns. "Heard you was back - I went in for the sale earlier. How did you get out to Petersens"? You didn't come by here!"

"Deputy Cowan told me the valley was fenced off. Warned me I might have trouble getting through. I wanted to get out to the homestead before anyone knew I was back, so I took the Fort Collins trail, to come in from the north."

"Huh. You took a chance. Watkins" men shoot on sight out thataways."

"Seems it ain't exactly peaceful anywhere in these parts."

Palmer nodded towards the dead man. "What happened?"

"Took a shot at me from up on the ridge."

"Tom here says you know him."

"Nope. Saw him yesterday in the Drovers, is all."

"So he knew you was back."

"He didn't know who I was when I saw him in the Drovers. That was before I met the Sheriff and Ben Cowan. When the sale was called off, Higgins and the land agent would have known though."

Palmer gave Judd a shrewd look and for the first time appeared to make an effort to be relaxed and easy with him.

"Well, I guess you came back just in time. You sure didn't hustle though."

Judd explained about the delay.

"Fran tell you about Sten's will?" asked Palmer.

Judd nodded.

"Place has grown a mite since you ran off. And you don't look like a farmer." He stared at Judd's firearms. "You gonna sell up, or what?"

"Are you interested in buying then, Mister Palmer?"

"Could be, if it was a straight up private sale."

"Well, you see, I was telling Fran I reckoned I should find

out why Sten was killed before I made up my mind what to do. Then this hombre took a pot at me and made it personal. The answer as of now is no I ain't selling up. As of now my only plan is to take this here in to Sheriff Kramer. I'll need a horse, though."

"Right. You want somebody to ride in with you?"

"No. Best I go in alone."

Palmer jerked a thumb at the man called Jim. "Saddle up one of the spares and bring it back here." Then to Judd, "Fran Healey's a brave woman. Takes a lotta guts to stay out there on her own with the little one an all. I offered her a chance to come in with us, did she tell you?"

"She did say something," said Judd. "What would it entail, exactly?"

"We've set up a community here, a kind of Cooperative, all for one and one for all. I'm running it. I'll explain how it works when we've got more time - if you're interested. Enough for now to say the big cattlemen can't push us farmers around no more. Time was they could pick us off one by one and make it just durned impossible for even the strongest to last out. Those days are over for us. We're staying for keeps. Your uncle was an independent cuss and it didn't do him no good. It won't do you none either. Think about it." He turned abruptly and went back into the house.

There had always been an awkwardness about Palmer but now Judd felt an underlying hardness as well, as if he was trying to prove something.

The man called Tom said, "Ya don't remember Jim and me, do ya?"

"Can't say I do," said Judd.

"Hallett. We had a farm coupla miles east of here. Till six years ago when they killed Pa."

"Hallett? Yes, I remember. It was Mrs. Hallett came over and nursed my mother in her last sickness," said Judd. "Who killed your pa?"

"Watkins, who else!"

"Would that be Butch Watkins of Double Diamond?"

"Mister, we didn't see who done the shooting, but the week before, Butch Watkins and three of his men came to the house at night and made us all watch while they beat up on Pa. Then they gave us a week to get out. One week to the day, Pa was shot dead." He paused. "Jim and me, we work as permanent guards on this community, and we're sure as hell looking forward to the day when Butch Watkins rides within rifle shot. We been practicing for six years and we won't miss."

"That'll be murder, Tom," Judd said.

"That'll be justice, Mister, and that's all we came back for."

"Did your ma come back with you?"

"Ma took us back east to her folks in Columbus, Ohio, and then she took and died, but she told us she'd left the title deeds of our land with Clem Palmer till such a time as we would be old enough to take over. Clem wrote us and we came back with him last Easter."

"Have any of the other original farmers come back?" asked Judd.

"Only the Morgans and the Canliffs."

Jim Hallet came up leading a saddled horse.

"Mount up and follow us on down to the trail," said Tom.

As they rode east of Palmer's farmhouse Judd saw that a number of sturdy, new dwelling houses had been put up, or were being built, each set in a large plot of land, with picket fences around. In the main street he saw a general store, a smithy, a corral, a church with a large meeting house, and

65

several part-finished buildings, mostly barns.

He could see the sense of it. Whereas formerly each family had its own house and outbuildings set in its own quarter section, and was therefore vulnerable, Palmer's community were grouping all the buildings together in one place for greater security.

Tom had said that he and his brother worked as permanent guards on the community, and Judd could envision these people's need for continuous vigilance. It also seemed to him that they would be unlikely to have time, or for that matter the inclination to be involved in rustling cattle. For the moment, at least, they were entirely inward-looking.

However, it looked as if whoever was stealing the cattle would be happy for the settlers to take the blame, and he wondered how long it would be before an attempt was made to furnish false evidence.

They came to the trail and rode on down to the gate. Jim Hallett dismounted and opened one side of the gate wide enough for the horses to pass through. He pointed to a big iron triangle and a heavy bar hanging by chains from a scaffold.

"When ya come back jus' whack it and someone'll come," he said

"Thanks," said Judd, "You boys want anything from town?"

"Coupla sacks of Bull Durham 'ud be 'preciated," said Tom.

"Okay, see you fellers later."

CHAPTER EIGHT

The trail to Twin Springs ran more or less due south through pleasant fertile country. In the low ground among the hills there were many large rocks and occasional clumps of trees, but generally the grass was good.

In the days before the homesteaders had arrived, all the land around Twin Springs had been free-graze. Matt Watkins had built up the M on W, Double Diamond ranch back at the beginnings of the territory, deep in the rolling grasslands north-east of the old army outpost, and when after a few years Todd Berman, his first foreman, had wanted to set up on his own, Matt had helped him establish the Star B about ten miles north-west of the town. Year by year others had come in: Kirk Barratt founded K Bar to the south and east, and farther east along the Fort Collins trail the Mannion brothers set up the Tomahawk. Pete Johnson's Oxyoke south of Star B completed the circle around what was by then a growing town.

The Petersens had been the first farmers to move into the area. They were tolerated because they had settled in an out-of-the-way part of the basin, but later, in the aftermath of the War between the States, a steady flow of homesteaders started coming in to take up the free quarter sections of land offered by the Federal government under the 1862 Act, and it was not long before three thousand acres had been taken over around Tinkers Creek. Good grassland was plowed under and fences put up on land that had always been used as free grazing by the cattlemen.

So far as old Matt Watkins was concerned all the land was free range; east of the creek was his, and west of it was Star B's. They'd been there first, they'd fought off the Indians and other rustlers, learned to survive summer droughts and winter snows, and built up large herds that depended on all that free grass. He just wasn't able to see that the free range would not last for ever.

Judd had been sixteen years old when the real harassment began. One by one the homesteads were attacked. Fences were cut, cattle driven in, crops destroyed, barns burnt, always at night and never in the same place twice. When the settlers went into town for supplies their menfolk would be set upon if they happened to meet up with cowhands. A few families were discouraged and moved out to try their luck elsewhere, but the majority just gritted their teeth and repaired or rebuilt, determined to hold on for the five years necessary before the land became theirs as of right.

The attacks had been going on for a whole year when old man Watkins decided to bring matters to a head. One pay day, when he had all his men together, he said he wondered if those damned sodbusters realized how lucky they were that none of them had gotten really badly hurt yet. He thought it was time they were made to realize.

The Petersens had not been directly affected by the trouble. They had always kept to themselves in their outlying homestead, and they had managed to avoid meeting men from the ranches on their monthly trips to Twin Springs. Their luck ran out on that payday, though.

Olaf and Sten had taken the buckboard into town to collect some new harness and a few replacement tools. They had just loaded up outside Joe Healey's saddle and harness shop, when Jack Watkins, Matt's son, and two of his hands, came out of the Drovers Saloon and sauntered towards them.

Olaf mounted the buckboard, taking up the reins, as Sten finished tying down the tarp over the pile of goods. Neither of them was carrying weapons, although they had a shotgun behind the seat.

Two of the men stopped in front of the wagon, grinning up at Olaf, while Watkins went round to Sten's side.

"Afternoon." he said, standing legs astride behind Sten as he tightened the last knot.

Sten ignored him.

Watkins poked a finger in his back.

"You know, you ain't very polite," he said. Then he turned to look up at Olaf. "Seems to me none of you dirt-scrabblers is too good at understanding either. A while back we told you to stay out of town."

"I reckon they just plumb forgot," said one of the others.

"Maybe if we gave 'em a hand it'd all come back to 'em," said the third.

He came forward and reaching up, caught hold of Olaf's leg, trying to pull him down. Olaf kicked out at him, overbalanced, and grabbed instinctively for the back of the seat. His hand clutched the shotgun, and as he straightened up with it, Watkins drew his pistol and fired point-blank, hitting Olaf in the back.

With a roar of rage, Sten leaped forward, fists swinging with all his weight behind them. He caught Watkins on the side of the head, knocking him to the ground.

The horse had reared up at the shot and the shotgun slid

from Olaf's hand. Sten grabbed it, and drew back both hammers. As Watkins started to bring his pistol up, Sten blew a hole in him.

Luckily for Sten, Joe Healey had seen everything that happened. What was more to the point, he was prepared to stand up and say so.

"It was self-defense," he said, and they had to let Sten go.

But Olaf died.

Judd had buried his bitter memories when he'd left Twin Springs, as he'd thought, for ever.

Riding down this trail now for the first time in ten years, he recalled happier times in his childhood. Like the times in the early days when they all camped out in the woodlands along the creek while they cut and dressed the timber for the cabin and the other buildings. Like the times when he and Pa used to go hunting in those same woods. And best of all, driving back from town through the summer twilight, when, sitting between Ma and Pa he'd learnt the old songs from England that Ma sang so well, and from Pa, the funny old Swedish folksongs that Pa's grandfather had taught him.

This could be a good place, he thought, if only folks would let it.

It was a little after four in the afternoon when he rode into town. People turned and stared as he walked the horses slowly up the street and drew up outside the sheriff's office. A few of the more curious followed and were gathering around as Judd went inside, ignoring their questions.

Deciding there was no reason anyone else should know about Fran's skill with a rifle - that could be a secret well worth keeping - he related what had happened in such a way that the lawmen assumed that he had fired the shot that killed Mason.

Sheriff Kramer and Ben went out to see the body for themselves. Ben told the onlookers to disperse.

"What do you know about him, Sheriff? Who did he work for?" asked Judd.

"He's only been around a week or so. Came in with another feller name of Voller. They never done any work that I know of, just hung around the Drovers, like they was waiting for something." He shrugged and turned away, "Well, he don't have to wait no longer. Take him on down to Sorrell, will you, Ben."

"There was a young dude who called himself Billy Bates with them in the Drovers," said Judd when they were back in the office. "What would their connection with him be?"

"That I wouldn't know," said Kramer. "Bates is a bit of a mystery. He lives in the hotel, plays cards there in the evenings, wins more than he loses but never wins much, not enough to live on in any style anyhow, throws his weight around. They say he fancies himself as a shootist, but he's never fired a shot in town since I've been here."

Judd told him about finding the stolen cattle.

Kramer considered for a few moments, then he said, "About three hundred to three fifty head, huh? DD must've lost about that many, I reckon, from what they've been saying. K Bar and Star B? I don't know. They both say they've missed plenty. See any Oxyoke or Tomahawk?"

"I didn't take note of any other brands especially," said Judd.

"How about the NHK? They reckon they lost some, too."

"No, as I say there were other brands but I didn't want to hang around there leaving sign."

"Yeah, sure, and thanks a lot. Uh, how d'you feel about

showing Ben where they're at?"

"Well, now," said Judd, irritated at the idea, "It's about half a day's ride from here, and I reckon I've got enough to keep me busy without that. I guess I can describe the place plain enough for you to go find them yourselves."

"Not your problem, huh?"

"You're damn right it's not."

"'spose I made it your problem?" said Kramer, looking Judd straight in the eye.

"Come again?"

"I could telegraph Ford County, seeing as how you're here an all, and ask for your help."

"Yeah, I guess you could at that. But I'm thinking I might want to give up on Marshalling. Besides, if you did you'd have to do it my way."

"Be only too happy," said Kramer. "Fact is, Petersen, I made a mistake when I took this job on. I should've found out who really runs this place. Old man Watkins. He believes every man can be bought, and it's getting mighty hard to keep turning him down, I'm telling you."

"Are you serious?"

"Yeah, I'm serious. Listen, I'm fifty-three years old. I've rid the range, ram-rodded a big spread down in New Mexico, bin trail boss on a coupla drives, rode shotgun for a stage line, an I've bin a deputy sheriff back east, where folks elect their lawmen. I never made a lot of money, but every job I done I played it straight, so now I reckon the time's coming for me to move on.

"I know a handsome little widda woman down south in Raton, runs a few freight wagons up through Trinidad to Pueblo and around. Promised her I'd come and give her a hand in a year or so. I doubt she'd turn me away if I made it a mite sooner."

"Why are you telling me this?" asked Judd.

"Only reason I've stayed on till now is I feel kinda responsible to the good folks in this town. Folks like the Cowans, Doc Campbell, Eddie Reynolds the barber, the Barratts out at K Bar, and all those decent hard-working farmers south of here. I could tell you a lot more if'n I thought it would help.

"Y'see I did telegraph Ford County after you left yesterday. Thought I better check up. From what they told me you're just the man this place needs - and you've gotten your own roots here as well. You've gotten a stake in this place, whether you like it or not."

"Feels like I'm being railroaded," said Judd.

"Waal, mebbe you oughta study on this: you and me and Ben can do together what Ben and me could never do on our own. We got to tackle that old man with a mite more than the local law behind us, 'cos that old devil can easy replace me with one of his own, and then where will poor old Ben be?"

Judd's first reaction had been indignation, but what the sheriff was saying was true, he did have an interest at stake, and if he wanted to get at the facts behind Sten's death, what better way than working officially within the law? He gave Sheriff Kramer a long, hard look while he thought about it.

"I've got to admit you make a good argument, Sheriff," he said. "But I reckon I ought to see how things stand at head office."

Kramers face split in a huge grin. "I already done that," he said, "You just got to bear out the facts is as I told 'em, and they'll give you the go-ahead."

"But what about the widow?" said Judd.

"Oh, she ain't expecting me for a week or two yet! Is it a deal?"

The sheriff stuck out his hand.

Judd grinned his lopsided smile. "Its a deal," he said, and they shook on it.

CHAPTER NINE

When Judd rode into town leading Mason's horse with a body face down across the saddle, thin, ginger-haired Sandy was among the curious half-dozen or so who followed him to the sheriff's office. As soon as Judd had tied up and gone inside, Sandy darted forward, grabbed the dead man's hair and lifted his head. Although the face was mutilated by the rifle bullet and covered in dried blood, he had no difficulty in recognizing the man.

"It's that Mickey Mason," he told the bystanders, "Shot through the head!"

None of the others had known Mason and they soon lost interest. Sandy loitered nearby after they had drifted away and when Ben came out to take the body to the mortician, he asked what had happened.

"It seems that he shot at Mr. Petersen but missed," said Ben, economically.

"Where'd it happen?" asked Sandy.

"Out at the Petersen homestead."

"What was he doing all the way out there?"

"We may never know," replied Ben, leading the horse away.

Sandy slid into lawyer Higgins office next door.

Cheswell was the name of Higgins's clerk. He and Sandy were cronies. They had found a shared interest in making a few easy dollars from Higgins from time to time by passing him odd bits of information they thought he might like to have. As Cheswell said, such bits of information need not always be strictly factual, but Higgins would pay anyhow.

Sandy sidled up to Cheswell's desk. "Your lord and master said to tell him when that Petersen came to town, didn't he. Well, he's in Kramer's office, just brought that Mickey Mason in, dead, shot in the head."

"Yeah?" Cheswell left his desk and went to the window. He looked out. "Where is he?"

"Deputy's just taking him down to Sorrell."

"That Mason feller was a pal of Billy Bates, wasn't he?"

"Yeah." Sandy nodded and grinned.

"And my lord and master had Bates back there in his office for quite a while yesterday after Petersen arrived in town, didn't he."

Sandy nodded and grinned again. "And not long after that I saw Bates talking to Mason, and then Mason rode out."

"So," said Cheswell, eyebrows raised, "Do we think my lord and master would want to know about him being shot?" His grin broadened. "I'll go tell him. You can wait here and we'll see what he does." He went through to Higgins's office.

Sandy and Cheswell were aware that there was a link between Higgins and Marburg, a fact which would have horrified Higgins had he known, although it shouldn't have surprised him. He'd encouraged them both to keep their eyes open and report to him on any interesting behavior by their fellow townsmen. They had seen no reason to exclude him from their observations, and although they didn't know what the connection with Marburg was about, they were sure the knowledge would come in useful some day and were just waiting their opportunity to capitalize on it.

To their delight, Higgins left the office almost immediately and scuttled across the road and into the Bank building where they knew he would go directly to the door marked Private and up the stairs to Marburg's apartment.

Marburg greeted him at the door and ushered him in with a friendly smile which faded rapidly as Higgins stammered out the news of Mason's failure. He'd never seen Marburg angry before and watched apprehensively as the big man, cursing violently, strode angrily around the room, his swarthy skin darkening even further as the blood rushed to his face. Higgins flinched as Marburg came and stood over him, eyes glaring.

"What kind of an outfit have we got here, Con?"

"Well, I ..." Higgins faltered.

"You are supposed to have all the local knowledge, so I rely on you to get the right men for the job!"

"Well, as I told you, Bates does have the reputation as the best around."

"Yes, you did tell me that, and you also said he could be relied on to be thorough!"

"Well, he certainly had that reputation, Mr. Marburg. And when I checked up on those men he brought in I was assured they really knew their business too."

"Con, I believed you when you said Bates needed more men, and I've been paying out good money for them. But what happens? The first time his so-called hard man sees Petersen he gets flattened, then next day Petersen shoots the other one dead!"

Higgins started to bluster but Marburg cut him short.

"Listen, Petersen is in the way, so this is what you do. You tell Bates there's a thousand dollars if he gets rid of him inside a week. He can do it any way he wants - shoot him, knife him, string him up, burn him out, it doesn't matter. Just get him out of the way. We need that land!"

"But what about the woman?"

"What about her?"

"Mr. Marburg, you have been out west long enough to know that people won't stand for a woman being molested, not even a rough kind of woman like her."

Marburg turned away with a dismissive gesture. "Leave that to Bates. Just make sure nothing leads back to you."

"Well, I don't like it, Mr. Marburg. She is the sister of Butch Watkins" wife, and we don't want them getting involved."

Marburg turned back angrily, stabbing his forefinger in Higgins chest. "You don't have to like it, Con. And if you and Bates play it right there's no reason why Watkins should get involved with you anyway." Then, seeing the frightened look on Higgins face and realizing he may have gone too far, he raised his hands in a calming motion and backed away. "Listen, we're nearly there now, and we can't let any penny-ante farmer's son get in our way. You can see that as well as me."

"Yes, but Petersen has already shown he's no pushover, and I just think it might be worth trying some other way."

"Some other way?"

"Well, I don't know. Make him an offer, maybe?"

Marburg looked sidelong at him. "What are you getting at?"

"Well, Shepherd could give us an idea of the going price for the land and we could figure it from there."

"You mean buy it all legit?"

"Well, look, I know we were hoping to get it cheap before he came, but as you just said we do need that land. Without it we're sunk."

Marburg considered himself a shrewd man but nevertheless he believed that when he trusted his instinct it would always pay off. Whenever he thought he was faced with strength he waited for opportunity, always trusting his instinct for survival to save him from over-reaching himself. With the government apparently inclined towards encouraging free enterprise on government land, he figured a man could get away with as much as he was big enough to handle, and Leo Marburg was, he acknowledged to himself, among the biggest, so when, as now, he saw weakness, his instinct was to act quickly and ruthlessly, because in his experience that led to success.

He looked long and hard at Higgins. Then he slowly shook his head.

"No. Wouldn't work, Con. We could have done that in the first place. Then, soon as the sale started to go through the whole business would come to light. No." He turned and went to sit at his desk. "Go tell Bates what's wanted and leave him to get on with it."

CHAPTER TEN

Sheriff Kramer agreed that Judd should work under cover for as long as he thought necessary. As far as they knew, the only other people who were aware that Judd was a lawman were Fran Healey and Clem Palmer.

"I dunno what to make of that Palmer," said the sheriff. "Ben's sweet on his daughter, Gwen, and Palmer makes no objection to 'em seeing each other. Probably thinks Ben's a catch not to be missed, 'cos she sure ain't no beauty to look at. But he just don't open up none, not to Ben nor to me."

"How d'you mean?" said Judd.

"Waal, he ain't said so in so many words, but I reckon he thinks he's the law inside that barb wire, and what goes on in there ain't nobody else's business. Another Watkins, on a smaller scale."

Judd related how Palmer had invited him to consider joining the Cooperative.

"Wouldn't do no harm to find out how it works," said Kramer. "From what I can make of it I reckon he's mebbe taken a leaf outa the Grangers" book. You ever come across them? Patrons of Husbandry they called themselves."

"I only ever heard of the cooperatives that failed. From what little I've seen of Palmer's set-up, I'd say he was better organized."

"That's a mighty big area he's got fenced off - a lot more than was first settled. He came in for the sale of your place, did you know that?"

"Yes, he told me," said Judd. "He didn't say he intended to buy, though. He knew Sten left everything he had to Fran Healey in his will."

"Is that a fact? He really did leave it to her, then?"

"She says she has the papers, and I believe her."

"But if it's bin left to her all legal, where do you come in?"

"I keep my folks quarter section."

"Uh-huh. " Kramer nodded. "Say, how'd you get along with her? She ain't no shrinking violet, that's for sure!"

Judd smiled. "I'd say she is tough, and honest, and no man's fool."

Kramer shook his head. "I can't see Lawyer Higgins being very happy proving that will."

"He won't get the chance," said Judd. "Which reminds me, I'll get on over to the telegraph and clear things with head office, and pick up any mail. Then I'd better get a few things from the store - the homestead's running out of basics."

"What about those cattle?"

"I guess we can take a chance on them staying where they are for a day or two. Is there anyone you can rely on to keep a lookout and maybe trail them if they're moved?"

"Waal, there's old Homer Foreman. Used to be a trapper, scout for the army. He's bin up the creek and over the mountain in his day. Works for Sam Cowan, helping out at the livery. He's a bit long in the tooth, but he's reliable alright."

"Okay," said Judd. "Swear him in and give him his badge but tell him not to wear it just yet. Folks might start to wondering."

At the post and telegraph office Judd collected a letter for

Fran, and sent a message confirming his intention to stay and help Sheriff Kramer.

Ben, back from the mortician, was waiting for him as he came out.

"Tom has just told me the good news," he said. "Now we'll be able to get something done! And if you'd like to come along to the livery with me, you can have a word with Homer Foreman yourself and see if you think he'll be up to it. And then you must come and have something to eat and drink with us before you go."

"Okay, Ben, and thanks, but first I've got to get me some supplies."

They walked the borrowed horse along to the cattlemen's store, where Judd bought coffee, sugar, salt, cornmeal, dried fruits, rice, and coal oil, some candy for Joe, and tobacco for the Hallett brothers. He was bending over, packing it all into a gunny sack when he heard footsteps coming towards him, spurs jangling. A pair of polished leather riding boots stopped immediately in front of him. He stood up, slowly, and found himself eye-to-eye with Butch Watkins.

"I heard you was back," said Watkins.

"And I heard you was still around," said Judd.

"Yeah, and I'll be staying around. You won't."

"Guess I'm in no hurry to leave just yet, though," said Judd.

"Take some advice, Petersen. Sell up and get out. Things are shaping up badly out your way. Palmer's squatters are making trouble."

"I've got no quarrel with Palmer."

"Well, we have and we ain't standing for it much longer. Be careful you don't get in the way."

Judd hefted the sack onto his shoulder, and looked Watkins

over. He noted that the five years and thirty pounds difference between them was now in his favor - Watkins was running to fat.

"Excuse me," he said, "I believe *you* are in *my* way."

He moved forward, and Watkins, obliged to step back quickly to avoid him, dislodged a shelf of patent nostrums and domestic items which scattered and rolled all over the floor.

"Oh, and uh, remember me to Mrs. Watkins?" Judd called over his shoulder.

Watkins glared after him in confusion as the storekeeper bustled over to re-set his display

Ben followed Judd out, grinning. "I think you may have unsettled Mister Watkins. And you homesteaders aren't supposed to use the cattlemen's store, you know!"

Judd tied his purchases behind the saddle, and as they walked together down to the livery, Ben told Judd how the Cowan family house had come to be built.

Sam, Ben's father, had passed through the town five years earlier on his way back from the gold fields. He'd been traveling in the area, looking at likely places where he might invest the profit from the sale of his gold mine, and was staying in the hotel the day Joe Healey was shot. He had recognized the potential of the place and before he left he'd bought ten acres of land behind a hundred yards of frontage along the south side of Main Street running west from the Stage and Telegraph office. This included the small drayage business, the saddle and harness shop and Joe Healey's livery stable and corral. He'd sent for Homer Foreman, whom he'd met in the goldfields, to look after his property until he could return with his family.

Ben said that his mother, Sarah, had been very patient when they had first arrived, putting up with all the inconvenience of living in the shacks behind the livery and saddlery. But once the repairs and enlargements that Sam wanted for the business premises were under way, she'd let him know that she hadn't left a civilized life in London, England, to come halfway around the world and live like a savage - it was time he built the fine big house she'd been promised.

"And that's the result," said Ben.

They had paused in the space between the drayage and the saddle and harness shop. A wide driveway led to a solid rectangular, two-story building of dressed stone, set well back. Polished, heavy wooden front doors were approached from stone steps via a porticoed entry.

Judd nodded. "Impressive," he said.

They left the horse with Homer Foreman at the livery. Judd watched the old man attending to the animal. Small and thin, Homer was quick and light on his feet, an alert, easy-moving man. He'd be okay. Judd nodded to Ben.

"Homer," said Ben, "How would you feel about doing a little job for the sheriff and me?"

"For the sheriff and you? The both of you?" Homer gave him a quizzical look. "Now, what would that en-tail, exactly?"

"You'd have to be sworn in."

"I figured I might."

"I expect you may have heard talk about cattle rustling?"

"Uh-huh."

"Some of the rustled cattle have been found," said Ben.

Homer gave a quick glance towards Judd. "So?"

"We need somebody to hide up in the hills and keep an eye on them. Somebody who could trail them if they were moved, and not be seen."

"This the gent that found them cows?" said Homer, indicating Judd.

"Yes," said Ben.

"And no-one else knows they been found?"

"That's right. What do you say?"

"Reckon I wouldn't object to a few days up in the high country."

"Good! Go and settle it with the sheriff then, and come back here afterwards. You'll get your directions from Mr. Petersen here."

From the rear of the stable Ben led the way along a neat gravel path with rows of bright green bay trees standing in tubs on either side. They passed through a gate in a picket fence, into a flower garden, laid out with shrubs and closely cut grass.

A wide, white-painted verandah stretched the whole width of the house along the south side, and as they approached, a young woman in a white cotton dress and wide-brimmed hat got up from a swing chair.

"Ruth," said Ben, "I'd like you to meet Mr. Petersen. He's come home to settle his uncle's estate. My sister, Ruth."

He took her hand and raised it to his lips and she bobbed him a little curtsey, and all the time their eyes held.

Her lips parted in a faint smile, "Please may I have my hand back?"

"Oh, uh, beg pardon, ma'am," he stammered, "But if you'll forgive me for saying so, I vow you have the prettiest eyes I ever did see."

Her response was warm and unhesitating. She blushed very slightly and inclined her head. "You are most flattering, Mr. Petersen."

She took her hat off and shook out her dark curls, She looked so cool and clean, and so pretty, that Judd wished he could have been more presentable than he felt in Sten's shabby work clothes.

Ben said, "Mr. Petersen has a long ride out to the

homestead, so I've invited him in for a little something to help him on his way."

Ruth smiled at Judd, "Well, you're very welcome, Mr. Petersen."

"Thank you, Miss Ruth," he said.

"The account of your arrival in town took up a large part of the conversation at dinner here last night," she said. "Isn't that so, Ben?"

Ben smiled. "I mentioned how you arrived just in time to stop your farm being sold. And Dan and Isaac, our brothers, decided that you must have been the Mister Judd who rather upset Ruth's friend Mr. Bates."

"Ah, yes, in the Drovers. Judd happens to be my given name. It's what my friends call me."

"Hmm, Judd!" she said as if tasting it, "Yes, it has a good masculine flavor. It suits you."

"Well, it's a real comfort to hear you say that, ma'am." he said solemnly, and they all laughed, "But as I recall, I was properly respectful to Mr. Bates, and if he truly is a friend of yours Miss Ruth, why, I'm real sorry! Yes, ma'am, I truly am!"

"Bates is a family joke," said Ben, with a smile. "The poor fellow has become such a persistent admirer!"

"One of many I'm sure," said Judd.

In the way she looked up at him, her head half turned away, the light glistening on her slightly parted lips, there was a hint of romantic and erotic invitation. Ruth Cowan, he decided was an interesting lady.

Ben said, "Ruth, why don't you take Mr. Petersen into the parlor. I'll go and find Mother."

The parlor was a large room, with thick decorative carpets, heavy velvet curtains, and stuffed with furniture: a huge leather-covered sofa and matching armchairs, glass-fronted china cabinets and bookcases, an upright piano, a longcase clock, several cushioned stools, and small tables, thickly draped with lace and bobble-fringed velvet, some bearing lamps, others displaying trailing plants, ferns or palms. On the mantleshelf over the massive fireplace were statuettes, figurines and framed lithographs, and in the center an ornate porcelain clock. Above the clock was a large picture of Queen Victoria. Gilded paintings on the wallpapered walls were mostly portraits, but there was one of a clipper ship, and another of spring in the Rocky Mountains.

Judd guessed it was probably the most richly furnished room in town, and he reckoned that the Cowans wanted to be seen to be comfortable.

As if reading his thoughts, Ruth said, "Many of the things in here came with us from London. Family heirlooms, you know, Mother's family mostly." She smiled, "Father would have preferred to buy new when we came out here. New things and new ways in a new land!"

"And how about you? Is that what you think?" asked Judd.

"Oh, well," she said, hesitating, as if surprised at being asked, "At first, before we actually came to America, I would have agreed with father. You know, everything new, a fresh start in a new life. It was an exciting idea. But now I understand how Mother felt. The things she made Father bring with us have a certain value. I mean, more than there would be in something similar but new."

Judd nodded, "I guess it must be kinda comforting to have something that's belonged in your family for years back."

"Yes, I think so. Although of course, we could well afford to buy new if we wanted."

Ben came in. "We're to have tea on the verandah. Mother is busy for the moment, but she'll try and join us later."

Judd followed Ruth and Ben outside. Four white-painted basket weave chairs had been placed around a glass-topped table, and a black woman in a maid's uniform was setting out cups and saucers and plates of sandwiches and cakes.

"Please take a seat, Mr. Petersen," said Ruth. "How do you like your tea? Mother always takes a slice of lemon with hers, but the rest of us take milk."

"Well, Miss Ruth, I haven't had tea with milk in it since I was a small boy, and it sure would be pleasing to taste it that way again."

The awkwardness he'd felt at finding himself in this unexpectedly elegant setting was soon dispelled by the open friendliness of the brother and sister towards him. Ruth clearly was curious to know more about him, but he succeeded in turning the conversation away from himself by expressing an interest in the family's prospering businesses and their position in the town.

They were more than happy to oblige, so that when the time came for Judd to leave he'd learnt that the Cowan family's chief concern was for the preservation of law and order, knowing that the future prosperity of the town, and therefore of their businesses, depended upon a firm stand against lawlessness. The townspeople generally were agreed on this, the majority being happy to go along with the initiative already taken by the Cattlemen's Association, led by old Matt Watkins, in installing Sheriff Kramer. There were some, however, including the Cowans, who recognized that the domination of the local economy by the big ranchers depended on the availability of free range grass, and they could see that new settlers would continue to move into the area, each having a legal claim to fence off one hundred and sixty acres of this free range. The cattlemen were reluctant to give it up and conflict seemed inevitable.

Ruth, meanwhile, had discovered only that Judd was unmarried, with which information she seemed contented for the present.

CHAPTER ELEVEN

Sandy was lolling against the doorframe of the lawyer's office, smoking a cigarette when Higgins came out of the bank building.

"Here he comes," he called over his shoulder to Cheswell.

"What's he look like?"

"Mighty troubled, I'd say."

Sandy levered himself upright and ambled away towards the land agent's office next door.

Higgins noticed him and called out.

"Can you spare me a minute of your time, please, Sandy?" he said.

Sandy turned back, smiling ingratiatingly. "Sure, Mister Higgins. What can I do for you?"

"I wonder if you'd see if you can find Mr. Billy Bates for me and ask him to come and see me as soon as he can? I expect he will be in the hotel if he isn't in the Drovers."

"Okay. Shall I tell him what it's about?"

"No. Just say it's urgent."

"Sure thing, Mister Higgins."

"Thank you." Higgins went in and paused by Cheswell's desk.

"I'm expecting Mr. Bates, Colin. Send him straight in when he comes, will you."

"Yes sir."

Higgins sat at his desk, resting his head in his hands, worried about what might happen to him and his lawyer's practice if his connection to Bates and his gang ever became general knowledge in the town. He'd taken risks before, of course, interpreting the law rather loosely when it was in his interest to do so, but he'd never even considered violence as a means to an end.

It had all started when he'd heard that Palmer was coming back to Tinkers Creek Crossing and seeking to buy land in the neighborhood. Shepherd, the Land Agent, had discovered that there was concern in Washington about the state in which government land stood, and there was a strong rumor that a change was due in the land laws, mainly because it was becoming difficult for railroads to dispose of their land.

The situation was complicated by petitions for and against the building of new railroads to link developing areas in the west with the successful transcontinental line, and the feeling was that there was a potential for massive profits to be made for those in possession when the land laws were changed.

This appealed to Higgins's instinct for a fast deal, but Marburg, having studied the topography around Tinkers Creek, decided there was a profit to be made without waiting for any legislative action. He'd made it all seem so simple and straightforward that Higgins had given in to his coaxing and one evening in the Drovers he'd hinted to Peretz that he had a client who needed somebody removed from the neighborhood. A few days later Bates had called at his office and after a brief conversation a sum of money had changed hands.

Higgins accepted that he should have guessed what was likely to happen, but it was still a shock when he heard the next day that Sten Petersen had been shot in the back out at his remote homestead. He'd been worried sick at first, but when a month had passed and nothing had happened he'd believed they'd got away with it. Then Petersen's nephew turned up and there was another killing out at the homestead, and now he was expected to ensure that the rest of the Petersen family would be disposed of. It was all going wrong and he didn't know what he could do about it. He was still worrying when his office door opened and Bates strolled in and sat uninvited in the visitors" chair.

Higgins decided to go on the offensive.

"My client is not very happy, Mr. Bates," he said. "He feels that he is not getting what he has paid for."

"Yeah, right." Bates leaned forward and scowled at him. "Mebbe you shoulda spelled out better just what it was your client wanted for his money."

Higgins frowned. "I thought I had made it quite clear."

"Listen! Micky Mason knew what he was about. He warn't no pushover. I just seen his body. There ain't no chance he'da let some little ole dirt farmer shoot him through the head that way!"

"What's that supposed to mean?"

"Your client is up against a mite more than he bargained for."

"Yes, well, I have to agree with you about that," said Higgins. "But he knows that now and he is willing to pay very well to get the matter settled."

"How much?"

"One thousand dollars, if it is done within seven days."

"No deal."

Higgins raised his eyebrows. "Should I look elsewhere then, Mr. Bates?"

Bates sat back, crossed his legs and smiled. "You could

sure try, but I guess your client would still want it all kept quiet. Right?"

"Yes, right." Higgins nodded, acknowledging that Bates was well aware who held the bargaining power here. "What would you suggest, then?"

"Well, if the job's gotta be done in a week, it'll take some setting up, I reckon." He thought for a few moments. "What about the woman?"

"He said to leave it to you."

"Okay. See, I reckon the only certain sure way is burn 'em out, and that'll take a bunch of fellas. Have to bring 'em down outta the hills. That'll mean leaving the cattle. They won't like that. How about your client? Will he like that?"

"No, I guess he won't. But if that's what it takes…"

"Sure. And - it'll take a thousand dollars before we start and another coupla thousand when the job's done." Bates stood up, the business finished so far as he was concerned. At the door he said, "Tell your client he can send the first one thousand dollars to me in my room at the hotel. When that's safely in the bank, he can leave the Petersens to me."

Sandy was sitting on the boardwalk outside the Drovers when Bates came out of Higgins's office and walked down the street and into the hotel. As expected, Higgins came out soon afterwards and trotted across to the Bank building.

Cheswell came to the door of the lawyer's office and beckoned Sandy to join him.

"Just what we thought, huh?" he said. "The three of them are cooking up something."

"Any idea what?"

"I reckon it's to do with the Petersen place. They called the sale off after that Judd Petersen turned up, didn't they, and it was just after that old Con had Billy Bates in last time, wasn't it?"

"Yeah. You reckon Bates is going to shoot it out with the Petersen guy? They say he's fast, got a rep down in Arizona, so they say."

Cheswell shook his head. "From what you said you saw when they met the first time, Bates was pretty quick to back off, wasn't he? No, I don't guess Bates would do much on his own. Keep your eyes open, eh? See what you can pick up around the Drovers." He went back into the office.

Rather to Higgins's surprise, Marburg accepted Bates's terms philosophically.

"Good," he nodded his approval. "At least the man's taking it seriously at last."

"But they'll have to leave the cattle. Is that alright with you?"

"Bates can use the men. Cattle can keep a day or so." He paused and drew on his cigar. "I did want to talk to you about that, though, Con. I want a proper tally done. See how we're doing. There ought to be enough young stock for a branding by now and then they can move on to the Tomahawk. Tell Lou Dessay to come and see me when this is over. I want him in charge. He knows what he's doing and I don't trust those Mannions."

"Alright. So Bates can go ahead, then?"

Marburg stood up and went to the window, waving vaguely towards Higgins in dismissal "Have your clerk, Cheswell, call at the bank in half an hour and collect a package. It'll have his name on it. He needn't know what's in it or who it's from, but tell him to hand it personally to Bates."

Later that afternoon, just as Higgins was contemplating going home Cheswell put his head around the door.

"Excuse me, Mr. Higgins," he said. "I've taken that

package to Mr. Bates."

"Alright. Thank you, Colin."

Cheswell remained standing in the doorway.

Higgins said, "Was there something else?"

"Yes, er, Sandy has just called in with some interesting news." He came fully into the room. "Tell Mr. Higgins what you've just heard, Sandy."

Sandy came and stood by the door.

"Fella come in the Drovers and wants to know about the Petersen place," he said.

"Oh? What sort of a fellow?"

"Fat, red face, fiftyish I'd say. Flashy dresser like a drummer and shoots his mouth off like one, too. Says his name's Hobbs and he's staying in the hotel and that's where Petersen can find him."

"I see."

"Thought you'd want to know."

"Yes. Thank you." Now what? Higgins thought. "Has he said why he wants to know about the Petersen place?"

"Says he's got a letter for 'em, something that'll shake up the whole town. Had a few, I'd say."

Higgins thought for a moment. "He looks as though he likes a drink, then, does he?"

"I'd say so."

Higgins took a key from his vest pocket, unlocked a drawer of his desk, and extracted a leather purse from which he removed a few small coins.

"Would you go back to the Drovers, Sandy, and ask Mr. Peretz if he would come and see me straightaway. Tell him it is urgent, please, and you might buy yourself a drink while you're there." He held out his hand and Sandy took the money.

"Thanks, Mr. Higgins." Sandy scuttled away.

Higgins said, "You can go on home if you like, Colin. Just leave the door open for Mr. Peretz, would you?"

When Peretz arrived he confirmed what Sandy had said.

Higgins said, "We need to find out what this fellow Hobbs has got for the Petersens, but we don't want it spread about. Who is in the saloon that we can use?"

"Carl Voller's there and Billy Bates has just come in. Other'n that there's a couple of guys from Double Diamond and a few regulars from the town."

"Good. This is what I want you to do. Let Bates make sure his drinks are topped up and when you think he's had enough, Voller can pick a fight with him and knock him out. Tell Bates to get one of the regulars to help him take Hobbs back to his room in the hotel. Then he and Voller are to go back later and search the room." Higgins took a golden eagle from his leather purse and passed it to Peretz. "This should cover the drinks."

The big barman grinned. "From what I seen of Mr. Hobbs already it should cover it easy."

CHAPTER TWELVE

As Ben walked back with Judd to the stable, he said, "I'm sorry you weren't able to meet my father. He and Michael have gone to Cheyenne to collect a windmill."

"A windmill?"

"Yes, it's for the K Bar ranch. They've had a mining engineer drilling for water on their land, and he says he has found a permanent supply. The trouble is it's an awfully long way down. This windmill is just the thing for bringing it up, apparently. It's called Halladay's Iron Turbine, and it cost a lot of money. Anyway, Michael got the job of transporting it from the railway at Cheyenne, and Father has gone along to help make sure it arrives safely."

"K Bar," said Judd, "That's east of here as I recall?"

"That's right. The Barratts. They have fenced off their land on this side from just outside the town, past the farm land to the south, and right along their boundary with the Oxyoke - that's over nine miles of barbed wire. On the far side it's still open range right over to the Mannion brothers at Tomahawk."

"They ever have trouble from the farmers?"

"No, their fence makes for good neighbors. In fact the only trouble we ever get from those farmers is here in town, when cowhands feel like letting off steam, and then it's only fistfighting and soon over."

As he saddled up Palmer's horse, Judd said, "Tell me about this Cattlemen's Association, Ben."

"Yes, it has been going on for about a year now. Matt Watkins started it up, and now all the ranchers around here are members, although I believe Ken Barratt wasn't too keen to join."

"So what's it all about?"

"Well, I don't know all the details, but one of their rules is that all cattle in the area are branded with registered brands - and the only registered brands are those of their members. They built drift fences along the boundaries of what they all agreed was their open range, and now they reckon any cattle found within those fences must belong to one of their members. They don't recognize any unregistered brand, and anybody who finds an unbranded animal is not allowed to keep it."

"That's hard," said Judd. "Branding mavericks is generally regarded as cowhand's bounty,"

"Not around here," said Ben, "In fact at first, they said that anyone who wasn't a member couldn't own any animals at all, but a lot of cowhands already owned their own horses, so they had to concede that point."

"But not having a chance at the mavericks could make any self-respecting cowpoke mighty sore, I'd say. Enough to reckon he was due some compensation, mebbe?" Judd suggested.

"Ah!" Ben was quick to see the implication. "You mean the rustling! Of course!"

"Well, it's a notion to study on. And there's another thing. Fran was telling me Sten's cattle have all gone, taken off when DD cattle came through our place. I doubt our old Circle S brand is registered. Guess I'll have to talk with the Cattlemen's Association before I get them back."

Homer Foreman came in from the street.

"Just been getting my warbag together," he said. "Sheriff told me to saddle up that horse you brung in, Marshall. On'y he said not to call you Marshall, right?"

Judd grinned, "Right," he said, offering his hand to the old man. "Judd is what I answer to."

"Glad to know you, son," said Homer, taking his hand in a surprisingly firm grip. "Your uncle and me was acquainted. We sat and smoked a pipe a time or two. He was a regular kind of gent."

"Have you got everything you need?" asked Judd. "There's no telling how long you'll be away."

"Well, as to that, I'm fixed like I was holing up for a siege," said Homer, "And I've got my old Spencer 56-56, and I'm taking along this here six-shooter." He handed an ancient Walker Colt to Judd for examination. "On'y one I ever had. A soldier gave me that back in eighteen and forty-seven, said he took it off a Mexican. Didn't say where the Mexican got it."

"Quite a few notches on the handle," said Judd.

"In memoriam. Injuns. `Paches mostly."

"Yeah? Well, you keep it holstered unless it's right-up necessary, you hear me? This is a real quiet little chore you hired on for. And that reminds me, talking of Indians, you got any renegades around here?"

"We haven't seen any for a couple of years," said Ben, "But Tom says he has seen tracks in the hills behind Double Diamond range."

"Todd Berman reckons there's a small band out north of his place," said Homer, "And a feller come into the livery a week or so back, said he was camped off the trail back of NHK and a coupla braves come nosing around. Scared em off, so he said."

"Todd Berman, that's Star B?" said Judd.

"Right." said Homer. "His range stretches from just north of here right up to Palmer's barb wire and then over the creek to the west of the ridge from your place."

"Yesterday I came across a young squaw, and I guess that would be some way north of Star B. She was hurt quite bad. She said she'd been set on by two white men but got away. She described them to me. One was short, fat and bald, with broken teeth, the other was younger, tall, with a big, black beard, and rode a white horse. Mean anything to you?"

Ben thought for a moment. "It could be Vin Foley and Lou Dessay. They were often seen together. Foley's short, fat, bald, with bad teeth, and Dessay is about six foot tall, long dark hair and beard, and rides a white horse. They used to work for Watkins but he got rid of them. They were trouble-makers. Foley has a reputation with a pistol, Dessay prefers knives. I haven't seen them around though and I assumed they'd left the district."

"Sounds as though maybe they didn't go too far." Judd stepped up into the saddle and looked down at the deputy. "Thanks for the tea, Ben. I guess I'll be back in the morning. Any messages for the Palmers?"

"Just say Ben sends his regards."

"Right. I'll ride on out of town, Homer," said Judd, "Give me about five minutes and then find your way by any roundabout route to the Tinkers Creek trail. It's not likely you'll be followed, but it's best we're not seen together in town. I'll lay up and wait for you someplace. Adios."

TINKERS CREEK

CHAPTER THIRTEEN

About five miles out from the town, at a place where the trail crested a low hill, Judd pulled off into a clump of trees and waited. Looking south he had a good view of his back trail for a mile or more, and almost immediately a rider came in sight traveling at a steady trot. Judd watched him approach, the horse making easy work of the long, shallow climb, its shoulders and legs relaxed and its hooves slapping down almost of their own weight. Homer was making time.

Judd pulled out to meet him as he drew level. "Nobody following," he said, "You made good time."

"This here's a mighty fine mount," said Homer. "I reckon he could trot along steady all day and travel fifty, sixty miles with no more than a healthy sweat, and then do the same tomorrow. Don't know how long a rider could stick it though. Makes your muscles ache trying to ease the jolts, and it warms up calluses on your ass you forgot you had."

Judd smiled, "Recognize his brand?"

"Hell now, you can't blame a hoss for his branding! But this here Ladder B could cover 'most anything."

"My thinking exactly. A genuine rustlers" brand. But if that's so, I'm puzzled why a rustler would want to take a shot at a little ole dirt farmer like me."

"Well, could be he was just one of them fellers that'll do

102

any dirty job if the price is right," suggested Homer.

"Yeah," said Judd, "But I reckon Sten was killed because somebody thought with him out of the way they could get hold of the homestead land. Then I show up so they've got to get rid of me in a hurry. Could be a connection, the folks that are after the homestead are doing the rustling too."

"Well, it's been spread around that them farmers from Tinkers Creek are to blame for the rustling," said Homer, "And it's no secret the Cattlemen's Association want 'em out."

"From what I've seen." said Judd, "Palmer's folks have been too busy of late to spend time away from the Settlement."

They rode on in silence for a while, and then Judd said, "It'll be nigh on dark when we get to the Settlement, so we'll ride on through to the homestead - you've hired on to work for me, savvy?"

"Well, it ain't too much of a lie."

"In the morning I'll take this horse back to Palmer, and you can pin on your badge and set off to find the cattle - if they're still there. If not you'll have to trail them. How well do you know the country up there?"

"Don't know it at all, but that don't signify. Most places I been to the first time I didn't know either."

As they crested the last hill before the Settlement, it was still light enough for Homer to be suitably impressed by the sturdy six-foot fence running for over two miles in each direction. Trees and scrub had been removed from the outside giving no cover within thirty yards or more, all the way along.

Judd gave the big iron triangle a couple of hefty blows, and after a few minutes Jim Hallett rode up to let them through. He took a long look at Homer's horse.

"Ain't that the dead feller's hoss?" he said.

Judd said, "Yes it is - on loan from the Sheriff's office.

And this here is Homer Foreman. He's taking a job with me. Say hello to Jim Hallett, Homer."

"Howdy, Mister Hallet," said the old-timer, "Mighty fine fence you folks have put up. How far does she run?"

"All the way round, 'bout fifteen miles, and every inch of it watched. We ain't invitin' company."

"What about the other end, Jim? Can we let ourselves out?" said Judd.

"Morgans and Canliffs look after that end. Milo Canliff's in charge. Their place is just off the trail. Ya see it just after ya come over the rise. They got orders to let ya through whenever."

"OK. Thanks. And tell Clem Palmer I'll bring his horse back in the morning. Oh, and uh," Judd dug into his vest pocket, "Have a smoke on me."

It was about four and a half miles through the Settlement lands to the boundary with the Petersen holdings. From the trail the buildings of some of the original homesteads could be seen from time to time. Many had been burnt down, none showed signs of habitation, although in places the land was clearly being cultivated.

Homer commented on this and Judd told him about the buildings back at Palmer's.

"But ain't they supposed to actually live on their quarter sections?" he asked.

"According to the 1862 Act," said Judd. "A man has to build a habitation on his land, live in it for certain months each year, and farm forty of his acres for five years. At the end of that time he gets title. Most of these homesteads must have been proved up by now. Palmer's Cooperative, as he calls it, must have bought them from the original settlers. Like Sten did with the two places south of ours."

"Uh-huh," said Homer, "Makes sense, I guess. If you're a settling man. Which I ain't."

Milo Canliff himself came out to intercept them as they came down towards the fence on the north side. He paused facing them at the edge of the trail, resting the stock of his carbine on the ground, both hands gripping the muzzle.

"Howdy," he said. "I'm Milo Canliff. I seen you coming. You the feller Petersen, kin of Sten?"

"Yeah," said Judd, "And this is Homer Foreman. He's hired on to work with me."

"Uh-huh. Tom Hallett said you was back. You gonna stay, then?"

"I guess I'll be around for a while."

"What about Fran? She staying too?"

"She hasn't told me she wants to leave."

Canliffe looked hard at Homer, and then at Judd's tied-down guns.

"If she's staying, she's sure gonna need a lotta help. She'd do better to come in with us. She needs proper protection, wouldn't keep on getting shot at. Besides, we could really make something of that place."

Judd smiled. "Yeah, Clem Palmer said something about that. I guess it's a thing we're going to have to study on." He edged his horse forward towards the gate. "This is one of his horses. I said I'd bring it back in the morning."

Milo took the hint and opened one side of the gate.

"Okay. Just tie it here to the gatepost. We'll pick it up. And any time you want to get through, just come down and holler or whistle."

Judd thanked him and they went on their way.

On both sides of the trail the land was divided into neatly fenced paddocks, all empty of stock. Judd said, "Fran told me

Sten bought this place and the one over there to the east when they left".

They came past burnt-out farm buildings. "Family called Manczur lived here, Grampa, Pa and Ma and two girls. Looks as if they were smoked out."

"I recollect Sten tellin' me about it," said Homer. "They woke up one night and found everything afire, house, barns, stables, the whole caboodle. Must have been done a purpose. The two younguns saved the plow horse and a yearling but they lost the saddle horses. Terrible thing. Sten took them in while they got theirselves together. I guess he gave them a fair price."

As they approached the homestead, Homer sniffed the air.

"This here's turning out to be a real interesting day," he said. "First I gets me a vacation in the hills and a badge to go with it, next I gets a mighty fine mount, and now I'm danged if I don't smell bear sign!"

Fran had been baking and she had a batch of doughnuts ready to follow pork and vegetables, with a pitcher of coffee, hot and strong, to wash it down.

Judd introduced Homer, who expressed his condolences about Sten's death.

"Him and me got along," he said. "He was real fond of you, ma'am, and mighty proud of the little feller."

"Thank you, Mr. Foreman," said Fran, "He spoke well of you, too."

The two men sat and ate, and while Fran unpacked and put away the supplies, Judd explained, between mouthfuls, how circumstances had changed since he'd left that morning. Then Homer went to see to the horses, before bedding down for the night in the room over the stable that had been Jack Marnier's.

Judd said, "Fran, that feller you shot, Sheriff tells me he'd only been in the area a few days. I'd seen him in the Drovers the morning before, but he didn't know me and I guess he didn't know you either, so someone else sent him. But, my, that was some shooting, Fran! He never knew what hit him."

"Well, I never wanted to kill no-one, but he was just a cold-blooded bushwhacker like the one that killed Sten, so I can't feel sorry. You know, when I came home that day and found Sten lying dead in the yard, and little Joe curled up beside him, something inside me turned to ice. I don't know if it'll ever thaw out."

"Joe was all alone with Sten?"

"Yes, and Sten had been dead some time. Joe must have cried himself to sleep. He didn't understand. He kept asking for Pa for some days, but I guess he's accepted now he won't see his Pa ever again."

Judd gave her the letter he'd collected from the post and telegraph office.

"It's from the lawyer in Louisville," she said. "It's dated just over two weeks ago so I guess they must have sent it pretty soon after they got mine."

She read it through a couple of times. "He says title has been established in my name for everything Sten left to me, and in yours for your folks" holding. So legally there is no problem over ownership and I was right in staying. And he says: In view of the manner of Mr. Petersen's death and of your anxieties about the reasons behind both previous and subsequent harassment, we will undertake to enquire on your behalf about the possibility of plans for development of Government land in your area. Meanwhile, in order to ensure that your interests are properly protected you would be well advised to show this letter to your local statutory legal authority".

She smiled and passed the letter to him. "I guess that'll be you now then, huh?"

"Well Fran, this letter and those deeds and things may turn out to be real valuable," said Judd. He was wondering how to put it to her that her home was no longer a safe place to keep such property. He need not have worried though, her thoughts were running along the same track.

"And this place sure ain't fireproof," she said, "And the cellar won't keep out the kind of varmint that'd want to get hold of them. But there's other places. When things started to get real bad a few months back, Sten reckoned we should have somewhere to fall back on if we ever got driven out of here. He showed me a good place up the valley a piece. He said me and the boy could hide out and be safe there for days, weeks maybe if right up necessary. I guess a strong box would be safe there, too."

"Well, it won't hurt to be careful," said Judd. He yawned suddenly and stretched. "Guess I'll turn in now, Fran, it's been a long day."

She smiled. "It's been a good day for Joe and me," she said, "Getting some support takes some of the weight off my mind."

Judd stood up and went to the door.

"I've aired the bed in your old room," she said, "And your clothes are washed and dried in the closet. Goodnight. And, Judd, thanks for coming."

Back in the room he'd used as a boy, Judd relaxed in the comfortable bed. He closed his eyes and reflected drowsily on the events of the past two days, but as he drifted into sleep the image uppermost on his mind was the smiling face of a pretty young woman with violet-blue eyes and dark curly hair.

CHAPTER FOURTEEN

A little head of curly yellow hair was peeping round the doorway when he opened his eyes in the morning.

"Howdy, pardner," said Judd, smiling.

Joe ran in and galloped the model wooden horse along the edge of the blankets right up to Judd's nose. Judd sat up and growled and the boy ran out of the room, laughing.

Fran called from the kitchen, "Hot water in the bath-house if you want to shave. Ham and eggs when you're ready."

Refreshed after a sound sleep, washed and shaved and dressed in his own clean clothes, Judd needed only a hearty breakfast to make him feel fully restored.

While he ate he told Fran that he wanted to get Homer out to the rustled cattle as soon as possible. "And on the way I ought to take a look at that safe place of Sten's you were talking about. Maybe take the strongbox with me, and any other valuables, what do you think?"

Fran agreed and said she would make up a bundle for him to leave there. This was mainly spare clothes for herself and Joe and a few household items.

She said the safe place was seven or eight miles beyond the great rock wall, one of a series of caves high up on the north-east side of one of the canyons that opened near the end of the valley. Sten told her he'd found it by chance many years before. He'd been hunting in the high mountains and was coming down the canyon on his way home when he was caught in a sudden storm. Looking for somewhere to shelter, he spotted a wide overhang in the canyon wall so he headed across, dismounted and led his horse under - it was just high enough to take a standing horse.

While he waited for the storm to ease, he went to sit on a rock at one end of the overhang where it went back about ten feet, and there, at the side, he noticed a large hole, like a doorway, partly blocked by rocks. Curious, since it looked as if the rocks might have been placed there deliberately, Sten started to clear them. As he worked he could feel a current of cool air against his face and he soon made an opening wide enough to squeeze through.

Inside he eased cautiously forward, into what appeared to be a short passage curving gradually downwards and widening, and he felt his way carefully along the rock wall until he could no longer see ahead. He struck a match and saw that he was at the end of a wide tunnel which opened out into a cave. The floor was even and quite smooth and the air, which seemed to come from the back of the cave, smelled clean and not at all musty or damp.

Fran said she'd been to the place a couple of times with Sten. The first time they had explored further into the cave and found an exit into a grassy hollow. There was about an acre of grass and a seep of water at one side, and it was hidden from sight except from the very top of the mountains to the west. The second time was a few days before Sten was killed. They had been able to clear enough space from both openings to lead a horse through to the grass, and they had left a cache of emergency items on a ledge high up on one wall.

She drew a map with directions to the cave, and then, as she made up a bundle for Judd to take with the strong box, she said, "It's real dark in there so we left a lamp on a big bit of a rock just inside."

Meanwhile Homer was taking Palmer's horse back. By the time he'd returned, Judd had saddled up the big buckskin and was getting ready to leave.

Fran brought the bundle and the strong box and a packet of sandwiches each for them.

Judd packed his saddlebags and as he mounted up, he said, "Fran, I'm taking Homer with me to that cave so he knows how to find it if need be. He'll go on to those rustled cattle from there. Then I'm going to ride on over and see Matt Watkins."

"Really?" she said, "You better be careful then. You won't get a friendly welcome."

"Yeah, well, I know there's always been ill-feeling between the Watkins and us but somehow I don't reckon any of the cattlemen would want this land bad enough to kill Sten for it. Bringing cattle here from Watkins side is a quite a trek over a deal of bad land, and as for Star B, they can't get to us without going through Palmer's Settlement."

"Butch was quick enough to take advantage soon as Sten was killed," said Fran.

"Their cattle didn't stay long though, did they. I reckon he was just making a point, or maybe he was being a bit hasty. In any case neither DD nor Star B used the upper valley before we came and as I remember they were always glad to buy the hay the farmers made. Saved them the trouble of making it themselves."

"So what do you reckon?"

"I don't rightly know, but it won't do any harm to clear the air with the old man. Besides they have eighty head of your cattle now."

"Yes, can't afford to lose them. Shouldn't worry though, they're all branded, Circle S."

"Registered brand?"

"Sure is. Sten made the Cattlemen see sense on that."

"That's good. And if they're out on the range they'll be okay, I guess. Anyway, there's no hurry to get them back here, is there." He looked down at her. "I'll be back as soon as I can. Meantime I don't guess I have to tell you to keep a real good look out."

For the first few miles Judd and Homer rode at a steady lope beside the creek. When they reached the place where Judd had found the injured Indian girl they crossed over and he told Homer all about the encounter, pointing out the route they had taken.

"About a mile upstream there's a wide bend to the west. You'll see a well-used game trail leading up the canyon wall. Follow it all the way up and over the ridge. My tracks are only a couple of days old, should still be plain to see until you come out of the trees. After that it's all rock and shale so just keep heading for a high spur right ahead. That's where I left the Indian girl. When you get near the base of that spur you'll make out a deep notch in the mountains to the south. You can't mistake it. Go through the pass and down the canyon headed due west. When you see the stream, that's when I reckon you should start keeping a sharp look-out. Follow the stream for about a half-hour and you'll come to where I found the first bunch of cows." He paused, "You get all that?"

"Follow your tracks, lose em in the rocks, head for a high spur, go through a pass in the south, west down a canyon, follow the stream and find them cows."

112

"You got it."

They crossed back over the creek and continued on their way to the hide-out cave in warm sunshine. After the end of the valley the going became much rougher and they walked their horses steadily up the steep incline for about half an hour until they found the canyon. Here they were several thousand feet up and it was cooler with a gentle breeze coming down from the higher mountains.

Fran's directions were clear and accurate and they had no trouble in finding the place. They dismounted, tethered their mounts to big rocks and went inside.

Judd struck a match, found the oil lamp, removed the chimney and lit the wick.

Sten and Fran had cached their emergency stores on a ledge high up at one side. Judd climbed up and passed everything down to Homer and they checked each item: two cooking pots and an empty canteen, Sten's old long gun, wrapped in two blankets bound up in a worn slicker, and an army issue haversack containing an oiled and fully loaded Colt .44, boxes of shells for the long gun, matches, candles, an old spyglass, a hatchet and a sheathed skinning knife. It was all in good condition.

Along the wall back from the entrance, there were heaps of logs and kindling wood.

"Looks like Sten thought of most everthing," said Homer, as he passed it all up for Judd to put back safely on the rock shelf, including the strong box and the bundle Fran had given him.

Judd climbed down and took the lamp. "Fran told me there's another way out."

He moved further in to where the floor started to slope gently downwards. Homer joined him.

At the back of the cave a wide passageway curved away to the right. The height varied considerably but was always well above a man's head, and the sloping floor was uneven and littered with rocks but the air was cool and fresh.

"I seen caves like this when I was prospecting for gold," said Homer. "They reckon some time hunderds a years back, flood waters from the winter snow-melt musta gouged out channels in the softer rocks, right through from one side of a ridge to the other. Don't look like there's bin much flooding here though for quite a while. These walls don't even feel damp.".

They went forward straight ahead for two or three minutes and then came to where there was a long bend to the left. After a while they could see a glimmer of light before them and soon the passage way opened out again into another cave. They took time to listen, then stepped out and looked around. There was no sign of recent occupation by anything apart from a few small lizards, basking in the sunshine just inside the wide opening. These scuttled away as Judd approached.

He looked down a gentle slope into a bowl-like depression in the hillside, about two hundred yards across. It was mostly rough grass and small bushes, with a bright green area to one side, which, upon investigation turned out to be moss and other bog-plants growing where water was seeping out. Homer made his hands into a bowl shape and pressed them into the seep until they filled with clear water. Raising his hands to his mouth he took in a mouthful, swirled it around and swallowed.

"Good water. Real sweet," he said.

"Sten sure found the right place for a hide-out," said Judd as they walked back up to the cave.

"Couldn't better it in the summertime. It'll be durn cold up here in winter though."

"Yeah, well, let's hope we never have to use it."

They went back through the cave. Judd blew out the lamp and put it back where he'd found it. As they unhitched their horses, he said, "I'll come back down the valley with you as far as the creek. Then I'll head off across to the hills and aim to hit the Fort Collins trail where I came off it. I've never been to the DD ranch, but I know more or less where it lies and I guess it'll be signed off the trail."

"I been there a few times," said Homer. "Hit the trail from the town as you say, and you can't miss it. You see it off the high points about a mile to the east, set in a pretty little dip in the hills. Big ranch house painted white. Been added to over the years, by the look of it. Picket fence all round. Corrals, stables and bunkhouses about coupla hunderd yards away, far enough for privacy, I guess. And post and rail paddocks on all sides. All of it looks well kept up too."

"Right, thanks, just a matter of finding the trail then," said Judd. "On my way to the homestead the other day I must have turned off too early to see it, I guess."

They rode back down the mountain in single file, Judd leading, until they reached the wide, shallow canyon from where Judd had followed the branch of Tinkers Creek downstream two days earlier.

He said, "This is where I'll leave you. Now, when you get to where I found that first bunch of cows – it's about a hundred acres of grass, roughly in a circle, with a few tall pines; if they're not there, there'll be plenty of sign – go "round to the south side and you'll see where they were driven in. Back-track their trail about a mile and there's another set of tracks branching off to the east. Follow them and you'll find where the second bunch was. I didn't look any further."

"Well, from what's been spread around, most every

cattleman has lost more'n a hunderd head. Chances are there's more stashed away nearby. I could scout around for sign."

"Okay, but make sure you don't leave any. Thinking about it, though, it makes sense for the rustlers to hold them in bunches up there till they've got enough for a big drive. To get them to market they'll have to drive them to the railroad and it surely wouldn't pay to make a lot of small drives."

"Be too risky, too."

"Right. So if the cattle have been moved, it'll be easy to trail them. If not, hole up somewhere and wait, see what happens. I guess a week wouldn't be too long. Whatever you do though, I'm counting on you keeping out of sight. Okay?"

"Nobody won't see me but the Good Lord Hisself, and He'll have to look good and hard. And I'll keep a weather eye out for them braves your young squaw said she was with, too."

"Yeah, but I shouldn't think they'd trouble you. I reckon they'd just want to be left alone."

"Mebbe, but Indians can be notional."

"Well, okay, I'll leave that to you. Let's hope you won't have to wait too long to see some action on those cows. Adios."

CHAPTER FIFTEEN

Judd set off across the valley, back-tracking the route he'd taken two days earlier. After about two hours he came into a region of long, rolling hills that broke into sharp bluffs and he recognized this as the area where he'd turned off the Fort Collins trail to avoid the Double Diamond land. This time though, the ranch was his objective and he pointed the buckskin to a fold of the hills in the north and set off at a fast lope. When he came closer he could see the trail going through the grass along the slope of the hill to his left, then climbing towards the summit where it entered a stand of evergreen trees. These stood out in contrast against the brilliant blue of the sky, with puff-balls of white cloud above.

At the top of the slope he halted in the shade of the trees, a refreshing breeze stirring the horse's mane. He looked down across wide meadows so green it almost hurt his eyes. There were no cattle to be seen, though, and he guessed this land would be left for winter pasture. Thinking about the rustling, and knowing that Matt Watkins claimed over sixty thousand acres as his range, Judd figured that the ranch would be hard put to spare enough hands to patrol such a wide area against organized rustlers who could pick and choose time and place at will. He wondered about telling old Matt about the cattle he'd found in the mountains, but decided that might hinder his plan to follow them when they were moved.

The trail appeared to continue straight ahead through the grass towards the next hill, about two miles away. On the slopes, pine trees and juniper were dotted darkly among bright greens of oak and aspen. A small patch of white just over the eastern rim of that hill caught his eye and he recalled that Homer had said the Double Diamond ranch house was painted white and he would see it from the high points of the trail. It was too far away to be certain and he urged the big horse forward once more.

When he came over the top of the next hill he noticed in the distance a wide track leading down off the trail in the direction of the white object. He dismounted, and trailed the buckskin's reins, allowing it to graze freely. Taking out his field glasses, he lay down behind a little grassy knoll and looked down over the gently sloping land along the line of the track. After about a mile a tall archway carried a large white, "M on W" facsimile of the Double Diamond brand. He'd found his objective.

Just beyond the arch the track divided. His eyes looked left to a wide triangular open space, and he identified stables, a big, open-sided hayshed and corrals along two sides, and a blacksmith shop next to a large combination bunkhouse and cookshack on the other. The right fork led upslope through an avenue flanking post-and-railed paddocks to the sprawling white house standing in splendid isolation against a dark backdrop of evergreens.

He'd not given much thought to how he would approach the Watkins family. Now he decided to make his visit look official and he took out his badge and pinned it on. Even so he knew they would be unlikely to welcome him. The incident involving the death of his father and Jack Watkins, Matt's eldest son, may have taken place twelve years ago, but it was still a painful memory. He just hoped old Matt would hear him out and maybe answer a few questions.

He went back to the buckskin and picked up the reins. The horse turned its head and pushed at him with its nose. He caressed it, saying aloud as he remounted, "Well, here goes, Buck old boy. I guess the worst they can do is turn me away."

As he approached the fork in the track to the ranch, two men walked out from the lefthand side. One stepped forward, raising his hand in greeting.

"Howdy, Marshall. What can we do for you?"

"Names Petersen. I'd like a word with Mr. Matt Watkins if at all possible."

"What's it in connection with?"

"In the first place it's about cattle rustling, but there's also a personal matter."

"Okay. If you'll just step down, Burt here will see to your horse and I'll walk up to the house with you. You won't need your guns."

"I'm not authorized to travel without them," said Judd, smiling as he dismounted. He left his Winchester in its scabbard, though, trusting that it and saddle bags belonging to a US Deputy Marshall would be safe enough in an establishment so clearly displaying its respectability.

"Mr. Watkins is a mite touchy about firearms in the house," the man replied.

"Yeah, I can understand that," said Judd. "I guess I would be too."

The man gave him a quizzical look as Burt led the buckskin down towards the stables.

"First time a Marshall's ever come out here, I reckon.

"Bout time something was done about the rustling. That sheriff sure ain't making no headway."

"What's the set-up here?" said Judd, as they moved off.

"I'm John Stainer," the man said. "I'm in charge around the home buildings. Foreman is Butch Watkins, he's the old man's son, but Rich Collins does most of the actual ramrodding. He reports to Butch and they kinda decide together what gets done. Rich'll be the one to tell you about the cattle."

"I understood Mister Matt Watkins was still in charge," said Judd.

"Well, gee, he's the boss right enough. I'm just talking of the day-to-day work. The old man gets out and about, same as he ever did, and he'll come down hard on Butch if things ain't as they should be."

For its last hundred yards the track to the Double Diamond ranch house widened, opening into a broad carriageway along the front of the main building. It was lined with well-grown oak trees, clearly planted to provide an avenue of shade for the future. At the far end of this driveway, a clump of mature cottonwoods was surrounded by mown grass, inset with well maintained flower beds.

The main structure of the house was a two-story block of stone, mortared and lime-washed, with a pair of tall windows at ground level either side of the central doorway, and five slightly smaller windows across the upper floor. Two single-story matching wings of heavy timber, painted white, were set back a few feet from the main building, the whole being built solidly into the slope behind.

Judd was highly impressed by the setting. He felt Homer had done it scant justice by merely saying it was pretty.

John Stainer led Judd around to a door at the side of the nearest wing of the house. He knocked hard, opened the door and called. An elderly man in a black suit came in answer. Stainer explained Judd's errand and then went away.

The door opened into a small room with shelves and coat-hooks along the facing wall. A large, bare wooden table was the only furniture.

"I must ask you to let me have those guns before you come in, Marshall," the old man said. "Mr. Watkins is most insistent. And please wipe your boots on that mat."

Judd wiped his boots carefully, unbuckled his two belts and handed them one by one to the old man who put them on a shelf.

"Follow me, please, and I will tell Mr. Watkins you are here."

He led the way to a pleasant sitting room at the back of the house, and invited Judd to take a seat.

Judd went to the window which overlooked yet more lawn and flower beds, bordered by a thick hedge beyond which junipers and tall pine trees covered the rising ground. He waited, feeling slightly apprehensive.

"Well, well," said a deep voice behind him. "I never thought to see a Petersen in my home."

Judd turned. He'd only ever seen Matt Watkins from a distance.

In the doorway stood a big man in his early seventies, over six feet tall, with wide, heavy shoulders, narrow hips, some thickening around the waist but in better shape than many men half his age. He had a large Roman head with thick white hair, pale blue eyes, deeply tanned skin, and, Judd thought, an oddly sensitive look like that of a man who had been deeply hurt.

"Good of you to see me, Mr. Watkins," said Judd.

"Curiosity, much as anything. Don't reckon a US Marshall would come out here just on a rustling matter. Wondering what's really on your mind."

Judd smiled, acknowledging the man's direct approach. "Yeah, well, I have been given leave to help Sheriff Kramer tackle the rustling, and I am interested to know what you think. But you're right, there is something else so I'll get right to it. I want to find my uncle's killer, but more than that I want to find out why he was killed."

"And you think I might know?"

Judd shook his head. "I guess it's more a matter of elimination. Alright, there's been bad blood between our families, but it was a long time ago and you've come a long way since then – what I can see here today confirms that - so it makes no sense to suddenly start it up again now for no reason."

Still standing in the doorway, the old cattleman looked back at him with hard eyes. "Go on."

"You see, it looks like whoever killed him wants our land, but I can't see how Double Diamond would benefit from it."

"Well, I can tell you that. I was going in for the sale. I had a notion to take it over and set up one of my men there to run it for me, separate from the main ranch. There's six thousand acres of good grass the other side of that rock wall and it could raise some prime beef."

"I see," said Judd. "Fran Healey thinks that way too. That's why she wants to stay."

"Yeah? What's she know about cattle?"

"I can't say, except she and Sten seemed to have given a deal of thought to it."

"Well, she won't be able to do it on her own. You gonna let her stay?"

"It's not up to me. It's her own land, everything except my parents" place. Sten left it to her. I've seen the will. And, she's put a claim in on the quarter section just north of the wall, too."

Old Matt raised his eyebrows in surprise. "Well, well. Sounds like she's quite a woman. Not one of your fancy gals like her sister." He nodded approvingly. "She did right not moving out. So what are you gonna do? You gonna go in with her?"

"I'm studying on it. But first I've got to find out who shot my uncle and why."

"Yeah, right." Matt looked hard at him for a moment as if considering, then he nodded, making up his mind. He came fully into the room and pulled on a red cord hanging by the side of the chimney breast. Then he took a box of cheroots from the mantleshelf, offering it to Judd who took one with thanks. They both lit up.

CHAPTER SIXTEEN

Moving to sit in one of the armchairs, Matt motioned to Judd to take a seat opposite.

The elderly gent came into the room.

Matt said, "Coffee?"

Judd thanked him and the old man retired silently.

"When I heard Sten Petersen was shot dead," said Matt, "I wondered. Couldn't figure it out. I sent my boy Butch – you met him yesterday, he married her sister – I sent him to see her, see what she would do. She told him you were a lawman some place, and he told her to send for you and sit tight till you came."

"So she said. And the same afternoon he drove a herd of your cattle right through the homestead, taking her cattle with them."

"Yeah, that Butch, he acts a mite hasty at times."

"Eighty head, she says, and she hasn't seen them since."

"Yeah, eighty head is right. Hereford crosses. Interesting. Mostly good young stock. Got them bunched in a canyon off our western range."

"What're you figuring to do with them?"

"Not sure now the sale's off. I would have taken them on - at a fair price. They're fine cattle, should do well. Make you an offer for em, unless you want me to drive em back?"

Judd smiled, "I don't think Fran would want to sell them, but on the other hand, short of turning them out on the grass beyond the wall, there's not much we could do with them as things stand. How would it be if we leave them where they are for now?"

"There's plenty of grass and water. Can't spare any hands to watch over them, though. Got enough to do covering all our range, and we're still losing stock."

"Yes, well, that's the other thing. Any ideas on that?"

"Nothing for sure. All the ranches have been hit, Star B, K Bar, Tomahawk, even Oxyoke and NHK. Trouble started soon after that farmer, Palmer, came back. Brought a lot of hard cases with him, look like they'd steal anything wasn't tied down. Got no way of proving it though, "less we catch em in the act."

"I doubt it's them," said Judd. "From what I've seen, they're too inward-looking. They seem to have one fixed notion, building their own township and fencing off all comers."

Matt snorted. "Nesters never minded helping themselves!"

"But Palmer's men just wouldn't have time for organized rustling, and that's what it looks like to me."

"I won't argue with that. We've lost over a hundred all told and Star B about the same, mostly twenty, thirty at a time. Some of the others say they've been hit more than once, too."

"So whoever is taking them could have a fair-sized herd by now. How do you reckon they get rid of them?"

"Well, they'd be plain foolish to try and sell them in any cattle town south of Cheyenne. All the brands are too well known. My guess would be they'd try the Oregon Trail, say, Ogallala to Laramie."

"Yeah, but they'd have to hold them until they had enough to make a drive. That is, always supposing they sell them for meat, which is most likely, I guess. But it could be someone wants to build a herd the quick and easy way, someplace way back in the mountains where they could use them for breeding stock."

Matt drew on his cheroot and looked hard at Judd. "Funny you should say that. My top hand says most of the rustled stock was heifers in calf. Very few steers or older cows have gone."

"Does he have any theories about who takes them – apart from nesters?"

"Well, yeah, a coupla times near where the cows were taken from he reckons he cut a fresh trail of a feller used to work for me. Followed it up but lost it in the rocks both times."

Judd took his notebook from his vest pocket and flipped through it. "Would the names Vin Foley or Lou Dessay fit?"

"Yeah," said Matt in surprise, "It was Dessay's horse. Got a long, uneven stride, puts down its near hind covering the print of its near fore every third time or so. You know him?"

"The names came up in the Sheriffs office."

"They would. They're a coupla trouble makers. I fired both of em."

"They'll know your range pretty well, then? Well enough to know good places to lay up in?"

"Yeah, that's right." Matt scowled. "And if it is them they'll know the trees they'll hang from when I catch em!"

"I dare say Sheriff Kramer will want any rustlers he catches to face a trial," said Judd, mildly.

"Well, he'll have his chance, but if my men have any say in it they'll hang any thieving critters we catch on our range. It wouldn't be the first time, either."

Judd raised his eyebrows. "Is that right?"

"Mebbe you think I shouldn't say that to a marshall, huh? And mebbe you're right, but we're out on a limb here and for a good many years we had to make our own justice. Habits die hard with some of us.

"Think on it. My men all ride for the brand and they're proud of the work they do. They sure as hell don't want to lose stock to these dirty, rustling coyotes, so when they find em on our range they'll shoot first and ask questions later, if at all. And if they catch any of em they won't want to ride miles looking for a judge."

Judd nodded. "I've rid the range and I know what you mean, but times are changing."

"Well, that's true, sure enough. When I came here in forty-one there was just the army, a few trappers, prospectors, drifters and the like, passing through. And Indians. Next nearest white folks was fifty miles away and they had to go another day's ride to find a sheriff. So when we caught thieves we hung em ourselves. The town grew some and we had a town marshall, Charlie Reynolds the barber, honest enough, but all he was ever good for was settling little arguments, jailing drunks, that kinda thing. Any real trouble, the town council would meet and talk it over, see what should be done. But the government opened up the country, and more and more settlers moved in. The town got to the size it is so the county agreed we oughta have a law officer. That's how we came to get Kramer."

"I understood that was your doing," said Judd.

"Town council decision."

"But you run the town council."

Matt ground out the butt of his cheroot in an ashtray and glared at Judd. "Mister Marshall Petersen," he said quietly, "I run Double Diamond ranch." He emphasized the words run and ranch.

"Yes, and it's by far the biggest ranch for miles around," said Judd. "I reckon it brings in a lot of business to the town. The town council would be respectful of that. They'd know that what's good for DD and the cattlemen is good for the town. That adds up to the same thing in my book."

"Listen, there's five other men in the council," He held a hand up, fingers extended and counted off. "Charlie Reynolds and me set it up, then there's Ken Barratt as the other cattleman, Sam Cowan as the other townsman, Bradman for the farmers, and Higgins as the lawyer. All of them can say their piece. I'm only one voice."

"So you're saying Tom Kramer has a free hand to run the sheriff's office as he thinks fit?"

"Sure he has. He's the government man. Else there's no point in having him."

"He says he thinks you believe every man can be bought, and he isn't for sale."

Matt frowned. "That what he told you?" He sighed. "That'll be Butch. He's gotten the idea that Palmer shouldn't fence off our range from Tinkers Creek Crossing, and he tried to get Kramer to raise a posse and pull it down. Kramer wouldn't do it, so Butch offered him a coupla hundred dollars. Trouble with Butch is he has the flint and steel to spark off an idea but he ain't got the kindling to fuel much thinking."

Judd was surprised at Matt's frank speaking. He said, "Does that mean you don't go along with that idea?"

"Listen, I can read sign as well as the next man. We tried for years to get rid of those farmers. Thought we'd won when Palmer moved out. Then he came back with papers showing he owned all that government land. Lawyer Higgins checked the papers and said it was all legal. Then Butch took a dozen hands over there to pull down the first lot of fencing they put up. Didn't stand a chance. Soon as they got within range, Palmer's men opened up with rifles. Three of my men were hit, not badly but they couldn't do any work for a while, and I lost two good horses. So, what do I read from that? I should hire myself some gunslingers and start a war? And lose more men and horses that I can't spare because I need em to stop my cattle being rustled, probably by the same damn farmers? And for what? We don't even need Tinkers Creek Crossing. Palmer can keep it. That answer your question?"

"Yeah, I guess it does, but it raises another - why you let your son loose in the first place."

Matt looked at Judd in disbelief. "You've got a damn nerve, marshall or no marshall."

"Okay, but on the one hand you say you see the need for law and order, and I believe that, but then you let Butch take a bunch of your men to break up other people's property."

"It wasn't a matter of letting him do it. Butch is hasty, acts on the spur of the moment. It was all over before I knew about it." He sighed, and then added bitterly, "Things might have been different if his brother had lived, but Butch is the only son I've got – your uncle made sure of that!"

Judd stood up. "While we're kicking over dead ashes we can recall that that was after your other son killed my father."

Matt stood and faced him. Both big men, they looked eye to eye with each other.

After a long moment Matt broke the tension. Turning away he said, "You and me, we both lost something that day." He touched Judd lightly on the shoulder and moved to the doorway. "Let me know how things are going with the cattle rustling – there's usually someone from the ranch in town. If you need any help, the Cattlemen's Association will back you up. I can let you have riders for a posse, and I'm sure Todd Berman at Star B will do the same."

"Thanks. Let's hope I have to take you up on that."

"Well, it's good to see the law taking some action. You

going back to town now?"

"Yeah, Tom Kramer will be glad to know he can raise a posse when necessary."

Matt nodded. "He can tell Todd Berman and Ken Barratt I suggested they join in, too. And listen, don't trust that Palmer. He didn't bring in those hard cases for no reason."

Judd was ready to accept that Matt was bound to be biased against the farmers. He said, "He offered to take us into his Cooperative, as he calls it, but I can't see him as any kind of threat."

"No? Well, think on this: there's just two ways now to get to your place if you don't go through Palmer's fence - from the top end of the valley the other side of that Rock Wall, or along the old Indian track that crosses the west of our range. When Butch went out the day after your uncle was shot he had a scout around. He said he picked up no sign as he came along the old track and there was none through the gap in the Wall. If I was you I'd wonder about that."

"I see," said Judd thoughtfully. "Yeah, that's sure worth keeping in mind. Thanks."

Matt paused as he started to leave. "You can tell Fran Healey her cattle can stay on my range till she's ready for 'em."

"Okay, thanks, she'll be glad to know that," said Judd. "Mind if I check up on them on the way to town?"

"Sure, but it's a far piece off the trail." Matt thought for a moment. "I guess you'll be going back to the homestead tonight?"

"Yes, Fran's still all on her own out there and I've got a feeling whoever wants us out ain't about to give up. They'll have another try and next time I want to be ready for them."

"Yeah, well, you could come back that way and you'd miss Palmer's place as well. The cattle are boxed in a canyon about a coupla miles off the old track. Over on your right you'll see a place where we burned off a big area of scrub a year or so ago. Two or three hundred acres. Can't miss it. Just after that there's a stream comes out of the canyon. I'll get Butch to draw you up a map."

"Thanks. Well, it's been real interesting talking to you Mister Watkins. I feel a lot easier in my mind now."

"The interest is mutual, marshall. You've come a long way in the ten years since you left. Oh. I nearly forgot!" His face creased in a slight, sardonic smile, relaxing for the first time since they had met. "Butch's wife saw you coming along the track. Said she'd like a word with you before you go. D'you want to see her?"

"Uh, yeah, okay, I guess so," said Judd in surprise.

"I'll send her in." Matt nodded a farewell and left him.

CHAPTER SEVENTEEN

While he was waiting, Judd wondered what Cassie could want to say to him. He had no particular wish to see her, any feeling he may once have had for her having long died away. At first he'd felt betrayed by the way she'd spurned him for the attentions of Butch, but he soon realized that to her he'd never been anything more than a casual friend, a boy whom she was pleased to think admired her. Now she meant no more to him than any other respectable married woman and he would treat her accordingly.

After a short while Cassie came in and walked directly up to him, in that quick, light-stepping way she always had.

"Hello Judd," she said, smiling, offering her hand.

He took her hand briefly. "Howdy, ma'am," he said.

She was much as he remembered her. The family resemblance with Fran was clear, but whereas Fran would be described as a big, strong, handsome woman, Cassie was dainty, soft and prettily feminine, like a fragile little doll. He could see what had attracted him when he was growing up, but she looked as if she belonged in a smart drawing-room in a big city, not here on a cattle ranch.

"It's been a long time," she said, looking up at him and smiling faintly.

"Sure has."

"I worked it out. It's ten years since we last met."

"Yes. What did you want to see me about?"

His abruptness startled her but she quickly recovered.

"Why, I thought we might talk a little, that's all. We were friends once weren't we?"

"I reckon I must have thought so."

"And my husband did say you asked to be remembered to me."

"So I did, ma'am, so I did." Judd smiled. He could hardly tell her he was only mocking Butch when he'd said that.

"You have come from Kansas, I believe."

"That's right, ma'am."

"And how long have you been marshalling in Kansas?"

"Long enough, I guess."

She looked disconcerted at his unfriendly answers and he was suddenly ashamed of his churlish behavior. He said, meaning it, "You know, you look just the same as I remember you."

"It's kind of you to say so," she said. "But I cannot say the same of you." She stepped back and looked him over appreciatively. "I remember a nice, polite, and shy farmer's boy who used to come and see me every time he came to town. And now look at you."

"Well, ma'am, I guess that nice, polite farmer's boy is still in here somewhere. He's just liable to forget who he is, time to time."

"Does he remember always asking for a drink of cool water every time he called?"

"Yeah, and you always fetched me a glass of your Ma's barley water. I loved that drink."

She smiled. "I can offer you something a little stronger nowadays."

She crossed the room to a highboy and stood on tiptoe to reach down a bottle and glasses.

"Armagnac brandy; Butch favors it," she said as she poured. "Shall we sit down?"

Judd murmured his thanks as she handed him the glass.

She sat in the chair her father-in-law had used, leaning back and crossing her legs, swinging her free foot back and forth. Although Judd knew she was several years older than Fran, she looked younger, more girlish, and demure in a neat white shirtwaist and full black skirt. The sunlight from the window behind her made a bright gold corona of her hair. But the faint lines around her eyes and mouth indicated sadness and disillusion, and he wondered about that.

She took a sip of brandy. "Did you come to see Butch's father about the rustling?"

"That's right, ma'am. And to clear up a question or two about my uncle's killing."

She took another sip and said, without looking up from the glass, "And how is my little sister?"

"Well, ma'am," said Judd, trying to choose his words carefully, "I guess Fran's as good as a body would expect, things being how they are."

"Yes, I suppose it must be difficult for her."

"Yeah, difficult about covers it. Could be easier, though, if she had a little more support."

Cassie looked up sharply. "It was her choice to side with the Petersens."

"I don't know that she took any sides, ma'am. As she tells it she didn't have many choices after your father died."

"She could have come here. Butch made the offer but she chose to listen to Sten Petersen. Much good it did her!"

"But your Pa and Sten were old buddies. You remember

that, don't you? You girls had both known Sten since you were little. He was like an uncle to you."

"Some uncle!"

Judd stared at her wondering why she was so ill-disposed towards her sister and Sten. Was it just bigotry, because Fran had had a child out of wedlock?

"Well," he said, "All I know is the Healey household was like a second home to me when we came to town, on account of our parents being such good friends. Seems only natural Sten would want to help."

"Yes, but that wasn't all he wanted, was it! Out there all alone on his homestead he took advantage of her. The least he could have done was marry her after the baby came along!"

Judd stood up, putting his brandy glass on a side table. "If this is all you wanted to say to me, ma'am, I'll thank you for the brandy and I'll be getting along."

"No. No, I'm sorry. Please don't go. I really would like to know about Fran." She smiled up at him through long eyelashes, "Does she know you were coming here?"

"Yes. I told her I was coming."

"What did she say?"

Judd shrugged and said, as he sat down again, "She just said to be careful."

"No, I mean about me."

"About you? All she's said to me about you is the two of you haven't spoken since before the boy was born."

Cassie looked down, toying with the glass in her hand. "We were never very close like sisters ought to be. She used to spend all her time with Pa and the horses, wasn't interested in anything else. Ma said one time, it was like she was trying to be the boy Pa always wanted. Anyways, she was not like me at all and we never did talk much. I guess I've never really known her." She looked up at him again, her expression intense, yearning. "But she is the only real family I've got. Her and the baby. What's he like, her little boy?"

"Why, he's a mighty good-looking little feller. Big for his age, I'd guess. Favors his mother for sure – got her blue eyes and yellow hair, and I'd say he'd be real quick to learn. He cottoned on to me quick enough. But I reckon he still misses his Pa."

"I wish I could see him!"

"You don't have any little ones of your own?"

She looked away. "No," she said, "No, it doesn't … I mean, we haven't, well, we've not been lucky, so far." She turned back to him with a slight smile, and shrugged. "But, who knows? Perhaps, one day?"

Judd realized that her seeming hostility towards her sister was possibly due to envy that Fran had so easily conceived a son, while she herself was still childless after nearly ten years of marriage. He got to his feet again. "Well, ma'am, it's been very pleasant but I ought to be on my way. You want me to take a message to your sister?"

"Could you tell her she's still welcome to come here to us if she wants? She'd be well looked after here. Her and little Joe."

"Alright."

Cassie pulled a red cord hanging by the mantleshelf. "William will see you out." She moved towards him and offered her hand again. "Goodbye." She turned and smiled over her shoulder as she went out. "I hope we can meet again," she said.

William, the elderly man in the black suit, came in and escorted him back to the room where he'd left his guns.

Judd was inspecting them before buckling his gunbelt back on when Butch Watkins came in.

"You sure musta sweet-talked Pa," he growled. "He told me to draw you up a map." He slapped a sheet of paper on the table. "This shows how to get to your place from town along the old Indian track across our west range. Take a look."

It was a neat, well-drawn map and Butch leaned over the table, pointing out various features along the route, including the canyon where he'd left the Petersen cattle.

"From there on," he concluded, "If you're going back to your place you can either follow the tracks the cattle left when we brought them back the other day," He swept his hand across the paper in a wide arc, "Or you could carry on another two, mebbe three miles and then cut across to the west about here, where the Indian trail bends north. That'd be quicker for a rider on his own." He pushed the map towards Judd and stood up. Looking Judd in the eye, he said aggressively, "Pa says you don't reckon on Palmer rustling our cows."

"I think it's unlikely to be his people," said Judd, mildly.

"Hah! You've only been back five minutes, what do you know!" He strode out of the room

"Thanks for the map!" Judd called after him.

William said, "There will be someone waiting with your horse at the stables, Marshall." He ushered Judd towards the outer door. "Good day to you."

CHAPTER EIGHTEEN

How far is it from here to Twin Springs?" Judd asked as he collected his horse. "I came here across country," he explained.

"I guess it must be the best part of twenty miles," said Burt, the stableman. "But the trail is easy and there ain't no call to stray off it."

Judd was puzzled. "Stray off it?"

"I mention it 'cos we've got most of the herd down that way now, Marshall, so you'd best ride careful. The hands will be on the lookout for any stranger crossing our range and they'll be trigger-happy, on the idea if you ain't one of our riders you must naturally be a rustler."

"I see. Okay."

This seemed to confirm that Matt Watkins had been serious about his men dealing with rustlers themselves, and Judd recalled Tom Kramer's warning to him when he'd set out for the homestead two days previously. But Judd had often known danger. In the western lands there was much to live for and gain from, but there were many ways in which a man could die: stampede, the bucking of a wild horse, long miles under a blazing sun without water, the settling of disputes by gun. It was a price a man paid for a way of life, the freedom, the space and the opportunities.

He had no intention of wandering away from the trail

though, and he set off at a steady trot. He knew the capabilities of his horse very well, and he reckoned that allowing for occasional changes of pace and a short stop to eat the sandwiches Fran had put up for him it would take him a little under two hours to get to the town.

The sun was high overhead as he came up to the rise with the stand of evergreen trees where he'd paused on his way to the ranch. This was a good place to stop and eat. He moved into the shade of the trees, dismounted and tied the buckskin loosely to a long horizontal bough.

Apart from a slight warm breeze which carried a scent of pines and occasionally cedar, it was utterly still, the only sound that of the horse as it snuffled among the stringy, dry stems of grass around the edge of the trees. Judd took off his Marshall's badge, put it in his pocket, and sat with his back against a broad tree trunk, facing the trail as he ate.

He was glad he'd had his talk with Matt Watkins. The man had impressed him as honest and straightforward. He'd agreed that the rustling appeared to be carried out in an organized way, but he'd not pointed a finger at any of the other ranches. Judd was pretty sure that if Matt had suspected any of them he'd have taken some sort of action himself by now.

So given that the rustling was organized, who was behind it? The two men Matt had fired, Foley and Dessay? But again, Matt would have said if he'd thought they were anything more than small fry.

What about others in Twin Springs? Bates, Higgins, Shepherd? He'd have to talk to Tom Kramer and Ben to get more background knowledge.

And then there was Palmer, of course. Judd just couldn't see how the Cooperative would be directly involved in stealing cattle, but what Matt had hinted to him about the possible route

139

taken by the gunman who shot Sten was interesting because it implied that Palmer had at the very least allowed the killer access through the Settlement, and therefore would be aware of who he was. If that was so, then Palmer was in some way connected with whoever had planned the killing. Maybe the killing, the rustling and the Cooperative were all linked in some way? It was something to study on, he thought.

He finished his meal with a drink of water from his canteen, untied his horse and mounted up. The buckskin was eager to go, and well within the two hours they were entering Twin Springs.

Judd rode through the town to the livery stable where he asked Isaac to feed and water the horse, groom him and put him in a stall for a while. Then he took his Winchester and saddle bags and walked back up to the sheriff's office. A thin gingery-haired man was lounging in the doorway of the lawyer's office next door. Judd remembered seeing him before and nodded a greeting.

Tom and Ben were drinking coffee as he entered. He put his gun and saddle bags in an empty cell while Ben went to the stove and poured a cup for him.

Tom said, "We was wondering when you'd show up. Palmer give you any trouble?"

"No. But I met Milo Canliff last night - he's in charge at the far end - and he brought up the Cooperative idea again. Pointed out that Fran wouldn't keep getting shot at if she went in with them."

"Sound like a warning, huh?"

Judd took a long swallow of coffee. "Yeah, kind of."

Tom Kramer shook his head slowly. "Palmer makes no secret he wants the place but I can't see him shooting your uncle Sten to get it, can you?"

"Well," said Judd, "I guess I'll keep an open mind on that for now."

He brought them up-to-date with Fran's situation and her wish to stay at the homestead even at the risk of being attacked. He described the hide-out in the hills and then went on to tell them of his meeting with Matt Watkins.

Kramer said, "You reckon Watkins could be on the level then, huh?"

"Yeah, I guess I do."

Kramer did not look convinced but was not going to argue the point.

Judd said, "I'd have thought you'd give him credit for offering us back-up from the Cattlemen's Association when we need a posse."

"Yeah, right. Talking of which we had Pete Johnson of Oxyoke in here earlier. He says he's lost more cattle and enough's enough. He wants the town council to meet with the Cattlemen's Association and decide what to do about it, and he wants me and Ben to be there."

"Did you tell him about the cattle I found?"

"Nope. Figured if you'd a mind to you'd tell him yourself. Had no call to mention you at all, him not knowing you're a Marshall an" all."

"Okay, but I wore the badge when I went to Double Diamond, so I guess it won't be a secret for long."

"Did Homer get off alright?" said Ben.

"Yeah, he's on his way to find the cows, probably found 'em by now."

"Good."

Kramer said, "We've had a happening here in town. Fella, called himself Hobbs, came in yesterday some time after you left, asking for the Petersen place. Said he'd come from

Louisville with something special and it was very important. Mean anything to you?"

"Hobbs? I don't know any Hobbs. From Louisville, you say?"

"That's where he said he'd come from."

"Must be something to do with Sten's lawyer that's acting for Fran over the will and stuff," said Judd.

"I told him you'd be in town today and he could leave whatever it was here if he liked, but he said he'd get a room at the hotel and wait till you came in. Only thing is, first thing this morning he was found there, dead of a broken neck."

Judd stared. "First thing this morning? And he was waiting for me? Seems mighty odd that he'd die right now. Any idea how he came to break his neck?"

"Yeah, I have, but Doc says he could have done it falling out of bed. Me and Ben asked around and it seems he was in the Drovers last night, drinking pretty good and talking more than was good for him. He kept saying he had a story to tell that would make a lot of folks in this town sit up and take notice. Then he got into an argument somehow with Carl Voller and Voller knocked him cold. So then Billy Bates called Voller off, and he got a DD cowhand who happened to be in there to help him get the Hobbs feller back to the hotel."

"I spoke to the Double Diamond fellow," said Ben, "And he assured me that Mr. Hobbs was quite alright when they left him in his room, just a bit groggy and feeling sorry for himself."

"And nobody saw him after that?" said Judd.

"Not till the maid found him this morn'ng."

"What about this 'something special' he's supposed to have had?"

"Well, we gave the room a good going over and searched all through his gear," said Tom, "Not that he had much, but what there was had nothing to do with the Petersen place." He paused. "So we kinda figure if he did have a special story to tell mebbe he didn't break his neck falling out of bed. Mebbe somebody didn't want that story to be told."

"Uh-huh. And who would that be?" said Judd. "Have we any ideas?"

"Well, yeah." Tom nodded, took out tobacco and papers and started rolling a cigarette. "Seems to me it's kinda interesting that it was Billy Bates took Hobbs to his room. Bates don't have no history as a Good Samaritan and I wondered about that, specially as it was his sidekick, Voller, picked the fight in the first place. Why would Bates take the trouble to clear up for him?"

"Yeah. Good point. Who does Bates work for, do we know?"

Judd was sitting facing the street door and he'd been aware for some time of an odd-shaped shadow on the floor just inside it. In view of the position of the sun at this time of day the shadow puzzled him. Then it made a small movement, and raising a finger to his lips to indicate silence, he moved swiftly to reach around the doorway, grab the listener by his vest and pull him into the office.

"Way, hey!" yelled Sandy, as he was propelled across the room and dumped into a chair.

"Well?" demanded Judd, standing over him. "You heard what we were wondering about. What do you think?"

Sandy cowered down, looking up at him, eyes wide in shocked surprise. "What?" He turned towards Tom and Ben. "Hey Sheriff, I ain't done nuthin'!"

"Now then, Sandy," said Tom. "It's a fact there ain't no law agin' listenin' at doorways, leastways not in this town, but it ain't a real neighborly thing to do, now, is it?"

143

"I warn't listenin', Sheriff, I jus' happen to be passin' by."

"Is that a fact? Well okay, now you're here mebbe you can help us some."

Judd stood back so that Tom could talk directly to Sandy.

Tom said, "We were talking about the fellow who broke his neck in the hotel last night. Mr. Hobbs. You hear about that?"

"Yeah. Got drunk and fell outa bed."

"Right. You in the Drovers at all last night?"

"Yeah. Had a beer and a game or two of cards."

"Did you happen to see the fellow in there?"

"Yeah. He kept shootin' his mouth off, somethin' about shakin' up the whole town." Sandy looked back at Judd, warily. "Said it was about the Petersen place."

"He got into a fight too, didn't he? How did that happen, d'you know?"

"Carl Voller said somethin' to him and he took a swing at Carl and Carl popped him one."

"Then what happened?" said Tom.

"Well, Billy Bates told Carl to knock it off. Then him and another fella picked the guy up and took him outside."

"Yeah, that's what we heard too. D'you have any idea why your friend Billy might go to all that trouble?"

Sandy frowned. "Billy Bates ain't my friend, exactly, Sheriff."

"Oh. Well, glad to hear that." Tom paused as if considering. "But you're a fella that don't miss much, Sandy You generally know what's going on around town. Now, suppose someone might have asked him to look after Mr. Hobbs, who d'you think that would be?"

It was Sandy's turn to pause and consider. He knew who he thought it would be of course, but should he tell them what he and Colin Cheswell had come to suspect about Higgins? After all, Higgins was a useful source of a few extra dollars from time to time and he was always easy to fool. On the other hand, Petersen, who was standing right next to him, staring at him menacingly, was a real dangerous kinda guy. Wouldn't do to cross him, specially, if he'd heard it right, as the fella was actually a US Marshall.

Anyway, there was no harm keeping in with the sheriff, so he said, "Well, I don't know it for a fact, Sheriff, but I figure mebbe Lawyer Higgins coulda ast him."

"Lawyer Higgins, huh? Don't see it myself," said Tom. "Why d'you say that?"

"Cos just lately whenever I seen Billy go in the law office, something happens right after."

"Yeah? How d'you mean? Give us a for instance."

"Well, okay," Sandy looked uncertainly at Judd. "When Mister Petersen here, uh, when he first come here and, uh, Carl Voller picked a fight with him in the Drovers, Mr. Higgins sent for Billy in his office and after that I saw Billy talking to Mickey Mason and then Mason rode out of town. Well, next thing was Mister Petersen brung him back, shot dead. Me and Colin Cheswell figured it out."

"What did you figure out?" said Tom.

"Well, we kinda thought it was all tied in, see."

"You thought Higgins told Bates to tell Mason to go after Mister Petersen?"

"Right."

Judd said, "Who's Colin Cheswell?"

"Higgins's clerk," said Ben.

"You're buddies, are you, you and this Cheswell?" said Judd.

"Yeah."

"So you get to know what goes on in the lawyer's office?"

"Not exactly. But we see who comes and goes, and we kinda watch and see what happens."

Tom said, "So what else have you seen that ties Lawyer Higgins in with Billy Bates?"

"Well after Mickey Mason was brought back, Mister Higgins sent for Billy again and they had another talk in his office. Then Cole Cheswell had to collect a parcel with his name on it from the bank and take it Billy's room at the hotel. We figured it was a parcel of money."

"Higgins was paying Bates to do something?"

"Yeah."

"Okay. Was this before or after Hobbs came on the scene?"

"This was early on. Hobbs didn't turn up till late, did he?"

"That's right. So it wouldn't be payment for looking after Hobbs?"

"I don't reckon Mister Higgins knew about Hobbs then."

"So how come you reckon Higgins asked Bates to take care of him?"

Sandy was beginning to enjoy being the center of attention.

"Well, see, it's like this, Mister Higgins and Vic Peretz is in cahoots."

"Peretz is the name of the barman at the Drovers," Ben interrupted, for Judd's benefit.

Sandy went on, "When this Hobbs came in the Drovers shooting his mouth off about the Petersen place, Vic sent me to tell Mister Higgins about it. So then Mister Higgins wants to talk to Vic. When Vic gets back to the Drovers again I seen him talking close with Billy and Carl. Then Carl starts the fight and Billy stops it and takes Hobbs back to his room. See? It all ties in, don't it?"

"It sorta follows," said Tom, "But what about the broken

neck?

Sandy shrugged. "Well, Billy'd know what room Hobbs was in."

"You mean if somebody went back later. Yeah, it all adds up." Tom looked at Judd. "Whaddya think?"

"I think Sandy here knows it pays to keep his eyes and ears open. Thing is though, who pays him and why was he listening at this door?"

"Ain't nobody pays me!"

"You run errands for Higgins and Peretz for nothing?"

"Well, Mister Higgins buys me a drink, time to time, that's all."

"You tell him what's happening around town and he buys you a drink, that it?"

Sandy shrugged. "Yeah."

"D'you have any idea why he wants to know what's going on around town, or what he does with the information you give him?"

Again Sandy wondered how much he should say. He decided on discretion, looked down at his boots and shook his head. "Nope. Not really."

"Reason I mention it is, according to what you've just told us, two people have died after you passed information on to Higgins, first Mason, then Hobbs. That make you feel good?"

Sandy looked up at Judd, startled at the thought. "I never meant nobody no harm!"

"But you're a part of it, like it or not. Now, I'll ask you again, why d'you think he wants to know what's going on?"

Sandy inspected his boots again. "It ain't just him. Cole and me, we reckon he's taking orders from someone."

"What makes you think that?"

"Cos whenever he thinks things ain't going his way he

scoots over to the bank building. And that's all I'm saying." Sandy got to his feet. "I never meant to come in here in the first place, Sheriff, and you can't make me stay here no longer."

"Okay, Sandy," said Tom. "And we won't tell a soul about our little talk, so long as you do the same. Get me?"

"Sure." Sandy sidled past Judd to the door and scuttled off toward the Drovers.

Judd said, "As you said, Tom, Sandy's idea about the Hobbs business makes sense. Someone went to Hobbs's room in the night, broke his neck to keep him quiet and took the letter."

"Yeah," said Tom. "I can't see Higgins as the boss man here though. He ain't got it in him. Sandy's right, he's working for someone else, and that bit about scootin' over to the bank building was interestin' 'cos he didn't mean he was goin' to the bank. There's a fella called Leo Marburg lives in the upstairs rooms. He owns the building. He came here about a year ago and nobody knows much about him but he gets on alright with the folks in the town. Reynolds, the barber, told me the other day he thought Marburg had bought the Tomahawk. I'd heard the ranch had money problems - the cattleman's store was owed a lot and the bank was gonna foreclose - but their bills are being paid on time nowadays. Maybe Reynolds was right."

Ben said, "Gwen Palmer has met Mr. Marburg. She says he is always very nice and polite when he comes to see her father. He talks like a gentleman from the east, she says."

Judd went to collect his gear from where he'd left it in the empty cell.

He said, "Well, fellas, I'll have to leave you to follow up on the Hobbs business. I came back to town to fill you in on Fran's situation and Matt Watkins" support for a posse. If the Oxyoke do get the Cattlemen's Association together with the town council, we might need to stall them until we hear from Homer, okay?"

"Sure," said Tom. "You two are the only folks who know where any of the rustled cattle is at anyway, so we won't let anything go off half-cock. But look here Judd, if what we heard from Sandy means anything, the Petersen homestead should be what matters most. Whatever Hobbs was carrying, Higgins and Bates are clearly in some sorta racket that means enough for Hobbs to be killed for it. We don't know who else might have a finger in the pie, and you might need someone to ride along with you back to the homestead."

"I guess I'd feel happier knowing you fellas are looking after things this end, following up on what we've found out," said Judd. "As I told you, we're ready to move out if right up necessary, and that'll be the time when we need back up. Anyway, I'm taking a roundabout route back through the DD range, calling in to check on Fran's cattle that Butch Watkins took away. I guess I'll be seeing you when Homer has some news about the cattle. Adios."

CHAPTER NINETEEN

Judd followed the clear directions on Butch Watkins's map and in due course came to the canyon where Fran's cattle had been left. It was still very warm in the early evening sun as he rode around, eventually accounting for all eighty of them. They had stayed at the far end of the canyon and seemed to be in good condition. There was plenty of water and enough grass to keep them there for several days yet, so he felt confident in leaving them for the time being.

Continuing along the route Butch had suggested, he came, after about three miles, to a curve in the trail where it headed north. Sure enough, a well-used game trail forked off westwards, dipping down for a couple of hundred yards through long grass before fording a shallow stream and leading up into pinewoods in the direction he needed to go. He turned on to it and dismounted at the stream.

The water ran fast and clear over rocks, and he let the horse have a long drink while he filled his canteen and studied for tracks. Indians still came this way occasionally it seemed, judging by faint marks of unshod hooves all but obscured by prints of deer and other creatures.

A short distance upstream a dipper sat on a rock next to a miniature waterfall. It cocked its head towards a potential meal at the stream's bottom, bobbed once and disappeared into the foam at the base of the waterfall, then came up suddenly almost at his feet.

Judd smiled at its tameness. He re-mounted and rode on and when he reached the shade of the trees, he slowed his horse to a steady walk and took off his hat to fan his face. It was cool here and very quiet, the only sound the soft thud of the buckskin's hooves on the dead pine needles. The trail was narrow but clearly defined, leading always upwards, and as they plodded along he recalled his brief talk with Fran.

Between the two of them they owned five quarter sections, or eight hundred acres, which in itself was quite a good-sized spread for a homestead. Add to that the use of ten square miles of grass in the upper valley, watered from the creek, and there would be a fair chance of building a prosperous future if only the current problems could be sorted out. This was good country. A man could make a good life here if he was strong and willing to work. Yes, he thought, his parents and Sten, had after all, chosen well, settling in this part of the land.

His thoughts thus distracted, he became aware suddenly of a subtle alteration in the buckskin's manner. The horse had noticed something different and it might be dangerous. Like any rider alone in the wild places of the west he'd learned to depend not only on his own instincts, but also on the sight and hearing of his horse, to know its moods and to be aware of any change in its behavior, however minor. He looked around carefully. About a hundred paces ahead of him, standing perfectly still against the trunk of a large tree near the edge of the trail, an Indian was silently awaiting him, rifle in hand. A little further along another appeared, then another ... then yet another. There were probably more back in the trees.

Judd slowed a little, shucked his carbine and laid it across his saddle. As he approached he made the sign for friend, lifting his right hand, palm facing out, making a fist, then raising the index and middle fingers together and placing them beside his face.

The first Indian stepped forward holding his right hand up, palm facing out, a universal sign for stop. The others waited, making no move.

Judd brought the buckskin to a halt.

The Indian moved closer, walking around the horse, studying it carefully. Apparently satisfied, he stopped in front of Judd, looked up and said, "Who you?"

"Petersen."

The nearest of the others grunted and said something in a low voice. Without looking back the leader replied with a monosyllable. Then, pointing at the horse, he said, "Snow Flower."

Judd nodded, looking serious. "She okay?"

"She good." The Indian nodded back, then said something in a loud voice.

The others approached and stood in a semi-circle a few paces behind him, muttering among themselves. There were seven altogether. Judd noted that two others also had rifles.

"Me Tutokwox," said the leader. "Your people say Bear Claw. Where you go?"

"Home. Back to homestead."

"Him Petersen, old man, young squaw, little man, bright hair, you brother?"

"Brother of my father," said Judd.

"Him dead," said Bear Claw. "No more beef. You man there now?"

"Yeah," said. Judd. He looked steadily at them all. Then, staring directly into Bear Claw's eyes, he said, "Their friends are my friends. Their enemies are my enemies. It is good if Bear

Claw is their friend and mine."

"It is good you speak peace with Bear Claw. This land is our land. You go now."

Bear Claw moved back and said something to the others, who clustered around him. They spoke among themselves, glancing at Judd from time to time, then moved off, back into the trees. Bear Claw turned at the edge of the trail and watched Judd ride away.

Relieved that there had been no trouble, Judd rode on up into the hills, through the tall pines, scattered here and there with birch or aspen along the slopes, until the land leveled out onto a plateau. Here the terrain changed, becoming full of rocks and shale and scattered dirty white bluffs and crags with long streaks of brown and rust-red, carved by wind and rain into strange shapes. On wide shelves of rock stunted trees grew from scattered crevices wherever there was space to take root.

He rode down long corridor canyons, his horse's hoofs echoing against the walls until finally, coming out around a finger of rock onto a wide slope of boulders and shale, the trail lost itself in tracks left by a herd of cattle. He guessed it must be the herd Butch had driven back from the homestead.

After a couple more miles something glistening in the far distance caught his eye. He drew up and took out his field glasses. It was light from the setting sun shining on a window in a small building, and suddenly he recognized Sten's original cabin nestling beneath the great rock wall north of the homestead. He had arrived.

After leaving Judd that morning, Homer had quickly picked up the tracks Judd had left two days earlier when leading his horse with the Indian girl on it. They were easy enough to follow up the length of the canyon, through the trees along the side of the ridge and over it until, as Judd had warned, they'd left the old track on the far side of the ridge and moved on to the rough, broken land to the west. He soon saw the tall, rocky spur Judd had described and headed out toward it. It was high up here, pretty close to ten thousand feet, or so he'd heard, but he'd spent a lot of time in the mountains, both as a trapper and in more recent times prospecting for gold in company with Sam Cowan, and he felt comfortable here, in fact, if truth be told, more at home in these places than he felt down in the towns.

Although he did not expect to come upon the rustlers just yet, he was mindful of the possibility that the band of Indians the girl had come from might still be around, and the region did seem to be perfectly laid out for ambush. He scouted every bit of country before he rode across it, looking for distant points from where he might be observed, and studying the lie of the land so that nobody might lay a trap for him. It took time but he was in no hurry, being only concerned with arriving alive and fully active at the place where the rustled cattle were hidden.

In due course he arrived at the pass through the deep v-shaped notch to the south and moved down the canyon to the stream, keeping an even sharper lookout now that he was getting close to the place where Judd had found the first bunch of cattle. Every now and then he picked up signs of Judd's progress. Judd had not known any reason to disguise his passage at the time and his buckskin's hoof prints were easy to recognize.

It was very hot in the bottom of the canyon. The sun was directly overhead and when Homer came up to an area of big, old trees he decided it could be a good place to stop for a while. He looked carefully around. Not far from the stream a few large trees had been blown down in the distant past, and there were tangles of fallen branches and some mossy old tree-trunks.

He watered the horse and picketed him on grass at the stream's edge. Then he took out the sandwiches Fran had put up for him and found himself a comfortable place to sit in the shade on one of the fallen tree-trunks. When he'd eaten enough he drank some water from his canteen, stood up, stretched, went back to his horse and packed his food away.

He was getting ready to re-mount and ride on when he thought he heard a cow lowing in the distance. He listened and heard it again and realized he must be close to one of the rustled herds. He led the horse back into the trees and tied it out of sight, took up his rifle and went on cautiously on foot.

After half a mile he saw that he was coming to the canyon's entrance leading out to the flat, grassy area surrounded by pine trees where Judd had found the first bunch of cattle.

They were still there and he approached slowly, watching and listening all the while, but there was no sign of human presence. Moving carefully among the cattle, he checked brands, keeping count as he went. Of the adults, all cows, he made it thirty Star B, and twelve Double Diamond and there were thirty-five unbranded youngsters of varying ages from a few days to several weeks. Obviously the rustlers were targeting young stock and pregnant females, no doubt intending to put their own brand on the youngsters in due course. All the animals looked to be in good condition and there was enough grass to keep them settled for a while yet.

He walked back to his horse, rolled himself a cigarette and lit it, leaning against the side of the horse while he smoked and thought about what to do next. Judd had told him to keep out of sight and watch and wait until the cattle were moved and then trail them, but the idea of waiting and doing nothing did not sit well with Homer at any time. He decided to focus on finding as many of the stolen cattle as there might be hidden away, and while he was doing that there was a good chance he'd find where the rustlers were camped too. Above all, though, he'd scout around for a good place to hole up.

He mounted up and keeping to the trees, he rode around the cattle and found the tracks they'd made when they'd been driven in. These sloped gently downhill, and after about half a mile another set of tracks branched off and up the mountain-side to the east, just as Judd had said. There were no signs that cattle had returned this way, but he decided to investigate.

The land here was a vast jumble of grass-covered slopes, pine-crested ridges and deep canyons, a wild and lonely place where no man seemed to have come, were it not for the evidence of driven cattle.

Aware that sound carries far in the clear mountain air, Homer moved cautiously through the trees, keeping his ears tuned for any unnatural noises, until he came to the edge of the thickly wooded area. Staying well back he looked down onto a long trough of grassland surrounded by trees and dotted with cows and calves. This must be the second herd that Judd had told him about and it was much bigger. He watched for several minutes. The cattle were too far away for him to identify brands and although there seemed to be nobody about in the long valley, the country was much too open for him to risk being seen riding amongst them.

He went back through the trees and continued, riding parallel to and above the tracks. until he came upon a place where the ground had been churned up a great deal. Various sets of tracks led into this central area and some were newer than others, but only one other set led out. It looked to him as if this was where the rustlers had brought each batch before moving them on.

Here the slope of the land was shallower and after

following for about half a mile he saw that the cattle had spread out more widely as they approached an area dotted with bushes and trees and occasional clumps of more substantial woodland. It was as if they had been left to find their own way from there on.

Homer had never been a reckless man, never taking any risk that was not demanded by circumstances. Much of his life had been lived where caution was the price of survival and being the man he was, he'd survived. He'd seen other men take chances and he'd helped to bury them, but he was reasonably sure that if he scouted around from here he would pick up the trail of the men who had herded the cattle and this would lead him to their camp, so he now rode very slowly, using every bit of terrain that offered cover, in case anyone should happen to be on the lookout.

But despite his best efforts the few traces of riders that he did find were widely scattered and led in no consistent direction. The cows had evidently moved on several weeks before, and Homer decided to follow their sign until he came in sight of them. He liked the clear, cold air and felt the excitement of the hunt, recalling his days as a trapper and later, scout for the army.

The way undulated but tended generally downward, and at last, coming out from a stand of pines he found himself facing a wide green slope, several hundred acres of grass, stretching away toward a dark canyon off to his left, and on his right, around a short promontory that rose upward from the lower slopes of the mountain and ended in a steep fall. Cattle were spread out around the mouth of the canyon.

That promontory would be a good place to look out over the lower ground, he thought, provided he kept under cover himself. He headed along the mountain toward it and tied his horse well back among the trees. Rummaging around in his saddle bags he found his moccasins and his old spy glass. He took off his boots, slipped the moccasins on his feet and set off.

The first part was difficult uphill walking through thorny scrub and broken rock. He crawled slowly up the last part and, flat on his belly, he peered over the rim - and there it was, only a quarter of a mile away to his right, a neat little camp tucked away among trees at the bottom of a steep slope, facing the grassland.

A couple of small wooden cabins were set at right angles to each other, about twenty feet apart and some fifty feet from a stream. Washing was hanging from a line stretched across the space in the angle between the cabins. He took out his spyglass for a closer look. There was a fire going in the middle of the open space, a blackened kettle hanging over it and a coffee pot in the coals. A tall man with long dark hair and a beard was leaning against the door frame of one of the cabins, smoking. Homer guessed it could be Lou Dessay. Another fellow was sitting against the wall beside him, dozing in the late evening sun, hat over his face. Three horses were picketed nearby. One of them had a snowy white coat like Dessay's horse.

It was a very quiet and peaceful scene. The cattle were scattered widely over the grassland across the stream from the cabins. Homer reckoned there could be about two hundred head, and although it was too far to see to be sure, he guessed they, too, would be in good shape. This was one of many mountain parks common in this part of the Rockies. The grass here would be about two weeks behind the lower valley grass and would not be as tall but it was just as nourishing.

He studied the situation with care and concluded that there was nothing to be gained by going any closer for the moment. He'd achieved what he'd set out to do and the best course of action would be to go back to his horse, hunt a good place to set up a base and return at first light.

CHAPTER TWENTY

Easing back off the rim of the promontory, Homer looked back at the mountainside. It continued northward as a hogback, a ridge several thousand feet high, mostly timbered with aspen and mixed conifer, the side facing him rugged and in places almost sheer. He had to find a way to get behind the rustlers" camp. It would not be easy.

He made his way back to his horse, taking his time. At this altitude it was not good for man or horse to hurry.

He stashed away his spyglass and his moccasins, put his boots back on and rode slowly through the aspen along the side of the ridge, studying the country for a place where he could set up a base. It had to be somewhere he could get into and out of without sky-lining himself or showing up plainly, where he could build a fire that could not be seen, and preferably not too far from a source of fresh water. It must also be safe to leave his horse to graze unobserved.

When he reckoned he would be directly behind the rustlers" camp he went toward the top of the ridge, but it was too much of a scramble for his horse to get up the steep rise and over the top. He dismounted and led the animal back toward where he'd noticed a mess of brush and rocks at what he guessed could be the head of a draw. The remains of huge fallen tree blocked his way and he had to maneuver his horse carefully around it on the steep slope. A game trail made by deer, elk and other creatures wound its way upward past the dead tree, which had been ripped open by a grizzly to get at termites. He could tell it was a grizzly, and not some other kind of bear, because its footprints showed very long claws on the forepaws.

A deer walked out of a clump of aspen some way ahead, stepping slowly along the trail, then suddenly catching a glimpse of him, it darted away, and he followed it through the brush and rocks to a gap leading down a steep slope onto the far side of the ridge.

He went a short distance down the draw, then remounted and wove his way carefully through the slim and graceful white trunks of the aspens. It was difficult going, though. For one thing, in places the trees were close together, and for another it was getting dark on this side of the ridge and there were many deadfalls and occasional boulders to be avoided, but eventually he came out into a small, grassy hollow surrounded by a few pines.

On examination it seemed an ideal place. It could be looked into from only one direction, that from which he'd come, and there was a trickle of spring water a little way down the slope.

He led the horse down into the hollow and stripped his rig. Then he let him roll before tying him with a slip-knot to one of the trees. It was cool now, but not uncomfortably cold, and in any case Homer had his slicker and his blanket roll and it was far from being the first time he'd slept out high up in the mountains.

Reaching into his saddlebag, he took out the remainder of the food Fran had given him, a large slice of meat pie and three doughnuts. She'd also packed separately a couple of fresh eggs, half a dozen biscuits and a chunk of bacon. He'd brought his own supplies of beans, crackers and coffee as well, and all this together with his emergency pack - a slab of pemmican, a small sack of cold flour and a tight coil of about ten feet of rawhide, always something handy to have, for, among other things, rigging snares to trap fresh food - left him, he felt, well provided for.

For his supper, Homer settled on the pie and two of the donuts followed by coffee. The rest of his supplies he packed away, hanging the saddlebag from a branch of the tree out of the reach of varmints.

He collected a large bunch of small, dry twigs off the lower trunks of the pines, the little branches that start to grow, then die, and then fetched some larger fragments of bark and fallen branches. Using a handful of dry grass as a starter, he built himself a small fire near the tree trunk so that the smoke would rise and dissipate through the leaves, leaving no rising column to be seen. Then he filled his coffee pot at the spring and when his little fire was going well, he put it on to make coffee.

When he'd eaten he hunted around for a suitable place to sleep, found what appeared to be a cozy spot under some low branches and after kicking around a little to discourage any snakes, he put his saddle down for a pillow and unrolled his bed. Then he smoked a cigarette, untied his horse, trusting that there was enough good grass to encourage him not to wander out of the hollow, took off his boots and, wrapping himself in his blanket, he curled up on his bed with his rifle beside him, muzzle toward his feet, and his old Walker Colt close to hand. He was tired after his long day in the saddle and fell asleep almost immediately, happy to leave the horse as lookout.

When his eyes opened, first light was filtering through the leaves. He sat up and looked for his horse. It was grazing on the far side of the hollow. Birds were singing and twittering all around and a breeze blew softly through the trees, otherwise all was quiet. For a few moments, Homer sat there listening and appreciating.

He rebuilt his fire on the cold ashes, made coffee, cut some strips of bacon and fried them, sopping up the bacon gravy with one of the Fran's biscuits. He ate the last donut and finished his coffee, then dowsed the fire, pulling the sticks away and scattering dirt over the ashes. This was a good hideout and he intended to return to it if necessary, but meanwhile he did not want traces of his overnight stay to be too obvious.

Saddling up and packing all his gear back on the horse, he back-tracked his route over to the draw and followed the game trail down past the dead tree until he came to an area where the forest was thinning out and he could look out through trees and brush across to the open grassland. The short promontory from where he'd spotted the rustlers" camp was now behind him to his left and he figured that he must be getting close. He stood up in the saddle to see along the slope to his right and made out the roof of one of the cabins about two hundred yards away.

He dismounted and led the horse up the slope until he found a safe place to leave it. Then he donned his moccasins once more, tucked his revolver into his waistband and set off.

The two cabins at the foot of the slope were in deep shadow. It was still very early and quite cold and Homer judged that the rustlers would not be up and about yet, but he took every precaution as he came down the steep slope behind the cabins, testing each step as he put his foot down for fear of treading on a fallen dead branch.

Finally he reached a big pine about forty feet behind the corner of one of the cabins. The ground fell away abruptly and Homer could see over the roof and directly into the doorway of the other cabin. He used his big skinning knife to scrape away the soil at the base of the tree until he'd made a trough deep enough so that when he was lying flat behind the trunk only his head showed.

Then he waited.

Fairly soon he heard sounds of life from the cabin beneath him, and Lou Dessay dressed in woolen underwear came around to the back and urinated against the steep bank, then ambled slowly down to the stream, where he had a half-hearted wash.

Shortly afterwards two men came out of the other cabin. One was an older man, bald and very big. His companion was short and stocky. Homer didn't recognize either of them. He watched while they went about their early morning routines, eventually joined by Vin Foley. They did not speak much but Homer could catch snatches of their conversation from time to time and he soon gathered, while they squatted around the fire eating fried bacon, that Vin Foley was grouchy and bored, and the others were irritated by him.

When they had all eaten, Lou Dessay saddled up his big white horse and rode off toward the cattle. The others went back inside out of Homer's view.

After two hours or more, by which time the sun was well over the top of the ridge, Homer noticed two riders rapidly approaching across the grassland, but it was not until they dismounted and called out that he recognized dapper little Billy Bates and the big red-head, Carl Voller.

Bates was angry. He yelled at the others for not keeping a lookout.

"We coulda been anybody. You're supposed to be watching them cows!"

Vin Foley answered back in a surly tone and Bates said, "Well, you can have something to do. We got us a good little chore, all of us. Where's Lou?"

Somebody told him.

"Alright, Vin, you want something to do so you go find him and bring him back, pronto."

"What'll I tell him?"

"We're gonna burn out a nester."

"Yeah? Where?"

"Tinkers Creek."

"Count me out," said the big man, making a dismissive sign as he walked away from Bates towards the cabin. "Me and Shorty signed up for a cattle drive, and that's all." He went inside.

"We want you there with us, Jonno," Bates called after him.

The stocky man, Shorty, followed his friend. When he reached the doorway he turned and said, "What's in it for us, Billy?"

"Fifty dollar bonus."

Shorty whistled. "Just for running out one nester?"

Voller called out, "This ain't just any ole dirt farmer."

"How come?"

"He managed to put a bullet through Mickey Mason's skull."

Homer's heart jumped. This must be about the Petersen place.

Jonno came back and stood behind Shorty. "Billy," he said, "D'you know what you're getting into here? I was in town and I knew that feller when he brung Mason in."

Foley was taking his saddle toward the horses. He said loudly, over his shoulder, "Leave him be, Billy. He's yaller."

Jonno called out to him. "Okay. You think you're good, Vin, but I seen Judd Petersen in action and he ain't no pilgrim."

Bates went over to him. He said, "You know Petersen?"

"Over in the Territory. Coupla years back. I was ridin' partners with Mick Farrell, the Laredo gunman? We was finagling a few steers out of a big herd. Marshall Petersen come up on us with a posse and took them steers back. We got out of there but Mick was real sore. Week or so after that we was in Abilene and we seen Petersen crossing the street ahead of us. He was carrying a gunny sack in one hand. Mick braced him." Jonno paused. "Nobody even seen Petersen draw, but you coulda put a silver dollar over the two holes in the left pocket of Mick's shirt. And you know somethin? Petersen still had that gunny sack in his other hand!"

Nobody spoke for a moment, then Bates laughed. "Okay, so that was then and this is now and there ain't no call for any of us to face Petersen on any street in Abilene or any place else, so it don't matter how fast he is with a gun." He turned to Shorty. "You're coming with Carl and me and I ain't takin' no for an answer, so go get saddled up."

Shorty looked at his partner. Jonno just shrugged and moved to let him pass into the cabin.

Bates said, "Jonno, you don't want no fifty dollar bonus so you can stay here with the cattle, and you can start by coming out with us as far as the rim and then driftin' all them that you've let wander out to there back to here." He called across to Vin Foley. "You and Lou follow along and meet up with us at Palmer's place, Tinkers Creek Crossing."

Homer waited impatiently until they were all out of sight. He didn't know the country too well, but he reckoned it would pretty likely take them at least as long to get back to Palmer's as it would take him to get to the homestead, returning the way he'd come. With luck he should be able to warn Judd & Fran in time.

166

CHAPTER TWENTY-ONE

At about the same time as Homer was watching Bates and Voller approach the rustlers" camp, a buckboard drew up outside the sheriff's office in Twin Springs, and a tall, thin young woman dressed in traveling clothes stepped down and tied the horse to the hitching rail. She walked briskly to the office door, tapped lightly and opened it.

"Good morning, Sheriff," she said, in a pleasant contralto voice as she went in.

Sheriff Tom Kramer was sitting at his desk, hunting through a pile of "Wanted" flyers and looked up as she entered. "Why, good morning, ma'am," he said with a puzzled smile. "What brings you to town this early in the day, if I may ask?"

She smiled. Tom thought the smile made her plain face look quite pleasant.

"I would like to speak to Deputy Cowan, if I may. Privately?"

"Oh, well, uh, Ben ain't here, ma'am, and I ain't expecting him back for a while."

She frowned. "Oh, that's a shame. I particularly wanted to ask his advice."

"Mebbe I can help?" said Tom, rising to his feet.

She considered for a long moment. "Well," she said at last,

"I suppose you would most likely give me the same sort of advice as Ben would. Only it would be easier with him, that's all."

Tom fetched a straight-back wooden chair from the row along the outer wall.

"Take a seat, ma'am," he said, placing the chair for her.

She sat, adjusted her skirt and took off her gloves.

"Can I get you anything?" asked Tom. "I got a pot of fresh coffee out back if you're thirsty after your long drive in."

"Thank you," she said. "A drink of water, perhaps?"

Tom went out to the washroom, came back with a tall glass half full of water and handed it to her, before sitting back down in his swivel chair behind the desk.

She thanked him, drank most of the water, and placed the glass on the desk top. Then she opened her purse, took out a small handkerchief and patted her lips.

After a long pause she said, sitting bolt upright, "This is not easy for me, Sheriff. Ben knows I have been unhappy at home for some time - since shortly after we came back, in fact - and he would understand what I am doing and why."

"Alright, ma'am." Tom was curious to know what had brought Gwen Palmer into his office, but he was happy to let her tell him in her own time. He nodded reassuringly.

"I've had enough. I've left!" She blurted it out. "And I'm not going back!"

"Okay," he said. "I guess you're of age and know your own mind."

"Yes, and I know what's right and I know what's wrong, but my stupid father…"

To Tom's consternation her eyes filled and she began to wail uncontrollably as the tears rolled down her face. He had no idea what to do so he sat still and did nothing until the wailing stopped as suddenly as it had begun.

"I'm sorry," she said, jerkily, mopping her face with her little handkerchief.

Tom leant forward across his desk. "That's okay, Miss Gwen," he said quietly. "You said it ain't easy for you. You want to talk about it?"

"Yes," she said with a final sob. She took a deep breath and let it out as a sigh. "I haven't been easy in my mind about the way my father has been behaving since we came back to our farm last Fall. He has never been easy to live with. He is cold and hard by nature and he became worse after Mother died. But now it's as if his success in starting the Cooperative has gone to his head, because he has become quite obsessed with the idea of taking over the whole of our valley. Do you know, when he heard Mr. Petersen had been shot dead, he was actually pleased about it? He actually said it would make it so much easier to expand. I was shocked." She paused. "But that's not the worst of it."

She rolled the damp handkerchief around in her hands, then looked directly at Tom.

"I believe that he and Mr. Higgins and Mr. Marburg are planning to do something criminal and it involves the land that belonged to Mr. Petersen."

Tom raised his eyebrows, sat back in his chair and stroked his chin with thumb and forefinger while he considered the implications.

"Something criminal, huh? With Mr. Higgins and Mr. Marburg?"

She nodded vigorously. "I believe so. I have suspected for some time that something was going on. Whenever Mr. Higgins came to see Father, they always went into our parlor and shut the door, saying they must not be disturbed. Sometimes Mr. Marburg came as well, but he never arrived with Mr. Higgins. They always came and left separately and I thought that was odd."

"Yeah, I can see why you'd think that," said Tom. "And, okay, they're meeting in secret, but why d'you think it's something criminal? I mean, that's a serious thing to say."

"Yes, I know. Well, last night Mr. Higgins came to see Father and he brought two other men with him. I didn't like the look of either of them."

"Why? What was wrong with them?"

"Well, one was big and rough-looking and I didn't like the way he looked at me. The other one was quite young, about the same size as me and very neatly dressed, and he walked with a funny kind of strut with short, quick steps. He had strange eyes too. They called him "Billy"."

Tom guessed they were Bates and his sidekick, Voller. This could be interesting.

"So what happened?" he said.

"Father and Mr. Higgins went into the parlor as usual, then Mr. Marburg arrived and he went in to join them. They all came out soon after and I could see that Father was very upset."

She stopped and her lips quivered as if she was going to burst into tears again. But she rallied, and taking a deep breath she went on.

"They had forgotten I was there, and the big man who came with Mr. Higgins was very abusive to Father and started pushing him around the yard. Mr. Marburg told him to stop, but then he said to Father, "Are you a complete fool, Palmer? We're going through here and don't you even try and stand in the way." He told the man called Billy to leave at first light and get the boys from the cattle. Then the Hallett brothers joined in and there was a lot of argument about who was going to do what, and I realized it was the Petersens they were talking about. And Mr. Marburg shouted at them, and he said, "Billy, I don't care how it's done, but by this time tomorrow I want that land - and no bodies, understand?" So I finally had to accept it, Sheriff, my father was involved with criminals."

Tom stood up. "Well, ma'am, you did well to get out of there. What was that about cattle?"

"I don't know but there was a bit of argument about it and Mr. Marburg was insistent. I don't want my father to go to jail, Sheriff. Something will have to be done to stop them, won't it? That's what I came in here for."

Tom said, "Yeah, and you did right." He went to the door and looked out. There was nobody about, but the side door to the Drovers Saloon was open. "'scuse me, ma'am," he said, "won't be but a minute."

He went into the Drovers. Sure enough, Sandy was in the saloon, sweeping the floor.

"Hey, Sandy," Tom called him over. "Here's a coupla nickels. Find Deputy Cowan for me and tell him I need him, pronto."

"Okay, Sheriff. Where should I start looking?"

"If he ain't at the livery they'll tell you where he's at. Most likely be at the K-Bar, 'cos they're bringin' in that windmill today. Tell them I said to lend you a horse to go fetch Ben back."

Sandy was delighted. This was something to boast to Cole Cheswell about. He dropped the broom, took the coins from Tom's outstretched hand and ran off down the street.

Tom took a look at Gwen Palmer's buckboard before he went back inside. He noted that it carried a sizable load under a tarpaulin; she'd had not left home in too much of a hurry, it seemed.

She was still sitting bolt upright on the wooden chair.

"Someone's gone to look for Ben," he said. "Anyone know you've come to town, Miss Gwen?"

She shrugged. "By now they'll be wondering why nobody had breakfast ready for them."

"But you didn't tell anyone you were leaving?"

"No I didn't."

"Reason I ask is I see you've brung a passel of stuff with you on the buckboard. You load all that your own self?"

"Yes," she said. "I did. I spent the night getting together all the things I didn't want to leave behind and as soon as it started to get light I harnessed the pony, brought the buckboard round to the back of the house and loaded up. I waited until I saw those two men leave and then I just set out. Nobody saw me. Nobody takes any notice of me anyway, Sheriff."

Tom had a thought. "What about Marburg and Lawyer Higgins? They still out there?"

"Yes, at least I didn't see them leave. They usually stay over in the guest house, just down the street from us."

"Okay. So, what are your plans now then, Miss Gwen?"

"Well, I've got enough money to last for a while, and I'm hoping Ben will help me. He's been a good friend to me and I thought he might be able to help me find a position somewhere. I'm a good housekeeper, been doing it more than half my life, I hope perhaps he'll know of places."

"You seem to have thought this through, ma'am."

"It's not as if I haven't thought about it before, Sheriff."

"Well, look, I'm gonna need Ben, so he won't be around to help you none just yet. Have you given any thought to where you'll be staying for the next day or so?"

"Yes. Mrs. Bradman usually has rooms to let. I'm sure

she'll have a place for me."

"Okay, good. Now, just so's I'm clear on what you're saying, you heard them decide to attack the Petersen homestead today, is that right?"

"Yes."

"And d'you have any idea how many of them are involved?"

"Well, I gathered it was the man called Billy and the other man Mr. Higgins brought, and Tom and Jim Hallet and the men from the cattle, whoever they are. I'm pretty sure Mr. Higgins and Mr. Marburg weren't actually going with them. Or Father, of course."

"Okay. Now, I'm gonna round up the town council and see about raising a posse, and when Ben gets in we'll decide what's best to do. One way or another we gotta stop them."

CHAPTER TWENTY-TWO

Judd's first feeling on waking that morning had been that something had been decided. The previous evening he'd told Fran all about his meeting with the Watkins family and his subsequent trip to Twin Springs. She had no more idea than he had what message the man Hobbs might have been bringing, but clearly it must have been important.

She told him she'd kept a good lookout as she went about her daily business on the homestead but had seen nothing to worry her all day. She'd been relieved to see him, however, when he'd arrived just before nightfall, and agreed that they must continue to be vigilant at all times.

After he'd eaten, the two of them had sat up late discussing her ideas for the development of the homestead. Judd had been very impressed by Fran's grasp of the business possibilities, and especially her understanding of the potential for cattle farming as opposed to ranching in the old open range style. He had retired to bed with a growing conviction that his thoughts earlier in the day had been along the right lines: this is good country and he could make a good life here, if only the present problems could be overcome.

Now, as he washed and shaved in the bath-house, under the solemn gaze of little Joe, he knew that when this was over he would not be going back to marshalling.

Over breakfast he told Fran his decision. She flushed with pleasure at the news.

"It really means a lot to me," she said. "Because it's what we wanted for Joe's future. And I reckon Sten would've been glad for you to be a part of it, too."

Judd said, "You know, when I left here ten years ago it was because I'd come to hate the place. Never wanted to come back. Coming back, though, has roused up some good memories. Musta been been buried pretty deep." He waited while Fran refilled his coffee cup. He thanked her.

"I guess Sten would have told you about why we left Kentucky?" he said.

"Your farm was burned down in the War Between the States."

"Right. Took us the best part of the summer of 'sixty-one to get this far west. We pulled in one day at an army camp - I guess it would be about where Fort Collins is - and Pa said we'd traveled far enough and him and Sten were going to look for our new home and they left Ma and me with the soldiers. Then, only a few days later they came back and fetched us, and we ended up here."

He paused and drank some coffee. "They were happy days at first. There was nothing here, of course. I'd had three years of schooling and Ma helped me study with reading and made me write a diary, and every Sunday morning, after Pa read from the Gospels, I had to read out loud what I'd been doing every day that week. Then, when I was coming up to seventeen, Ma took sick and died. A few months later Pa was shot and killed. After that Sten moved in here and my life became nothing but work - 'from see to can't see', as he put it." Judd shook his head. "Turned me against farm work, as I thought, for life."

Fran said, "Sten did tell me once that he knew he'd pushed

you too hard."

Judd drained his cup and stood up. "Mebbe," he said, with a smile. He buckled on his right-hand gun belt. "But at least I learned that I could do hard work, and there's plenty of that needs doing around here. Where'd be a good place to start?"

"How about the bridge over the creek? I put up everything I could lay my hands on quickly to try and keep Butch's cattle out. It worked, but it sure is a muddle, and there's no way to get even the buggy out."

It took Judd less than half an hour to clear the makeshift barrier and he was walking back to the stables to see to the horses when he heard the sound of hoofs rapidly approaching. He paused, right hand near the butt of his gun, as the rider came up to the other side of the bridge.

It was Tom Hallett.

"Hey! Petersen! Get your horse," he called out. "Clem Palmer wants to see you."

Judd looked at him calmly. "If Clem Palmer wants to see me he can come here any time."

Hallett looked surprised. "You want me to tell him that?"

"You can tell him if you like," said Judd. "But he should know it anyway."

"He said I had to fetch you straightaway."

"That so?" said Judd, irritated by the idea he could be summoned just like that. "Well, you can come and fetch me if you've a mind to."

Hallett hesitated a moment, then said, "If you don't want to come that's your hard luck, Petersen!" He yanked on the reins and wheeled his horse's head around sharply all in one movement.

Judd winced at the effect on the animal's mouth. He watched, puzzled, as Hallett galloped off.

He worked steadily around the homestead buildings all morning, mainly under Fran's guidance as to what needed doing most urgently, all the time keeping a watchful eye open.

Then, just as he was thinking of stopping for a bite to eat, Fran called out from the kitchen doorway, "Rider coming! Through the gap. Looks like Mr. Foreman."

Judd ran across to join her. He could see the rider coming at a steady lope, but it took him a good minute to make out who he was. Once again he was impressed by Fran's keen eyesight.

"It is Homer. I told the sheriff he'd be watching the rustled cattle."

"I never pegged him as a man to leave a job he'd been given," said Fran. "Mebbe they've been moved on."

They watched as Homer approached without slackening speed until he came to the bridge over the creek. Judd went to meet him and held the horse as Homer dismounted in the yard.

"My, but them mountain trails sure get rougher as the years pass," he said, breathing heavily and stretching to ease the stiffness in his ageing limbs. "Looks like I got here in good time, though."

He quickly told them what he'd overheard at the rustlers" camp.

Fran hustled him into the kitchen and poured him a cup of the coffee that she'd made ready for their nooning.

He said, between sips, "I figured to get here before they did, but we won't have a whole lot of time. I don't guess they'll be expecting any kinda fight, and one thing I learnt when I was scouting for the army was they tried not to let the enemy fight in a situation of his own choosing."

He looked up at Judd. "Any ideas?"

"They're planning to burn us out, you said?"

"Well, that's what I heard. And leave no bodies."

"So if that's what they'll try first they'll have to come right up to the house. I reckon they'll just ride straight up the trail from Palmer's. It's the easiest and most obvious and they'll think to take us by surprise. Fran, soon as you've put little Joe safe, I want you in the back room lining up on the other side of the bridge with your Henry rifle. Okay?"

Homer looked at Judd with raised eyebrows.

"Don't worry, she can outshoot you and me any day, Homer. Now, I want you in the stable with Sten's long gun. I'll leave it to you to choose your spot, but let the horses out in the paddock first."

Fran said, "Where will you be, Judd?"

"I'm going to take my Winchester and hole up in the rocks where I can see all round. And, Homer, I don't think I need remind you these men are killers. They shot Sten and they killed another feller in town on Tuesday night because he was bringing us some letter or other. What I'm saying is if we gotta shoot we shoot to kill. It's us or them, and there ain't any rules."

"I been shot at a time or two, young feller, and I'm still here. If I pick up a gun and aim it at someone, I'm aiming to kill him. That's what a gun's for, so that's how I use it. And I knew that while you was still on your way from Kentucky!"

Judd grinned. "I stand corrected. Okay, let's you and me make sure we've got all the water and ammunition we need. We may have a long wait, but the sooner we're in position the better."

Fran was wrapping up beef sandwiches from the lunch table. She passed one pack to Homer as he went to fill his canteen with water from the pump before heading off to the stables. And another to Judd.

He said, "Fran, I guess this is what you and Sten were half expecting but hoping would never happen. I'm sorry it's come to this, but we'll give them a good fight and thanks to Homer, we stand a good chance of sending them away."

CHAPTER TWENTY-THREE

At about the same time as Fran was pouring Homer his first cup of coffee at the Petersen homestead, Bates and Voller were arriving back at Tinkers Creek Crossing with the three men from the rustled cattle. Leo Marburg was waiting for them.

A few hours earlier he'd learned of Gwen Palmer's absence and he was unconvinced by Clem Palmer's forceful denials that he'd sent his daughter to warn the Petersens.

"Con, the man's a liability," he'd said to Higgins, as Palmer strode angrily away from them. "We're going have to part company with him just as soon as we can."

A man with a rifle had ridden into the yard at that point and they watched Palmer go across and speak to him.

"That's one of the Hallett brothers he's talking to," Higgins had said. "Tom, I think. He and his brother patrol the Settlement boundaries and are said to be crack shots."

Marburg had merely grunted. He'd told Palmer that for the attack on the homestead he needed any of the Settlement men who could be trusted to shoot and ask no questions. Presumably that had been what Palmer was telling Tom Hallett about.

Now, before Bates even had time to get out of his saddle, Marburg caught his eye, indicated with a jerk of his head, and set off down the track toward the ford. Bates dismounted and still holding the reins, followed Marburg.

When he was far enough away from the others, Marburg

paused, letting Bates come up to him. "There's a complication. Palmer's daughter has run off. He says he knows nothing about it, but I reckon he might of sent her to the Petersen place to warn them."

Bates swore.

Marburg said, "This is how I want you to play it. We'll make Palmer go with you. Let him think we want him to negotiate, let him think he's in charge." He paused. "Just between the two of us, when it's over we won't need him anymore."

Bates met Marburg's eyes and nodded, "Alright, then." He hitched his gun into a firmer seating on his thigh.

"But watch your step. Two of his men are going along too."

"That'll make eight, then. Should be more than enough."

"Right." Marburg turned away "And remember," he said over his shoulder, "No bodies."

Marburg walked quickly back to Clem Palmer. "Get these men something to eat and drink, and then get going. I want this over and done with before dark."

"You don't mean you want me to go with them?"

"Sure I do." Marburg pretended to look surprised he should ask. "You're the only one who could talk them into getting out without a fight, aren't you? It's up to you. You're in charge."

Judd had settled himself into a comfortable position in the rocks where there was a good view all around. He didn't know it but he was in almost the same position as the gunman who'd shot Sten.

The house was well situated for defense. It had been built on a low mound in a loop of the creek, which was about twenty-five yards across here, slow moving and too deep to be crossed easily on horseback. The bridge was the only quick way across and Fran could cover that from the house.

Behind Judd to the west the rocky ground rose toward the base of the ridge. To his left was the house, the yard and the barn, and he could see part of the stables from where Homer could cover everything to the north as well as the house and yard. Directly ahead, the creek came under the bridge some sixty or seventy yards away and flowed straight toward him before veering off to his right between steep banks lined with cottonwoods and scrub oaks. In places on the far side of it he could see stretches of the trail that led through the Settlement to Twin Springs.

After little more than an hour, Judd heard the sound of a group of horsemen trotting from the Settlement. He caught glimpses of them through the trees along the creek and counted eight riders bunched together. He recognized Tom Hallett and Clem Palmer among them.

As soon as the riders came in sight of the bridge they accelerated, whooping and yelling and firing pistols at random.

Immediately a shot rang out from the farmhouse quickly followed by another and Judd saw large splinters fly off the parapet of the bridge as the bullets ricocheted. The riders wheeled around and drew up in the trees about fifty yards downstream, not far from Judd's position across the creek.

He waited. After a couple of minutes he saw Clem Palmer approach the bridge slowly with Tom Hallett riding beside him. When they about twenty feet away Fran called to them to stop.

Palmer called out, "You've got to get out, Fran, you and Petersen. Come on now, see sense! The Bank's taking over and there's nothing you can do."

Judd could not hear what Fran's answer was, but Palmer shouted, "You don't stand a chance! There's eight of us here!"

This time Judd did hear her, "But only one of them is you, Clem. Get back where you belong or I'll shoot you out your saddle!"

Palmer turned his horse away quickly, but Tom Hallett whipped up his Winchester and fired at the house. It was the last thing he did. Fran replied in kind and before the echo of his own shot died away he was dying with it as he his horse threw him and galloped off.

Palmer raced back to the others.

Judd watched as they gathered together. From what he could see it looked as if it was Bates who was giving the orders.

Eventually two men rode out of the trees away from the house and made a wide circling movement which brought them to the north of the homestead. There, they could cross the creek through the shallows where it came out of the great rock wall and then attack from that direction.

As soon as the two men were across, three other men came out of the trees at the edge of the creek and headed down the steep bank as if intending to cross it in front of Judd. He recognized two of them: Jim Hallett and the big red head, Carl Voller.

He waited until they were in the water, then opened fire with his Winchester. He hit the man he didn't know, and Jim Hallett, and they both fell into the creek. Voller grabbed Jim Hallett, struggled back to the bank and took shelter back in the trees.

Meanwhile, Homer had opened up on the two men coming from the north and Judd saw one of them fall to the ground. The other one, on a white horse, turned back to help. As he reached his companion, a volley of shots rang out from the top of the great rock wall and both men and their horses were hit. One of the men tried to rise but more shots came and he fell back.

Judd was puzzled. Who could it be up on the wall and why were they helping?

His attention returned to the remaining men across the creek from him and he saw that Palmer was racing back along the trail to the Settlement, with Bates not far behind him, followed a little later by Voller who had Jim Hallett clinging on behind his saddle. The attack was over.

Then he became aware of riders approaching from the direction of the old Indian trail in the east and slowly made out Tom Kramer and Ben with four others.

He stood up and made his way back to the yard, calling out to Homer that it was over.

Fran met them at the kitchen door. She was wiping little Joe's face. "I put him in the pantry and he found the jelly," she said.

Judd said, "Sheriff Kramer and Ben are heading across from the old trail. They've got some others with them. I guess the sight of them coming was enough to finish it off." He picked Joe up and put him on his shoulder.

Fran smiled. "Kramer's more or less on time for once," she said. "What will he do when he finds Hallett's body out there?"

"He'll ask me what happened and I'll tell him, like a good US Deputy Marshall should. Why? You bothered by it, Fran?"

She looked at him and shook her head, slowly. "No, I'm not. He shot at me and I shot back."

"Right. There's another of them in the creek and two more across the paddock he'll want to know about, too."

"Wasn't them firing from the top of the Wall, was it?"

"Couldn't see who they was," said Homer. "But they was three of them, mebbe more, and they could shoot alright."

"It couldn't have been them," said Judd. "They would have

184

been too far away to the east."

"Well, whoever they were, thanks," said Fran. "And thanks to you, Mr. Foreman. If you hadn't gone to look over the rustlers" camp and got back in time to warn us, we coulda been in deep trouble."

Homer smiled, "If I hadn't been blessed with too much curiosity I guess I coulda just done as I was told and set and watched the cattle, but it paid off and I'm real thankful. And if I may mention it, ma'am, I believe we're well enough acquainted now for you to call me Homer."

Fran laughed. "And I'm Fran."

Tom and Ben rode over the bridge and into the yard accompanied by four men, two in range clothes, one of whom Judd recognized as John Stainer from the Double Diamond, and two in broadcloth.

Tom said, "Howdy folks, good to see you all looking alive and well. We heard shooting from way back and wondered. Looks like we're too late to join in, though." He waved a hand toward the men with him. "John and Ed from DD happened to be in town and came along to help. Doc Campbell was the only one of the council I could round up in time, and this other gent is George Pitt and he's come all the way from New York City." He paused. "So, what's been going on here? We saw the body out front. What happened?"

Fran said, indicating the bench around the big tree, "Light and set if you will, gentlemen. I'll get coffee." She took Joe from Judd and went into the kitchen, tugging a reluctant Joe with her; he was having an interesting day and didn't want to miss anything.

The riders all dismounted and Homer went to help Ed Flynn, the DD hand, with the horses.

Judd started to describe how they had been able to prepare,

thanks to Homer's warning, and what had happened once the attack started.

Tom interrupted. "You sure the feller you hit in the creek is dead?"

"I saw him float off downstream," said Judd. "He wasn't swimming."

"Anybody check on the other two?"

"Not yet."

"Homer," said Tom, "Show Ben where they're at, will you, so he can bring them in."

"I'll come with you," said Doc Campbell, "Just in case."

As the three men left Judd said, "We're sure glad to see you, Tom, but what brings you folks out here, anyway?"

Tom Kramer recounted all that had happened after Gwen Palmer had come into his office first thing that morning. "Then just as we was leaving," he concluded, "Mr. Pitt here turned up and after we filled him in he wanted to come with us."

George Pitt was a tall, well-built man of about Judd's age, dark haired, dark eyed and handsome with a neatly trimmed moustache and beard, and dressed in a well-cut charcoal-colored suit and matching fedora. He stepped forward and shook Judd's hand.

"It appears that your troubles and mine are connected, Marshall," he said. "I have an interest in the fellow calling himself Leo Marburg, who, it seems, is behind this attack on you."

"Marburg? That's the fellow Sandy said Higgins was in cahoots with, isn't it, Tom?"

"Yeah, but before we get into that, I've got an idea who was shooting from up on that rock wall. When we came along the old Indian trail we picked up the tracks of your buckskin, then after a mile or so they was joined by fresh tracks of leather-shod ponies. We thought mebbe you'd been followed by Indians. Then we lost the tracks in the rock and shale, but Ben pointed out a couple of riders, looked like Indians, up on the Wall. Right, fellers?"

The others nodded.

John Stainer said, "They were Indians for sure. There's been a small band of braves around our west range for some years. They're led by an older guy, calls himself Bear Claw. Never give us any trouble and Mr. Watkins says to leave them be."

Judd said, "I met Bear Claw on my way back from checking Fran's cattle last night. That was back in the pinewoods just off your west range." He smiled. "Asked me who I was and where I was going. He obviously knew this place, described Sten and Fran and Joe well enough. Mebbe you're right, Tom, they trailed me to see if I was who I said I was."

Fran arrived with her big coffee pot. Joe came behind her very cautiously, carrying a wooden tray with several cups on it. She put the pot down and motioned to the men to take cups.

She'd overheard what Judd had just said. "I know Bear Claw," she said. "The winter after I came here four years ago, we had a long spell of real bad weather and when it eased off Sten went out hunting up in the high country and he came across a small bunch of Indians. They'd run off the reservation and they were starving. Sten had a deer carcass he was bringing home, but he gave it to them instead. Then in the Spring, Bear Claw rode in one day with one of his braves and brought a freshly killed deer carcass for us. After that we'd see them from time to time up on the ridge."

Judd said "Did I tell you about the young squaw I found injured along the creek the first day I came out here? I know I told Ben and Homer. Anyway, she was one of Bear Claw's."

Ben and Homer, with Doc Campbell rejoined them.

Ben said, "Those two men were Vin Foley and Lou Dessay. Homer recognized them as two of the rustlers. They are both dead and so are their horses."

Homer said, "Didn't we say they coulda been the ones that squaw you found said attacked her?"

"If they were, Bear Claw would have had a good reason for shooting them. Seems you could be right, Tom," said Judd.

John Stainer said, "Sheriff tells me you've found some of our cattle, Marshall."

"Right," said Judd, "And Homer, here, went out to keep an eye on them and found some more. Did you get an idea how many head there was, Homer."

"I found a couple more herds. Didn't get a close enough look to check all the brands but there was some DD and Star B among them. I guess I saw six or seven hundred head, all told, a lot of them young stock."

"Well, that's good news," said Stainer. He stood up and replaced his cup on the wooden tray. "Thanks very much for that, ma'am. It was real welcome. If you fellers don't need Ed and me anymore, we'll be getting back to the ranch. Mr. Watkins will want to organize a drive to get those cows back where they belong. I guess he'll be in town to see you real soon, Sheriff."

"Okay, John, and thanks for coming."

CHAPTER TWENTY-FOUR

Higgins was scared. Suppose something went wrong and the raid failed! Or, even if it worked and there actually were no bodies left to show what had happened, how sure could they be that there would be no investigation? The sheriff was no fool and he'd certainly hear about it and come out and check, like he did the first time. Then, if what Sandy had said he'd heard was right and Petersen was a US Deputy Marshall, Kramer would most likely report it to his superiors, and all hell could break out.

And in any case, what about Palmer's daughter? Why had she run off? Had she heard anything? How much did she know? She certainly knew he and Marburg had visited with her father several times.

He was trying hard to hide his anxiety, but he suspected that Marburg could see it, and that gave him even more cause to worry because he now realized how ruthless Marburg was. He had no doubt what the man had really meant when he said they'd have to part company with Palmer. He shuddered at the thought.

The two men were in an ante-room of the newly-finished building designated as the Co-operative's Assembly Rooms, where the day-to-day running of the Settlement's affairs would be dealt with. It had been agreed that the raiding party would report there on their return.

Marburg was sitting at a table reading a week-old newspaper from the east while they waited. He was outwardly calm, but Higgins believed he must be anxious too.

Higgins was standing by a window facing the street. Suddenly he saw a horseman coming at speed down the street from the direction of the trail. It was Palmer.

"Palmer's back," Higgins called across the room to Marburg. "He's on his own."

"What!" Marburg came off his seat and joined Higgins at the window. "The lily-livered coyote! He's run out on us!"

Palmer clattered to a halt outside the building and fairly leapt off his horse. He charged up the steps into the building and burst into the room, gun in hand.

"Marburg, you damned fool! You've ruined everything!" he yelled, brandishing his six-shooter. "They were waiting for us. We didn't stand a chance. Now you get the hell out of here! Both of you! You and your damned schemes! Go on, get out! Out!"

Higgins needed no further urging. His worst fears realized, he ducked around Marburg and scuttled out of the building. He set off down the street in a blind panic, his eyes fixed on the Settlement stables where he'd left his horse the night before, so he didn't see Bates arrive and stare after him before running up the steps into the Assembly Rooms.

Marburg was failing to register what had happened. It didn't occur to him that anything could have gone wrong with his plan, and he was furious with Palmer for waving a gun at him and shouting at him to get out. He shouted back, and Palmer, losing control completely, took a shot at him, catching him a glancing blow on his hip bone just as Bates came through the door.

Seeing Marburg fall to the floor, Bates called out, his voice high-pitched, "Hey, Palmer!" and when Palmer turned to face him, Bates drew his gun and fired twice, hitting Palmer in the chest. Palmer staggered and fell backward against the wall, his face showing shock, then pain, then collapsing as the life left his body.

Bates, still holding his gun, went toward Marburg who was struggling to his feet.

"You okay?" he asked.

"No, I'm not," growled Marburg, loosening his belt and pulling out his shirt to examine the wound on his hip. It was a long, deep gash and it was pouring blood.

Bates re-holstered his gun. "Nasty scratch," he said, helping Marburg to a chair by the table. He took out his knife and cut a strip off Marburg's shirt to make a pad to cover the wound. "Put that on and tighten your belt around it. Better sit still a while till the blood clots."

Marburg winced as between them they fixed the pad in place.

"What happened out there?" he said. "Palmer said they were waiting for you."

"Yeah. You told us there was just a woman, the old feller from the livery and Petersen, right?"

"That's right, and there was eight of you went to burn them out. More than enough, I seem to remember you saying."

"Would have been if that's all we were really facing. I don't know how many they were but we only got one shot off. After that, a shot from the house killed one of the Halletts. Another gun on the side of the ridge somewhere killed Shorty and hit the other Hallett, someone in the stable shot Vin Foley out the saddle and when Lou went to help him a bunch of them up on that rock wall shot both of them to rags. Then the sheriff came from over the east with a posse. That's when Palmer lit out, and I followed him. I don't know what happened to Carl."

Marburg swore long and hard. "Palmer's daughter! She must have told them!"

"Don't think so, somehow," said Bates. "Palmer told me on the way out there she was sweet on that deputy, and he was scared she'd gone and told him."

"Gone to Twin Springs?"

"Yep."

"Hell! She'll have told them about me being here. No one else knows I'm involved in this." Marburg looked around the room, suddenly aware that apart from Palmer's body, they were alone. "Where's Higgins?"

"Seen him running up the road like a scared jack rabbit just as I got here."

Marburg groaned and leant forward on the table, head in hands.

"And just to round it all off," said Bates, as if relishing the thought, "Now you've lost Lou, Vin and Shorty, and there's only Jonno out with the cattle."

Voller appeared in the doorway. He looked from Palmer's body to Marburg to Bates, and raised his eyebrows. "Billy," he said, "Looks like this here situation's turning out like a busted flush."

"Sure does. Don't know about you but I reckon we can have more fun with less trouble some place else."

The big red-head indicated Marburg. "What about him? He owes us, don't he?"

Marburg looked up. "I don't owe you a plugged nickel."

Bates said, slowly and in a reasonable tone, "The job was three thousand dollars, Mr. Marburg. You've paid one thousand, so there's two thousand to come."

"When the job's done," snarled Marburg. "But it's not done, is it!"

"And whose fault's that, then?"

"The hell with whose fault! I gave you a thousand dollars and what have I got for it? Nothing! In any case, you don't think I carry that much around with me, do you?"

"How much have you got, then?" demanded Voller.

"Go to hell!"

Bates said, still with the pretense of sounding reasonable, "Mr. Marburg, if you hand over your billfold, Carl won't have to break your neck and I won't have to shoot you."

Marburg put his hand into his jacket. It came out holding an ugly, snub-nosed, automatic pistol. "You may be fast with a gun, Billy, but you won't be faster than this. Now, get out."

As he spoke there was the noise of people shouting outside in the street. Bates and Voller exchanged looks and backed over to the door.

Voller said, "That Jim feller. He was shot up some. I dropped him off at a place up the trail a piece. I didn't give 'em no whys nor wherefores." He shrugged. "I guess they've come a-looking."

Bates said, "Time to go." He waved airily in Marburg's direction. "See you around, when you haven't got a gun pointed at me."

A minute or so later Marburg heard them riding off. He put his gun away and tried to ease himself off the chair but the pain in his hip was too much. He groaned and sat back down.

The voices outside came nearer and three men, all in bib-overalls, came into the room.

The first fellow saw Palmer's body crumpled against the wall, blood all around. He ran across and called out. "It's Clem!

193

He's dead! Get Milo, quick!"

One of the others left and the third went towards Marburg, who was still sitting at the table.

"What's been going on here?" he said.

Marburg put his hand back inside his jacket and gripped the butt of his gun. He said, "You got a doctor here? I've been shot."

"Hey, Barney," the fellow called to the man who had stayed by the body, "This guy's shot, too."

"Hell of a thing," said Barney. "Milo didn't say anything about shooting. He just said round up who you can and see who's in the Assembly Rooms."

More men arrived, Milo Canliffe at the head of them. He took one look at Palmer's body, then turned to Marburg, "What happened here?"

Marburg said, "Palmer went crazy. He shot me. Bates shot him."

"Bates? Who's Bates? And who are you, anyway?"

"Look, I need a doctor. I've been shot."

"Yeah, but you can still talk! Who are you and what are you doing here?"

Marburg realized he was in trouble and there was not much he could do about it. None of the men were carrying guns, as far as he could see, but in his present state he could not shoot his way out of the Settlement. He decided to bluff his way out of it if he could.

He said, "I've been doing a business deal with Clem Palmer. I thought we were friends. But something must have gone wrong, and Clem got hold of the wrong end of the stick. He got mad at me and took a shot at me, hit me in the side." He started to indicate his wounded hip.

Milo interrupted him. "I know who you are! You're

Marburg, aren't you?"

"That's my name, yes, but..."

"One of your bully boys left Jim Hallett at my place. He's badly hurt, but he told me enough!"

Milo turned to the men who were now crowding into the room.

"This guy got Clem and Tom Hallett killed!" he said.

There were angry and indignant reactions. Barney said, "Tom Hallett dead, too?" Someone else said, "What did he do?"

"The way Jim tells it, this feller here got Clem to try and talk Fran Petersen into selling up, but he sent his gunmen along to make sure, and there was a gunfight. It looks to me like Clem came back to have it out with him."

There were more and louder protests and calls of "String him up!"

"Alright! Alright, listen!" shouted Milo above the din. "There's gonna be no lynching, okay? We could send someone into Twin Springs for the law, but that could take the rest of the day and we don't want their meddling anyway. I say we put him on his horse and turn him loose as he is. Let the law catch up with him if it can. What do you say?"

There were shouts of agreement. Milo sent someone to the stables for Marburg's horse.

Marburg finally took his hand out of his inside pocket; no sense in letting them know he had a gun. He started to bluster but Milo cut him short.

"Get him outside," he said to the two men nearest him.

Marburg was hauled none too carefully to his feet and bundled out of the building. He could feel his wound start to bleed again. When his horse came they lifted him onto it and then gave its hindquarters a hard smack and chased it up the street until it was out of sight.

CHAPTER TWENTY-FIVE

Sandy had found Ben at the livery just about ready to set off for the K-Bar ranch to help his father and brothers install the new windmill. He was disappointed in a way because he rarely managed to get out of the town and he'd hoped he'd have the chance to borrow a horse and have a good ride all the way out to the ranch to fetch Ben back for the Sheriff. However, over the next half-hour or so some interesting things happened which helped to compensate.

On arriving at the sheriff's office and discovering that Gwen Palmer had left home and why, Ben had taken her to the Cowan house and left her in the care of his sister Ruth.

Sandy had been sent to find various members of the town council, but without success; even Mr. Higgins was not to be found. Then the stranger, Mr. Pitt, had come in on the morning stage and Sandy had been able to eavesdrop when he and the sheriff discussed Mr. Pitt's interest in Leo Marburg and follow them to the Bank building where they found that Marburg was also not at home.

Finally Sandy had watched the posse form and ride out of town to the Petersen place, so when his pal Cole Cheswell arrived for work at the law office Sandy had plenty to tell him.

Nothing much happened after that until late in the

afternoon when lawyer Higgins came dashing down the street and pulled up in front of his office. Both he and his horse looked ready to drop. Higgins flung the reins at Sandy and told him to wait there. Then he rushed inside past a startled Cheswell, slamming the inner door behind him.

No more than five minutes later Higgins reappeared carrying a bulging Gladstone bag which he strapped behind his saddle, then snatching the reins from Sandy's hands without a word, he leapt on the horse and galloped off down the street, heading south.

Sandy and Cheswell didn't know what to make of it, then Cheswell had an idea. He opened the door to Higgins's room and they both looked in. There were papers all over the place and the door of the big safe stood wide open.

Cheswell said, "He's done a bunk!"

Shortly after this Billy Bates and Carl Voller rode into town and tied up outside the Drovers.

Sandy sauntered into the saloon after them and stood behind one of the card players at a table not far from the bar as if intending to watch the game, but he was actually watching Bates and Voller walk up to the bar in silence.

Peretz, the big barman, greeted them and poured them both a whisky. He guessed something must have gone wrong and waited for them to speak, but he couldn't restrain his curiosity for long.

"What happened?" he said.

"Petersen's there for keeps," Bates said with a wry smile. "He sure showed us he aims to stay there." He tossed off his drink. "Gimme another."

While Peretz poured, Bates continued. "He was ready for us. He had men all around the place. We lost Shorty, Lou and Vin, and a coupla Palmer's men were hit too. Then would you believe it, the sheriff turned up with a posse."

"How did they know?"

"Good question. Palmer's daughter ran off last night. Palmer told me she was sweet on the Deputy."

Peretz nodded. "Yeah, well, she came in first thing with a buckboard and the Deputy took her down to his place."

"She's at the Cowan place, huh?" Bates smiled. He looked in the mirror behind the bar, removed his hat, took out a comb and drew it carefully several times through his hair until he was satisfied it was perfect, then he downed his second whisky and walked jauntily to the door, swinging his hat by the chin strap. "I got me a little courting to do before I leave town. See you around."

Voller waited until Bates had left, then he swallowed the last of his whisky and set the glass down gently on the bar. "Gimme a beer, will you," he said.

As Peretz placed a glass in front of him and opened a bottle, Voller told him about Marburg.

Peretz swore. "That's me finished here, then."

"Why's that?"

"He owns the place. Pays my wages. Least that'll happen is he'll be run out of town."

"You don't know that."

Peretz grunted. "What about Lawyer Higgins? He was there, wasn't he?"

"Billy said soon as Palmer showed up, he ran off."

Sandy resisted the urge to tell them what he knew, but someone sitting at one of the few other occupied tables called out, "I saw him on the trail just as I was coming in. He was riding as if he had the devil on his tail. I said hello, but he never saw me first nor last."

"Well," said Peretz, "Town's gonna need a new lawyer,

then, 'cos he won't be back."

He turned back to Voller. "What're you and Billy gonna do now?"

"Dunno about Billy, but soon as I've finished this beer I'll be hitting the trail. Just gotta pack my warbag."

Sandy reckoned he'd heard enough. He sidled out of the saloon and went back to his pal Cheswell in the lawyer's office.

Cheswell was a married man with a baby on the way and he was worried that not only did he no longer have a job but that the authorities might think he was implicated in some way in whatever Higgins had been up to.   Over several cups of Higgins's coffee, Sandy tried to reassure him and eventually they agreed that the best thing they could do would be to tell the Marshall everything they knew.

The five men rode at a steady trot down the trail to the Settlement. They had found Shorty's and Jim Hallett's horses tied up in the trees, and Judd and Tom Kramer were leading one each. Ben was leading Tom Hallett's horse which he'd caught easily enough. Hallett's body was draped across it. George Pitt and Doc Campbell were riding side by side.

Judd had told the others that he'd not seen either Marburg or Higgins on the raid and he was sure only Palmer and Bates, and then Voller with the injured Jim Hallett behind, had returned toward the Settlement.

Judd and Ben had buried Foley and Dessay near where they had died. They'd made bundles of their possessions, which they'd left with Homer, who had agreed to stay with Fran for the duration.

When they came to the Settlement boundary, the gate on the trail was wide open.

Judd reined in. "That's the Canliff place down there," he

said, pointing to a track off to their right. "We'll leave Hallett and these horses with them."

He took his Marshall's badge out of his vest pocket and pinned it on, then led the way down the track for about two hundred yards until the Canliff buildings came in sight. As they were about to enter the farm yard, a woman and a tall youngster came out of a barn and approached them. They were both carrying shotguns, the boy's pointed in their direction.

Judd said to Tom Kramer beside him, "They look nervous." He dismounted and handed Tom the reins. "The rest of you wait here. I'll go talk to them."

"Howdy, ma'am," he said, walking across the yard. The boy had moved to one side, still pointing his gun towards the others. "Name's Petersen. We've had trouble at the homestead."

"We heard about it," she replied. She stared at his badge. "You really a Marshall?"

"Yes, ma'am. And Sheriff Kramer and Deputy Cowan from Twin Springs are with me."

"I'm Betty Canliff," she said. She peered at the body on the horse behind Ben. "Is that Tom Hallett you've got there?"

"Yes, ma'am. I'm sorry to say he's been shot dead."

She shook her head, sadly. "His brother's inside," she said. "He's in a bad way. We're doing what we can, but…"

Judd said. "One of these men is a doctor. Maybe he can help." He turned and called out. "Doc, there's an injured man here."

Doc Campbell rode forward.

Betty Canliff said, "Luke, put that gun up and take the doctor to Jimmy."

"Now, Mrs. Canliff," said Judd. "Do you want to tell me what's been happening here? Eight armed men, including Clem Palmer, came from this Cooperative and attacked our homestead today. What can you tell me about that?"

"Can't tell you anything, Marshall. First thing we knew about it was when we heard shooting in the distance, up the valley. Then some fellow came in with Jimmy Hallett and just dropped him off here in the yard. My son saw him ride off. Jimmy told my husband what had happened and he's gone down to the Crossing to find out what's going on."

"Your husband, that'll be Milo?"

"Yes."

"I met him Tuesday. He suggested to me if Fran joined your Cooperative, she wouldn't keep getting shot at." He raised his eyebrows. "See what I'm getting at?"

Betty Canliff looked flustered and then indignant. "My husband is a law-abiding Christian man, Marshall. I can assure you he knew nothing about this until Jimmy Hallett told him. If he had, he would have put a stop to it. He was shocked, as we all were."

"Okay, ma'am, I'm happy to take your word on that. No doubt I'll see him at Palmer's and we'll see what has to be done." He started to turn away. "That's Jim Hallett's horse I was leading," he said. "We're going to leave it here, and the others too, while we go on to Clem Palmer's place. You folks will know what to do about Tom Hallett. Would you tell Doc Campbell we're going and where?"

"Alright, Marshall," said Betty Canliff. "If it helps, I heard Jimmy tell my husband they were all meant to meet at the new Assembly Rooms."

"Okay, thanks."

When they had handed over the horses, Judd said, "We'll keep together and stay on the trail 'til we get to the turn-off down to the Crossing. I don't know what kind of reception we'll get at Palmer's place, but with the Halletts out of the action I guess if there's any shooting it'll be mainly down to Bates and Voller, if they're still there."

"Shooting or no shooting," said Tom, "They're both "Wanted" men, and so's Palmer, so he can forget those "Keep Out" notions he's always had."

George Pitt said, "I want first turn at Leo Marburg, as he calls himself these days, if that's alright with you guys."

"Well," said Judd, "We've got nothing definite on him as yet. I guess if you've come all the way from New York specially, you're entitled. But I've got a few questions for Higgins to answer and if Marburg's involved with that I'll want a piece of him, too."

He led the way back to the trail, then set off at a fast lope for Palmer's place.

As they arrived they saw that a small crowd had gathered. Judd slowed to a walk and the four of them drew up in a line across the street. The crowd, mostly men, were standing around a farm cart in front of what he guessed would be the Assembly Rooms, and they watched two men carry a body down the steps of the building and lift it onto the cart.

Judd recognized Milo Canliff standing at the top of the steps. He called to him.

"What's going on here?"

Milo came down and walked quickly across to him. "That's Clem Palmer," he said, indicating the body on the cart. "Shot dead. Seems there was a gunfight up the valley. Jim Hallett was hurt, too."

"We've just come from there, and I spoke to Mrs. Canliff on the way here. Who shot Palmer?"

"According to Marburg, a feller called Bates."

George Pitt said, "Marburg's still here, is he?"

"No, we sent him on his way. About ten minutes ago. We

didn't want any part of him. According to Jim Hallett it was him that was behind it all."

"Damnation. Which way did he go?"

"We just sent him up the street. I'd guess he'd head back to wherever he came from."

Pitt wheeled his horse around.

"I'll come with you," said Kramer.

Judd said, "See you back at the office, Tom. We're going after Bates and Voller."

Pitt and Kramer set off at speed in pursuit of Marburg.

Judd turned back to Milo. "We left Tom Hallett's body at your place, with his horse and Jim's horse, and another horse that belonged to one of Marburg's men who got shot and fell in the creek. I'll leave you to handle that." He paused and raised his voice so that others standing nearby could hear.

"Now, before we go, take a word of advice. With Palmer gone I guess you folks are going to have to reorganize things here. I'll have to send in a report of what's happened, so the best thing you can do is make sure this Cooperative is on the right footing with the authorities. These days they don't take kindly to armed patrols on government land. I know Palmer thought differently, but if you're not stealing their cows you folks really have nothing to fear from the cattlemen.

"And there's another thing, on a more personal level. I'm going to be settling on my folks" land pretty soon so we'll be neighbors and I truly hope we can all get along from now on. Okay? Be seeing you."

Judd and Ben rode side by side up the street and back to the trail to Twin Springs.

Judd said, "Some good may come out of this in the end. This Cooperative could be the base for a new township if they go about it in the right way. They stand a better chance with someone like Milo Canliff than they ever would with Palmer."

Ben said, "Poor Gwen. She would have had no idea when she left this morning that she would never again see her father alive."

CHAPTER TWENTY-SIX

Gwen Palmer and Ruth Cowan were from entirely different backgrounds, but as they began to get to know each other after Ben had introduced them, they soon discovered similar interests, particularly in literature and music.

Ruth was an accomplished piano player, and Gwen had a fine contralto voice and had benefitted from singing lessons during the short time she'd spent in the east.

They were in the Cowan's music room, practicing a song from a book of lieder, when the French windows opened and Billy Bates stepped quickly in from the verandah.

"Howdy, ladies." He gave them a mocking bow, sweeping his hat across his body.

He centered his eyes on Gwen. "I didn't come to see you, but I got some news for you. You can go back home. Your Pa's dead."

"Dead?" she gasped, horrified. "How? Did he go on the raid, then?"

"Yeah, he did, but that ain't how he died. I shot him."

"You? Why? What for?"

"He went crazy, shooting his gun off. He hit Marburg and he would of shot me too, but he wasn't quick enough."

"Father - dead." Gwen was shocked.

Ruth got up from the piano stool. "What about the Petersens?" she said as she moved to comfort Gwen. "What happened to them?"

Bates stared at her, a strange, wondering gaze as if he was not sure why she'd asked. "They're okay. They whipped us." He turned to Gwen. "Thanks to you." He took tobacco and paper from his vest pocket and started to make a cigarette. "You can get out," he said. "I want to talk to Ruth."

"You can leave us," said Ruth. "We do not wish to talk to you."

He ignored her, touched his tongue to the cigarette paper and stared at Gwen, his eyes flat and expressionless. "You heard me," he said. "Get out. I'd hate to have to treat you rough."

"Mr. Bates, we do not want you here," Ruth said firmly. "Will you please leave us."

Bates struck a match and lit his cigarette. "You can stop playing high and mighty," he said. "It won't do you no good. Come on, you're coming with me."

"You're talking nonsense." Ruth was angry. "You had better leave. Now!"

Gwen moved a couple of paces to the small table where she'd left her purse. In it was her derringer.

At the same time Bates started toward Ruth, but whatever he intended never took place. Gwen put her hand in the purse, gripped the derringer and fired it without taking it out. The first bullet hit the toe of Bates's left boot and the second took the lobe off his right ear.

He yelped in surprise, clapped his hand to his damaged ear and leapt through the French window onto the verandah.

Ruth stared in amazement at Gwen. Her gaze dropped to the little gun that Gwen had now drawn from her purse. She laughed, a little shakily. "You shot Billy Bates, the gunfighter!

And with that! He'll never live it down!"

Judd and Ben rode into the town at a fast trot. As they were coming up to the sheriff's office Ben pointed to the horses tied to the rail outside the Drovers saloon.

"That black one belongs to Bates," he said.

"Right," said Judd. "Do you see Voller's?"

"No. It isn't there. You can't mistake it. It's a really big bay mare, a good seventeen hands."

"Okay, so mebbe Bates is in there on his own."

Judd swung down and tied the buckskin to the rail.

Sandy and Cheswell hurried out from the lawyer's next door.

Sandy called out, "Lawyer Higgins has gone! He's run off!" Excitedly, he started to explain what had happened, Cheswell interjecting from time to time.

Judd cut them short. "Whoa there, hold it! Ben, you take care of this, will you? I'm going after Bates." He hitched his guns into place and walked quickly to the batwing doors of the Drovers.

About a dozen men were standing at the bar talking to the barman. Peretz saw Judd come in and said something in a low voice. All the men turned and stared.

Judd said, "I'm looking for Billy Bates."

"Ain't here," said Peretz.

"So I see. But his horse is outside. Anybody know where he is? Or his sidekick, Voller?" Judd looked them over and recognized Ike Sorrell, the mortician. "You seen either of them, Mr. Sorrell?"

"Yes, they were both in here earlier, Marshall. Mr. Peretz was just telling us about the gunfight up at Tinkers Creek."

Peretz scowled. "You just missed Voller. He lit out. Won't

be back." A sneering look came to his face. "And if you're really sure you want to find Billy, he said he was goin' courtin'."

"Did he say where?"

"Well, it's well-known he fancies his chances at the livery." He laughed. "Me, I wouldn't want to get in his way, but it's your funeral."

Judd turned on his heel and hurried down the street. Just as he came to the pump outside the livery he heard a couple of shots, which sounded as if they came from the back of the house. He ran through to the rear of the stables, calling to Dan and Isaac on the way.

As he came to the gravel path, Bates, clutching his bloody ear, was stumbling toward him from the direction of the verandah. Having reached the gate in the picket fence, Bates fumbled with the latch and had to use both hands to open it. His face twisted when saw the blood on his right hand. As if amazed at the sight of his own blood, he stared at it and didn't notice Judd until the gate was pushed open against him.

For an instant he froze, then stepped back and grabbed for his gun, but he'd lost his chance.

In that split second Judd jumped, his right hand grasped Bates's gun wrist, pulling him forward and down over the top of the open gate to land flat on his back on the gravel path, winded.

Judd hauled him to his feet as Isaac came running from the wagon yard.

Judd said, "I heard shots. Go see if your family need help. Quick!"

He frog-marched Bates through the livery stables and out into the street, where a crowd was gathering, the men from the Drovers having followed to see the action.

Judd called out. "Okay men, take a look. This is Billy

Bates, the gunfighter. Somebody has already bled him a little," he twisted Bates around so that his bleeding ear was clear to see. Bates, furious, struggled against the stronger man's grip.

"Mebbe he's not as fast as he thinks he is," said Judd. "Let's see, shall we?"

He spun Bates around, back-handed him across the mouth, and shoved him away.

"Okay, Billy, you've got your gun. Reach!"

Almost crying with fury, Bates flashed his left hand down and whipped out his gun, but the events of the past few minutes had wrecked his timing and Judd's own left-hand gun belched flame smashing the gun from Bates's hand before he could pull the trigger.

Bates staggered back, staring at the blood welling from a massive wound where his thumb and forefinger had been. Maddened beyond control, he dived for his fallen gun, reaching for it with his right hand, but again Judd was too quick for him, and his heel came down on Bates's knuckles with a sickening crunch.

Roughly, Judd grabbed him by the back of his collar and hauled him upright. The normally immaculately dressed, swaggering dandy was now a tattered, trembling wreck of a man. Judd held him up and shook him. He said, "This is what a gunfighter really looks like."

Somebody called out, "String him up!" There were murmurs of assent.

Judd raised his voice. "There'll be no lynching!" he said. "We've got no evidence against him, for one thing. All he's ever done in this town is scare people."

In the forefront of the watching crowd was Charlie Reynolds, the barber, attracted from his shop opposite the livery by the sounds of gunshots.

Judd shoved Bates in his direction. "Mr. Reynolds," he said, "We'll take him inside your place and fix up his hands - Doc Campbell is out of town."

"Then what are you going to do with him?" said Reynolds.

"Take him through the town so everyone can see him as he really is. Then turn him loose."

"Turn him loose? You must be crazy!"

"No. He'll leave this country far behind him and we'll never see him again. Losing his gun hand and being shown up like this is worse than death to him, believe me. I've seen his kind before. They teach themselves to be fast and accurate with a gun and think that makes them tough. All they need is someone to face them who isn't afraid. No, he knows now what he's really worth."

Pushing Bates ahead of him, he followed Charlie Reynolds into the barber shop and the crowd started to drift away.

CHAPTER TWENTY-SEVEN

The next morning Matt Watkins arrived in town early. He had his son Butch with him and a half-dozen hands. Judd and Tom Kramer were just coming back from breakfast at the Drovers.

Matt hailed them from his horse. "Howdy Marshall, Sheriff. We've come to fetch our cows back. John Stainer tells me you found em. You just point us in the right direction and we'll go get em."

Judd walked up to Matt's horse. "Howdy Mr. Watkins. Good to see you and your men. Sheriff and I have just been talking about it. Step down and come in the office, will you?"

"Butch," said Matt, as he dismounted, "Take the men and wait in the Drovers. Beer! Or coffee!"

In the sheriff's office Judd and Tom explained their plan to go back to the Cooperative Settlement at Tinkers Creek Crossing and follow the trail Bates and Voller and the three rustlers would have left from their camp.

"Should be easy enough," said Tom. "They wouldn't have tried to hide their tracks and there's been no rain to wash em away."

"It'll mean going through Star B range," said Matt.

"Yeah, and part of NHK, we think. We was figuring to

pick up a few hands from Todd Berman on the way, and mebbe send someone to NHK, too."

"Yeah, Todd will want to come along, and so will Newman and Harrison. One of my men can go fetch em. How many of those coyotes are still out there, do we know? Seems we were right about Dessay, Marshall. John said he and Foley were both killed. By Indians he said. That right?"

"Yeah," said Judd. "We reckon it could have been Bear Claw's men."

Matt shook his head. "Bear Claw keeps himself to himself mostly." He shrugged. "Indians can be notional."

Judd privately thought that, watching the attack on the homestead, Bear Claw and his men had recognized Foley and Dessay from Snow Flower's description of the white men who'd attacked her four days earlier. They'd then taken the opportunity to shoot at them.

But he merely said, "As for how many rustlers there are out there, Homer Foreman said there were four at the camp he found. Only one of them stayed behind."

"Hmmn." Matt frowned. "Judging by how many cattle we reckon have been taken all told, they'd need more than four to move a herd that size any distance."

"Well, the sooner we get after them, the sooner we'll know" said Judd. "I'll go get my gear." He went towards the door at the back of the office which opened into the block of cells. He'd spent the night in one of them. "Tom," he said, pausing in the doorway. "You've got plenty to do here in town. I guess now Mr. Watkins is here with a posse all set to go there's no call for you to come along."

"Sure," said Tom. "Lawyer Higgins ran off yesterday," he explained to Matt. "Emptied his safe and left his office in a clutter, papers all over."

He went on to tell how, very late the previous evening, he and George Pitt, having failed to hunt down Leo Marburg, had returned to the town and found Judd and Ben with Cheswell's help, trying to make sense of the chaos in the lawyer's office.

"It turns out that George Pitt is a lawyer too," said Tom. "Last night he was too tired after a day and a night on the stage and a long day in the saddle, but he's goin' through it all with us today."

"John Stainer told me about this guy," said Matt. "From back east, right? Went with you straight off the stage, John said. Seemed mighty hasty. What's his concern here?"

"He's after Marburg. It seems a year or so ago Marburg ran off with a passel of money from a bank they both worked for in New York. He's been trackin' him down ever since, so now he's set on findin' out what happened to that money. And, it seems, from what Ben could make out from the papers Higgins left behind, Marburg was the drivin' force behind the whole Petersen caboodle, too. He wanted that land, but we still don't know what for."

Judd came back into the room. "I'm all set," he said. "Any good trackers among your men?"

"Butch is a fair hand," said Matt, "And Charlie Gomez. They won't miss much."

"Okay, good. Let's head on out. We've got a lot of riding ahead of us."

The sky was clear blue and there was very little breeze. The day was turning out to be warm and on the way out to Tinkers Creek Crossing, Judd let the older man set the pace. As they rode side by side Judd brought Matt up to date with what had happened since the raid on the homestead, finishing with his account of escorting Bates out of the town.

Matt said, "Yeah, that Bates. Couple of my hands stopped

going into town on account of him."

"Oh? Why was that?"

"They knew him from Arizona. He'd picked a fight with a buddy of theirs down there, beat him to the draw and shot him dead. When Bates saw them in the Drovers the day he arrived, he dared them to do something, but they had more sense."

"Well, the town will be more pleasing to them now," said Judd.

"And what about the troubles out at the your place? Do you reckon they're over now?"

"I guess so. Palmer's dead, Marburg and Higgins are on the run, Bates is out of it. Yeah, I guess so, though it'd be good to know what it was all about."

They were quiet for a few miles, then Matt said, "I don't get over this way much these days. It's good country, isn't it? I guess I think of it as the south-western edge of my range, but in recent years we've tended to keep east of here. It's even better over there, least ways it was before the rustling started."

They continued in companionable silence for a while. Then Matt said, "The range life is wonderful. I still get out, time to time. Never miss a round-up." He paused for a minute or so before continuing. "Didn't you tell me you'd spent time out on the range?"

"Yeah. First real job I had after I left the homestead was on a drive from New Mexico up through the Panhandle and on to Abilene."

Matt said, "Along the old Coronado Trail?"

"Right."

"That was, what, ten years ago, then?"

"About that."

"Indians were real bothersome down there at that time, as I remember. Have any trouble?"

"Not till we reached the North Canadian and then we had to fight off a bunch of em, wouldn't let us cross the river."

"That would be about the time of the fight at Adobe Walls, wouldn't it?"

"Well, that was a year or two later, I think. Probably the same Indians, though."

Matt said, "I went up the trail three times in the early years. Out in the air all day and all night for weeks on end. Going through country you'd never seen before, open country mostly, miles of it. And in the evenings, after bedding down the herd for the night, setting around the fire with good companions, dog-tired but happy, the old-timers telling their stories, and always someone with a guitar or a squeeze-box, singing the old songs."

Judd grinned across at him. "And then getting in your bed-roll. There's never any sleep like it."

"Right. It's a good life. Nothing to beat it in the world."

Judd found himself warming to the old rancher, and wondered at the feeling. He would never have thought it possible.

When they reached the Settlement, they went through the open gate and down the street past the Assembly Rooms and Palmer's house. The few people who were about watched them curiously as they continued over the ford across the creek and through the gate in the fence. There, Butch and Charlie Gomez dismounted and cast about for sign. Butch soon looked up with a satisfied smile.

"Got it!" he said. "Dessay's horse."

"How many others?" asked Judd.

They both searched all around and then had a short discussion.

Butch said, "We make it five altogether. What it looks like, two sets of prints went out and came back with Dessay and two others, then it looks like one of the first horses went back again."

Judd frowned, "Five would be the right number though: Dessay, Bates and Voller, Foley and another from the rustlers" camp." He had a thought. "What can you say about the one that went back?"

"Big horse, heavy rider, I'd say," said Charlie.

"That'd be Voller," said Judd. "He went back to town with Bates, then packed up and left. I reckon he's gone back to the cattle."

"Okay, let's get after them," said Matt, "Mount up you two and lead the way."

Butch said, "I'll go get Todd. He'll want to come along for his cows, too."

"No," said Matt. "We'll follow these tracks till we know where they're going. Then you can fetch Todd."

Butch reluctantly agreed.

As his son remounted and took the lead, Matt said to Judd, "Todd Berman was my foreman when the boys were kids. Butch has always idolized him, and Liza, his wife. She took him under her wing when his mother died. Butch'll take any chance that comes along to visit with them."

The terrain was different this side of the creek, reddish granite rocks laid bare in helter-skelter stacks and piles with a scattering of yellowish lichen on them. Between the rocks grew Douglas fir, ponderosa pine, lodgepole pine and juniper, with occasional sloping pastures of tawny grass dotted with choke cherry and holly, but these didn't mask the underlying rocky character of the land.

The trail was easy to follow and they traveled mostly northwest and at a good speed through the foothills for several miles until they came out on the edge of a wide, rocky plateau.

Here they had to slow down as the sign was more difficult to read, and after about a mile Butch signaled a halt and spoke with Charlie Gomez. Then he looked at Judd and nodded straight ahead to where the land began to rise sharply toward high mountains, three or four miles away.

"We reckon we're headed directly toward that fold in the hills," he said, "And that will lead us up into the high country south of NHK. That set right with you?"

"Yeah, that'd tie in with what Homer Foreman said."

Butch turned to Matt. "It's about ten miles to Todd's place from here. I'll go fetch him along. You'll be okay with Charlie from here on."

He put spurs to his horse and set off at a fast pace before his father could argue.

Matt watched him go, a trace of a smile on his face.

CHAPTER TWENTY-EIGHT

With Charlie Gomez leading the way the posse picked as straight a path through the rocks as they could until they came to the rising ground. There, Charlie scouted around and soon found the tracks of the rustlers again, leading, as expected, through the fold in the hills.

From here on the trail was clear once more, always leading upwards, and with Charlie some distance ahead, they were able to continue at a good speed for several miles until, after a long, straight run through shade thrown by a mixture of Ponderosa pine and Douglas fir, they came to a steep passage through rocks and stunted pines. This led them up onto a high ridge where they could look down over a wide grassy area.

Charlie reined in and signaled a halt. He waved his arm, pointing ahead along the side of the mountain at the far end of the ridge, and they saw in the distance the first of the cattle.

About half an hour later they came down the side of that mountain and approached the cattle. They reckoned there were about two hundred all told and they were well spread out, but all the nearest cows had either Star B or NHK brands and it was obvious they were part of the rustlers" haul.

Matt said, "Charlie, you stay with me and the marshall. We'll carry on, see where the tracks lead to. The rest of you men bring these cows along behind, quick as you can."

Matt said, "We're looking for a couple of cabins, right Marshall?"

"That's what Homer saw, set at an angle to each other among trees, close up against the mountain and facing a big, open area of grass. Look out for a short, high spur, between a canyon on one side and a curve in the mountainside on the other. The cabins should be in the curve."

The tracks continued along the mountainside and eventually through a rocky valley where there was plenty of sign that this was the way the cattle had been driven in. The far end of the valley widened out onto open country again, mainly poor quality grass among rocks, sloping gently upward and surrounded by high land. Judd reined in, dug in his saddle bag and took out his field glasses. He scanned the land ahead of them, then grunted in satisfaction.

Matt said, "What do you see?"

"Another herd, coupla miles, could be, over to the right, and looks like there's a big canyon further on, mebbe coupla miles more, and what could be a high spur in back of there."

"I guess we're getting near," said Matt. He paused, eased his position on the horse and put both hands on the pommel, considering. Then he said, "I reckon the three of us could gather those cows up and hold them until the boys come up with the others. What do you say, Marshall?"

Judd grinned. "I guess ol' Buck and me can still bring in a few cows, eh old feller?" He patted the buckskin's neck.

The cattle were spread out for over a mile, back in the direction of the canyon, and as the three men got closer Judd became convinced that the canyon and the high spur were those that Homer had described. The rustlers" cabins would be just beyond.

First, though, they had to round up the cattle. The grass was much better here and these cattle were in good shape. Some of the cows were clearly not far off calving, so they tried to avoid too much chasing around and by the time they had them all gathered, the other, smaller herd were coming to join them.

When the two herds met there was a short spell of confusion as they mingled, then they settled down and the men moved them along again slowly, toward the mouth of the canyon. The herd was now two hundred and thirty cows with fifty or so unbranded young stock. The adult animals were mainly Star B and NHK, with only a dozen Double Diamond.

Leaving a couple of men to keep an eye on the cattle, Judd and Matt led the rest out and around the high spur to search for the rustlers" camp.

As they set off Matt said, "It's clear we were right. They've been taking cows in calf. Must be plenty more some place else, though. We reckon to have lost over a hundred head ourselves and I know Ken Barratt lost about the same."

"I saw a few of yours in the first lot I came across," said Judd. "I didn't check brands on any others and Homer didn't either, but he did find two more bunches of cattle and plenty of sign. I guess this is the third bunch he saw, so there'll be at least another two."

"How many in the other two herds?"

"About sixty, seventy in the first one," Judd paused, trying to visualize the second lot of tracks he'd seen. "About the same in the second bunch, probably."

"So we've got to search around for at least one more big herd," said Matt, "Tucked away somewhere back in this godforsaken mountain country."

"Unless they've moved some on," said Judd. "The way I see it, if they ever did try to move them all together it wouldn't be more than a day or two before someone noticed, would it?"

"What are you getting at?"

"I reckon they've been bringing them here and holding them 'til they're ready move them on a few at a time. That would account for why they wouldn't need many men."

"Okay. So where would they move them to?"

"Tell me something," said Judd. "Where we are now is just off the south east of NHK range, is that right?"

"Yeah, I guess so."

"And who is NHK's neighbor to the east?"

"Well, allowing for a few miles of scrub land it would be the Mannion brothers at Tomahawk, I guess. The western part of their range butts on the north of ours, but it's poor land and they never made a lot of use of it."

"Until now, perhaps," said Judd. "See, Tom Kramer told me there'd been talk of Tomahawk going bust not so long ago, but lately their bills are being paid on time and he'd heard that Marburg had bought the place."

Matt said, "Well, I wouldn't know about that, but I've seen the Mannion brothers at sales several times lately."

"Buying or selling? said Judd.

"I only saw them selling. I figured they were selling stock to pay off their debts."

"No question about the origin of the cattle they were selling?"

"No, none at all."

Judd was quiet for a moment, thinking. "Well, okay," he said, "I wouldn't mind placing a bet with you that if any of the young stock we find here are branded, it'll be a Tomahawk brand."

Matt stared at him. "You mean they're replacing the cattle they've sold with stock from here?"

"That's exactly what I mean."

"Well," said Matt, sadly. "I never would have pegged the Mannions as cattle thieves. I've always thought of them as friends and neighbors. But it kind of figures, and if it's true I don't like to think about what could happen to them."

Judd said, "That'd be for a judge to decide."

They had rounded the spur and there ahead of them were the two cabins. They soon saw that they were deserted.

Matt called Charlie Gomez to him.

"Charlie, see if you can find fresh tracks of that big horse and rider - what's his name?"

"Voller," said Judd. "And there was the fellow that stayed here, too."

"Their tracks will be fresh. Follow them, see which way they went. We'll go back to the cattle and wait for Butch and you can join us there."

Charlie Gomez soon found the tracks Voller and Jonno had made when they'd left in a hurry, and the others watched him follow their trail back around the promontory and onto the long slope of grassland that stretched away from the mouth of the canyon where the cattle were being held, until he passed out of sight up into a gully.

One of the men left with the cattle had made a small fire to brew coffee, and they all sat around taking a welcome break. Then Butch arrived with Todd Berman and a couple of Star B riders. They all stepped down and helped themselves to coffee. Matt brought them up-to-date with the ideas he and Judd had been knocking around.

Soon after this Charlie Gomez returned. He had news.

"You're gonna love this," he said. "They led me to where they been bringing the cows in. But first they swung off a little ways to a pretty little valley with mebbe fifty head of young stuff, mostly yearlings, and they took a coupla dozen with them. Left as easy a trail as I ever followed. But," Charlie paused dramatically, "Them yearlings was all fresh branded." He stopped again and smiled broadly at Judd. "Mr. Marshall, you know what the brand was, don't you?"

"Tomahawk," said Judd.

"Right."

Butch swore and stood up. "I'm going after those two! Charlie, you just point me in the right direction." He strode over to his horse.

Matt said, "Charlie, I'll need you back here to show us where those yearlings are. Ed and Pete, you can go along with Butch if you've a mind to. Butch, you be sure to bring those yearlings back here, you hear me?"

CHAPTER TWENTY-NINE

Ben and George Pitt came out of the Cowan house and started up the street just in time to see Judd and the posse leaving the Drovers and heading out the other end of town. George Pitt was carrying a leather document case. He'd spent the night as guest of the Cowan family.

By the time they reached the sheriff's office, Cheswell had arrived, keen to help sort out the muddle left by Higgins. He wanted to make a good impression on this newcomer, who, he'd learnt, was also a lawyer and might therefore be in need of a clerk.

But Pitt's overriding concern was Marburg, not Higgins, and he wanted the sheriff's help to search Marburg's apartment over the Bank for evidence of the stolen money. Leaving Ben and Cheswell to deal with the lawyer's office, Tom Kramer accompanied Pitt across the road to the Bank building, where they made their way upstairs to Marburg's rooms.

They were surprised to find the door unlocked, but they soon discovered why; the place was in some disarray, not as bad as the lawyer's office, but it was obvious Marburg had returned, taken what he needed and left again in some haste.

"Goddammit!" Pitt shouted, "The bastard's been back here! He couldn't have gotten here before us yesterday, could he? We were only minutes behind him at the Settlement."

"He must have crept in during the night," said Tom.

Pitt ground his teeth in frustrated anger. "I knew we should have checked as soon as we got back! Hell! I was too damned tired to think straight!"

"Let's take a look-see," said Tom. He went to the open safe, pulled out a few envelopes and began looking through their contents. "What are we lookin' for, exactly?"

"Anything to do with bank accounts for a start," said Pitt. He moved over to Marburg's big desk and started opening drawers. None were locked.

They looked through documents in silence for a while, then Tom said, "Well, well. Here's somethin' interestin'. Not bank papers, but the deeds of the Tomahawk ranch. That answers the question how they suddenly started payin' their bills lately."

Pitt quickly joined him. "Let me see."

Tom passed him the sheaf of papers and he flicked through them, stopping with a grunt of satisfaction. "Well, here's eleven thousand of the money accounted for. That's good, Sheriff." He smiled. "I guess that makes my employer the legal owner now. I can't see any court disputing that."

He put the deeds in his pocket and they continued their search.

Among the other documents from the safe, Tom also found deeds of the hotel, the Drovers and adjoining offices, and the building they were in, the total value of which, Pitt estimated, would, together with the Tomahawk, account for more than half of the original amount stolen.

When they had finished with the desk and safe they searched the remainder of the apartment, but the only item of interest they turned up was a large map showing the Tinkers Creek Settlement and the valley to the north, including the Petersen homestead and the upper valley. There were no marks on the map to indicate what Marburg may have wanted it for, but Tom thought it would be interesting to see what ideas Shepherd, the land agent, might have about it.

Although they found no money and nothing at all relating to bank accounts, Pitt expressed himself well pleased with what they had achieved so far. He put all the relevant documents into his case and they went back across the street to the lawyer's office.

Ben and Cheswell had made good progress. They had sorted the papers into separate stacks and Cheswell was busily filing away items from the biggest of them.

Ben was sitting at Cheswell's desk in the outer office and looked up as Tom and Pitt came in.

"This is all business Higgins was taking care of for Marburg," he said, indicating the untidy heap of documentation he was sorting through."

"Any references to bank accounts?" asked Pitt.

"I haven't seen any so far." Ben picked up a batch of files. "But this is intriguing. It appears to be correspondence with a railway company, Greeley, Salt Lake, and Pacific Railroad. I've just been looking at a letter enquiring about purchase of shares in the company."

"May I see?" said Pitt. "If Marburg bought any it would show how he paid for them."

Ben stood up. "You'll know better than I do what to look for," he said, and moved away from the desk to let Pitt take over.

He said to Tom, "My father and my brother Michael were talking the other day about a rumor of a new railway line from Greeley through Fort Collins and continuing west. They were speculating on how it might affect the drayage business. I suppose such a line could go through somewhere near here, couldn't it?"

"Well, I dunno. It would depend on the lie of the land. There's some mighty rough country between here and Fort Collins."

Ben said, "When we first came here four years ago, there was talk of a branch line coming to the town. The Union Pacific Railway lines from Cheyenne had just reached Fort Collins at the time. They went ahead with the telegraph lines but then the railway was cancelled. Father was disappointed because he'd thought the railway would bring more business."

"I'd say he wouldn't have bin the only one," said Tom. He paused, considering, then he said, "We found a map over the road showing the country around the Petersen place. Could be a connection. Let's drop in next door, ask Shepherd about it. I've got a hunch he may have a few answers."

Shepherd stood up from his desk as Tom entered his office with Ben. He was a heavy-set man in his fifties, balding, with a round red face, a thick mustache and glasses. He looked apprehensive.

"Good morning, Sheriff," he said nervously. "I was wondering if you might call in."

"Oh, really?" said Tom.

"Yes," He chewed his top lip and his bottom lip alternately, staring from Tom to Ben and back again. "I understand Con Higgins has left town."

"Right," said Tom. "And it so happens that Mr. Leo Marburg has skedaddled as well."

There was a long pause. Ben smiled encouragingly at Shepherd. Shepherd cleared his throat.

"What was it you wanted, Sheriff?" he said.

"Marburg left a few bits and pieces behind him. Like this map, for instance," said Tom, tapping the map with his fingertips. "And I figure you'd know what he'd want with it."

"Ah, yes. Well, yes." Shepherd sat down carefully behind his desk. He linked his fingers across his belly and looked down at them, tapping his thumbs together for a few seconds.

"I suppose Mr. Marburg won't be coming back any time soon?" he said at last.

"He'll get arrested if he does," said Tom.

"Alright. I gave him the map. Well, he paid me for it." he said. "He wanted to know about the ownership of the land, what sections had been taken up, who had title and what land remained the property of the federal government."

"And you told him."

"Yes."

"So he would know who owned the Petersen land."

"Yes."

"And you did nothin' to stop that land comin' up for sale."

Shepherd stared up at him, a pleading look in his eyes. "Con Higgins told me it would be best if I said nothing in case an accident was arranged for me," he said. "And then that man Bates went to my house and frightened my wife. I was scared, Sheriff."

Tom Kramer looked at him in silence for a long moment. Then he said, "So why did Marburg want to know about that land?"

"Well, Con Higgins told me he and Mr. Marburg had shares in a railroad company that had been incorporated to build a line from Greeley to Fort Collins and westward to Salt Lake City. He said the company expected to get a free right of way through Fort Collins, so Mr. Marburg wanted to know what government land the railroad company would be likely to claim west of there. I found out that Tinkers Creek Valley was on the most favored route."

"But Clem Palmer's Cooperative owns a big part of the valley," said Ben.

"Yes, well," said Shepherd, "Palmer's in partnership with them."

"Was," said Tom. "He's dead. Bates shot him."

"Oh. Well, I suppose that's the end of it now then." Shepherd looked from one to the other of the again, hopefully, eyebrows raised.

"Not quite," said Tom. "So, tell me, what were you figurin' on gettin' out of it?"

"Con promised me shares in the company when it's all set up."

Tom shook his head at Shepherd pityingly. He said, "I guess you must be thinkin' it was just bad luck Judd Petersen happens to be a Deputy US Marshall, huh?" He went to the door. "If I was you I'd be lookin' to my hole card, "cos it's certain sure he'll be sendin' in a report on this whole rotten business and it won't be easy for you to keep this job when it all gets known. C'mon Ben, we got what we came for."

Doc Campbell was waiting outside the sheriff's office.

He told them that the settlers at Tinkers Creek Crossing had elected Milo Canliffe as their new leader, and it was agreed that there would be no further armed patrols of their fences, and the trail through the Cooperative would remain open at all times. He also said he'd patched up Jim Hallett and thought he had a fair chance of surviving, but might well end up a semi-invalid.

Ben asked him if he knew if anything was being done to settle Clem Palmer's affairs.

Doc said, "Milo asked me to let his daughter know she's welcome to go back and help them if she will. The sooner the better, he said. You'll pass the message on, I trust. Now, I must get along. I've got a few patients to call on."

Tom and Ben looked in on George Pitt but he told them he was managing well enough with Cheswell's help. He hadn't found any link to the remainder of the missing money yet, but it was probably only a matter of time.

Tom said, "We're goin to put out "Wanted" flyers for Marburg and Higgins. You never know, sometimes it gets results."

Back in their own office, Ben and Tom talked about Judd's handling of Bates, agreeing that it did not seem a wise decision just to turn him loose, incapacitated or not.

Ben said, as if in Judd's defense, "We could have put him in a cell, I suppose, but what could we have held him for?"

"Shootin' Palmer."

"But we have no evidence. All we have is Milo Canliffe's word that Marburg told him Bates had done it."

"Well, okay, but it would of kept him out the way for a while."

"Still, he won't show his face in town again anyway, after what Gwen did to him."

"Yeah, what actually happened there?"

"According to Ruth, she and Gwen were trying out some songs together and Bates interrupted them. He told Gwen quite casually that he'd shot her father dead, and then tried to make Ruth leave with him." Ben smiled, and there was a hint of pride in his voice when he added, "But he underestimated Gwen. She'd brought a little two-shot pistol with her when she left home, and she shot at him, and made him run off, straight into Judd, it seems."

"Yeah, she's got a lotta spirit, that young lady."

"She certainly has."

"Stayin' over for a while at your place, is she?"

"Well, Mother and Ruth seem quite taken with her and they have invited her to stay for as long as she likes."

Tom smiled at him. "You've been sweet on her for some time, haven't you? You figurin' on gettin' together on a regular basis any time soon?"

Ben grinned self-consciously. "When things have settled down a bit I'm going to ask her to marry me and live here in town."

CHAPTER THIRTY

Three days later a rider came up the trail from the Settlement toward the Petersen place. Judd saw him first. He and Homer were fixing the final section of the fencing that Butch's cattle had broken, and Judd had just stepped back from hammering in the last nail when he caught a glimpse of movement through the trees down where the trail ran alongside the creek.

"Somebody coming," he said.

His Winchester was leaning against the fence rail a few feet away and he moved quickly to pick it up. He was wary of going far without it, although nothing had happened to disturb the peace at the homestead since he'd returned after leaving Matt Watkins and Todd Berman up in the mountains. By the time he'd led them to the small park-like area where he'd seen the first of the stolen cattle, they'd agreed they'd found all that there was to find and he'd been anxious to get back.

The two ranchers had started planning how to get all the rustled cattle back on their rightful ranges, so Judd had searched around and found the tracks left by Homer the previous day, and he'd followed them, reasoning correctly that they'd show a good route back.

Now, Homer came to stand beside him, holding his Spencer 56 in one hand and shielding his eyes with the other as he peered down toward the trail.

The rider came out of the trees half a mile away and Judd said, "Whoever he is he's got something shiny, probably a star, on his vest. Tom Kramer or Ben, I'd guess."

"It's the sheriff's horse," said Homer. "Big, bay gelding, know him anywhere."

Judd said, "Let's pack all this gear and go see what news brings him all the way out here."

They loaded their tools and the spare posts and rails onto their cart, and Homer led Betsy, the plow horse, back across the pasture and down to the yard.

Tom Kramer had dismounted and Fran was welcoming him when they arrived.

Homer said he'd see to Tom's horse, and Fran invited them all to sit on the bench under the cottonwood. "I'll bring coffee," she said, and went back to the kitchen.

"I've got a fair passel of news for you," Tom said to Judd, "But the best of it'll wait till Fran Healey comes back. And first, I got to thank you for all you done to put a stop to the rustlin'. Much appreciated. Just to keep you in the picture, the Cattlemen's Association are makin shift to get all the stolen cattle back where they belong, and they've taken over the Tomahawk ranch and put Matt Watkins in charge there for the time being."

Judd said, "I guessed right, then, did I, about them replacing their own cows a few at a time with rustled youngstock?"

"You did, and they had a coupla hundred K Bar and DD cows and calves on their range as well."

"What about the owners, the Mannion brothers? They must have been in it, too."

"In my jail. And their foreman and a couple of their hands. We've got a judge comin' some time later in the week."

"Good," said Judd. "And there was a couple of rustlers Butch Watkins went after up in the mountains. Bates's sidekick, Voller, was one of them. Did he catch them, do you know?"

"He did. They were up in that scrub land on the edge of the Tomahawk with a dozen or so branded yearlings. And would you believe it, they tried to brave it out, saying they were just roundin' up strays, but Butch wasn't havin' that. Voller drew on him and there was a shootin' match. Voller bought it. The other one scooted out of it and they let him go."

"Well, that about accounts for all of them, then, except Higgins and Marburg."

"Yeah. Nobody's seen hide nor hair of Marburg since Milo Canliffe ran him off from the Settlement. As for Higgins, I heard this morning his horse was found at Loveland. Been tied up outside a store for several days." Tom shook his head in disgust. "In the end somebody took notice of it and they found his address in the saddlebag. Seems he most likely caught a train."

Homer came to join them. He said, "I guess my short run as a lawman is over, Sheriff." He put his hand in his vest pocket, took out his Deputy's badge and handed it to Tom.

"You did a real good job, Homer," said Tom, taking it. "Job's still open if you want it."

"Waal, if it means I get to spend a day or two up in the high country, time to time, I'll think about it."

Fran arrived with the coffee, followed slowly by little Joe carrying a plate piled with doughnuts. She'd heard Tom's offer to Homer.

"Now, Sheriff Kramer, don't you go undoing all our hard work," she said. "Joe and me, we've been trying to sweet-talk him into staying on here and I was beginning to think we were winning."

Homer said, indicating Joe and the doughnuts. "I reckon I'm gonna have to give in to her, Sheriff. How can a man put up a de-fence agin' two powerful agents like these?"

Joe put the plate down firmly on Homer's lap.

"See?" said Homer, taking a doughnut in one hand and riffling Joe's curly hair with the other.

Fran's face lit up. "You really mean that?"

"Sure. If you'll have me."

He took a bite and smiled appreciatively, and passed the plate to the sheriff.

Then he said. "It's nigh on forty years now since I lost my family and my farm to the "Paches. After that I guess I just wanted to be fancy-dancin' along the trail. I just knew there would always be something better over the next hill, and when they told me a rolling stone gathers no moss, I'd say: "a setting hen loses feathers". But, you know, in the end the day came when I got wise to the fact - it was always the looking that was good, not so much the finding. That's how it didn't come too hard for me to stay on and look after things for Sam Cowan while he went back to England for his folks. And now? Well, I feel like I've found me a new family, and I guess I'm good and ready to set and moult."

Fran stood and went to hug him. Then she said, "There won't be a lot of setting, though!"

Tom said, "Ma'am, I was telling Judd what's been going on in the last few days. But I wouldn't come all the way out here just for that. See, George Pitt - you met him when we came out last Thursday - he's spent the last three days going through all the papers Higgins and Marburg left behind, and he found out why they wanted this land." He paused and they looked at him expectantly. "It's clear they believed there was going to be railroad built through here and they thought if they owned the whole of the valley they could hold the railroad company to ransom over access, and then, after the lines were laid, they would make another killing because land values would shoot up. This morning, though, George heard that the railroad company have made their plans public and the lines will not be coming through here."

There was a brief silence.

Judd said, "Why didn't we hear anything about this railroad?"

"It was all rumor and hearsay," said Tom. "There never was any actual plan to bring a railroad through here. Okay, this valley and all the way down through to Twin Springs would be easy enough, but they'd have to get here first and if you know the country at all, it's plain why they wouldn't want to try. And in any case, where would the line go after Twin Springs?"

Fran said, "So it was all for nothing, then? Sten got shot for nothing in the end."

Tom said, "Sten Petersen got shot because some schemin', power-hungry varmints thought he was in their way. I've seen this sort of thing happen too often, a decent, honest citizen leadin' his own life in his own way is pushed aside just so others can take what they want. It's the main reason I took this job, to try and stop it happenin'. I know it ain't much comfort, ma'am, but in this case the varmints didn't get what they wanted."

She said, "It's no comfort at all, Sheriff, because they didn't get what they deserved, either. Well," she paused, "Clem Palmer did, I suppose, but I don't guess he was the one who shot Sten. And Marburg and lawyer Higgins are still on the loose, right?"

"Yeah. I've sent out fliers for both of them, but I'd say Higgins is well and truly out of sight by now. Marburg, though,

I dunno. He was hurt so he'd have a tough time travelin' very far. Palmer threw a shot at him and hit him in the leg apparently."

"What's this fellow Pitt doing about it, then?" said Judd. "He's supposed to have trailed him all the way from New York, why ain't he out looking for him?"

"It appears it ain't Marburg he's so set on catching up with as much as the money he took from the bank. That's why he's been digging through all that paper, and now he thinks he's found where it could be, or what's left of it, in a bank in Cheyenne. He set off on the stage first thing this morning to check on it." Tom paused and looked at Judd. "He took Ruth Cowan with him, too."

Judd raised his eyebrows. "Is that so?"

Tom shrugged. He said, "Ben thought you might be interested to know that."

Judd smiled his lopsided smile. He hadn't realized he'd shown that much interest in Ruth Cowan for others to notice it. Sure, she was a fine-looking woman, and her beautiful, violet-colored eyes had fascinated him, but that was as far as it went. From their brief conversation in the Cowans" grand parlor he'd got the idea she was by nature somebody rather more conscious of her social standing than were any of those few people he was glad to call friends, and in truth, during the days following their meeting, his mind had been fully focused on other events, and he'd not thought about her at all.

He said, "Well, you thank Ben for me, will you? And you can tell him, if you will, that I'm not positive I appreciate how he was able to peg me as a man interested in town gossip."

Tom laughed. "He figured you wrong, then?"

"Oh, I wouldn't swear to that. Sometimes it's handy to know what's going on in town, right folks?"

Fran nodded. She said, seriously, "I grew up in the town, and I'll allow there's been times when I felt a mite left outa things, way out here."

"Okay, then," said Tom, "Here's somethin' else for you to know about. Ben went out to the Settlement yesterday with Gwen Palmer to help her settle her father's affairs, and afterwards she agreed to marry him and live in town."

Judd said, "Well, good for them. How's she feel about him staying on as a Deputy, though?"

"Ain't been nothing said as yet. But, on that subject, you'll remember I told you about that widda woman down south in Raton? I'm thinkin' now's a good time for me to get ready to hand in my star and go give her a helpin' hand like I promised."

"What would the town council think about that?" asked Judd.

"When I told them, they said to tell you if you ain't going back to marshallin' in Kansas, the job's yours."

Fran looked at Judd anxiously.

Judd took a deep breath. This was it, then. Decision time.

Over the past three days, working with Fran and Homer about the homestead, he'd come to fully appreciate the potentiality in the place. Now, from what Tom had just told them, the threat over ownership had been removed, so there was a chance to make that potentiality into more of a certainty. It would need a great deal of hard work, but it shouldn't be too difficult now to hire on a few skilled hands. It would take a fair amount of capital, too. Well, he had savings which would get them some way, and in all likelihood he could raise a loan if right up necessary. And besides, he'd grown fond of little Joe, and his respect for Fran was growing by the day. He had no doubt they could work together to develop the homestead to give them all a good living.

He said, "When I came in your office a week ago today, I thought all I'd have to do was sign a few papers and arrange to close up or sell this place, and then do just that, go on back to marshalling. I didn't even expect to come out here. What would I want with a two-bit farm? But I won't be going back to Kansas, and I won't be settling in Twin Springs as their sheriff either." He looked at them all in turn. "Fran has already told me she wants to stay here and carry on with the plans she made with Sten. They're good plans, but she can't do it all on her own and she needs my land anyway. So I guess I'm going to stay here and help her make my fortune out of farming."

He smiled at her. He'd come to think of her as a serious, steady kind of person, worried, naturally enough, about the future for herself and her little boy after losing Sten, but determined to make the most out of whatever came along. Now though, her bright, sparkling blue eyes and her broad smile of pure happiness as she looked up at him gave her a kind of radiance that he hadn't seen in her before.

Homer was nodding his head, smiling in a satisfied way as he scratched his whiskers.

Tom Kramer said, "Waal, I guess the town will find some one. What d'you think of Ben for the job? Think he'd make it?"

"Yeah, he's a good man. I wouldn't put him up against a gunslinger like Bates, but then, there's not so many like him around these days. In any case, I guess he'd find a way around gunfights. He's got a head on his shoulders. But find him a good deputy before you go, will you?"

CHAPTER THIRTY-ONE

For three weeks life at the homestead went along peacefully. Judd had sent a report to his superiors in Kansas and included with it a letter informing them of his decision to hand in his Marshall's badge.

One of his first actions after his decision to stay had been to put in a claim on the quarter section north of Fran's along the creek, and he'd persuaded Homer to do the same on the next section along as well, thus confirming his partnership with them. This would bring the total amount of land actually belonging to the homestead to eleven hundred and twenty acres, next to about ten square miles of mainly well-watered grass land available to them on which to graze a future herd.

Tom Kramer had sent out a couple of men who had arrived in the town looking for jobs, and Judd had hired them to work on the farm along the creek between the homestead and the Settlement fenceline. They had started by renovating the burnt-out buildings so that they had somewhere to live while they reinstated the land.

It was this part of the holding that Fran saw as the main area for managing the breeding stock from which their herd would develop. She'd decided to leave the eighty cows which were to be the foundation of the herd on the Double Diamond range until this land was ready, or at least, for as long as Matt Watkins would let them stay there.

Judd was still using his old bedroom and he was beginning to find living in close proximity to Fran unsettling, not least because he was becoming more attracted to her day by day. She'd made no sign that she would welcome advances from him, however, and he felt she was still mourning the loss of Sten. He found himself starting to hope that perhaps in due time things might change.

Meanwhile, he and Homer had completed all the restoration work needed around the main house, so now he decided they should set to and repair the buildings on Sten's original homestead to make them fit for him to live in. They were about half a mile away across the valley to the east.

The two-room cabin had been used as a store for various items that might come in handy one day and the lengthiest job was clearing it out and cleaning up afterwards. The stables needed some repairs too, but the buildings had been well-built originally and after a couple of days everything was ready for Judd to move in.

Fran had told him she was quite happy for things to go along as they were, but if that's what he wanted then she'd take it kindly if he were to agree for her to carry on doing his laundry and cooking his meals in the main house. And she'd do the same for Homer.

"That way," she'd said, "We'll get together at the beginning of each day, so we all know what we'll be doing, and at the end so we all know what's done."

Judd and Homer were only too happy to agree, and late one evening Judd harnessed Buck, loaded his few belongings on the buckboard, and moved out of his family home.

His first night in Sten's old cabin was not uneventful, however. He awoke suddenly about an hour before first light. He wasn't sure what had woken him, but he thought it might have been a gunshot, and the more he thought about it the more certain he became. He listened, took up the six-gun by his pillow, and fumbled his way in the dark through the cabin to the door. He opened it and looked out. It was a clear night, stars but no moon, and all was silent.

He went out onto the stoop and listened again, turning his head this way and that, and he thought he caught a glimpse of light through the trees to his right, in the direction of the main house. When Sten had built this cabin it had been in direct line of sight from his brother's, but in the intervening years since he'd moved into the main house after Olaf's death, trees and scrub had been allowed to grow unchecked close by, and the cabins were now hidden from each other.

Judd was puzzled by that light. He went back indoors, found matches and lit the lamp. Then he put on his pants, gunbelt and work boots and went up the slope behind the cabin to get a better view. When he was high enough he could see that there was indeed a light in that direction and it seemed to be flickering. Suddenly he realized. He was looking at a fire.

He turned and ran back down to the track that led to the bridge over the creek and as he ran three booming gunshots, equally spaced, one after the other, echoed around the valley. It was Homer's Spencer 56 rifle and he was signaling for help.

When Judd came past the trees, he saw flames coming from the window in the wall of the main house facing him. That was the room where Fran and Joe slept. He felt a jolt of fear that made him run as fast as he'd ever run. Then, as he came closer he could see Homer on the bridge struggling with a rope, hauling up a pail of water from the creek.

"Where's Fran and the boy?" he yelled.

"Joe's safe," said Homer, "Back of the yard."

Judd grabbed the pail and rushed to hurl the water through

the window.

"Fran's in there, though," called Homer, "Tackling it from inside."

"Hell's bells!" Judd turned, threw the empty pail back to Homer. He rushed around to the yard and opened the kitchen door, expecting to find smoke but there was none. The door to the parlor was closed but the one to the bath house was open and the lamp was lit. He called out, "Fran!"

"Here!" she gasped, coming to the doorway of the bath house. "Stand clear! I've got a full pail!"

"Out!" he ordered. He stepped forward and grabbed the pail. "We'll all tackle it from outside."

He ran back to the flames and again threw the water through the smashed window.

"It smells of oil," he shouted. "Fran, fetch the old tarp, will you, and hammer and nails. We'll try and smother it."

He went back to Homer and took his refilled bucket, handing him the empty one.

The solid outside timbers around the window frame were well alight and flames were still spurting out from inside but the fire had not yet taken a good hold on the roof. He threw the water as high as he could to drench the nearest shingles, then, as he returned to the creek he heard approaching hoofbeats. It was the two new hands, Pedro and Ike, coming to help.

He sent Pedro to find Fran and help her with the tarpaulin, and told Ike, a big, strong young man, to swap places with Homer at the creek so that the three of them could make a bucket chain.

"And fetch more buckets!" he called after Pedro.

The bucket chain worked well. Ike stood on the bank of the creek, dipped the bucket and passed it up full to Homer, who met Judd on his way back from the house with the emptied one, which Homer passed on to Ike. After several repetitions, with Judd throwing the water at the fire inside, they were rewarded by more smoke and less flame, and Judd started concentrating on the wall around the window.

By the time Fran and Pedro arrived with the tarp, the area around the window was no longer blazing but still smoldering red and smoking.

Judd's idea was to soak the tarp and fix it over the window frame to contain the fire within the room. Then with two men continuing to soak the outside, the rest could try to put out the fire from inside the house. They formed a chain of three from the bath house, through the kitchen, into the parlor, where Judd threw water at the flames through the doorway to Fran's room. Several times he had to step outside when the dense smoke threatened to overcome him, but eventually, as dawn broke over the eastern rim of the valley, he doused the last smoldering ember in the room and called a halt. He was exhausted.

They gathered together out in the yard, and after detailing Pedro to make coffee, Fran went to comfort little Joe, whom she'd wrapped up in her quilted bedcover and left just inside the barn. Then she joined the others as they took stock of the situation.

By smothering the window frame with the tarp and keeping all inside doors closed as much as possible, they'd managed to confine the fire to Fran's bedroom.

"Let's go see what can be salvaged," she said. "Look at me. What can I look like!" She was in her night clothes covered by an old slicker, her feet in work boots. Her hair was all awry and her face smudged with soot. She picked Joe up and hitched him onto her hip.

"I guess we could all do with a cleanup," said Judd as they went back into the house.

Ike and Homer took the tarp off the window frame. In the early morning light Fran's bedroom was a blackened ruin.

She stared in silence from the parlor doorway while Joe looked on with a puzzled frown.

The bedroom window and the wooden chest that also served as a simple dressing table beneath it were burnt beyond repair. There was a large hole in the wooden floor close by. Next to it was a blackened can of the type used for coal oil. It was obvious how the fire was started.

Fran nodded toward the remains of the chest. "Most of our clothes and linen were in there."

Her bed, which had originally been that of Judd's parents, had been built in a corner with the interior cabin walls forming two of the sides. The posts and rails forming the other two sides were badly charred, and the webbing supporting the mattress and bedding had collapsed on to the remains of the rag rug that Judd's mother had made. The whole room was a smelly, soggy ruin.

Judd put his hand lightly on her shoulder. "We'll rebuild," he said.

She nodded and turned to go out, noting the smoke damage in the parlor.

"I guess the rest of the house'll be big enough for Joe and me in the meantime."

They went through into the kitchen just as Pedro was taking out the coffee pot and cups. He'd found a plate of doughnuts, too, which Fran had made the day before, and she and Judd followed him to the bench under the cottonwood where he set it all out.

Everyone helped themselves to coffee and doughnuts.

Fran said, "Thank you, all of you, for saving the house." She took a sip of coffee and broke off a piece of donut to share with Joe. "This is the second time they've tried to burn us out," she said. "There won't be a third. Those dirty coyotes are going to pay, even if I have to do it my ownself!"

Pedro said, "You think it's the same ones you had trouble from before? Sheriff told us it was all over, finished. What happened?"

Fran said, "There was a crash and something came through the window and hit the end of the bed. Then the room sorta filled up with flames. I grabbed Joe and wrapped him in the quilt and got out of there, yelling for Homer. Then I heard his Spencer rifle, so I knew he was on to it."

"I heard a noise and got up to look out," said Homer. "I see a flame start up and a shadow cross the bridge, so I up with my rifle and let fly. Dunno if I hit anything. Then I see Fran come out with the boy. She said to fire off a few shots so I did. Then I took a bucket from the stable and run to the creek, then you come along." He looked hard at Judd. "Y'know, I'm thinking mebbe Bates shouldn't have been turned loose."

Judd stared back. "You think it was Bates? I don't see it. Bates was thoroughly whipped when he left Twin Springs. I reckon he ran like a scared rabbit. If he did want to settle the score he wouldn't be ready yet. In a few month's, who knows? But not so soon. And, anyway, this wouldn't be his style. He'd use a gun. No, this is somebody else."

Fran said, "Marburg. It's got to be him."

Judd nodded. "Yeah, you're right."

He'd been worrying about Marburg. The man had got away scot-free and nothing had been seen or heard of him. It was as if he'd dropped off the end of the world. But he'd put a great deal of effort into the land swindle and it had not only failed but he'd lost all his other ill-gotten gains as well. He might well be looking for revenge.

"Nobody else is hunting him," said Fran, "So we're gonna have to, right?"

"Guess so," said Judd. "And sooner the better."

CHAPTER THIRTY-TWO

Fran Healey was consumed by a cold, hard fury. The anger she'd felt when she'd found Sten's body that day was as nothing in comparison. This cowardly, unwarranted attack on herself and her little boy, just as their lives were beginning to start afresh, had to be avenged. Marburg - she was sure it was him - must be dealt with, once and for all.

"I meant it," she said to Judd, as she came out of the bath house, dressed in what she'd worn the previous day, the only set of clothes she still possessed.

Homer was making pancakes for them all, feeding little crispy bits to Joe.

Ike and Pedro had returned to their base, with instructions to come back with tools and lumber and start repairing the main house immediately.

Judd, being the one who'd borne the brunt of the smoke and soot, had been the first to wash. He sat, eating his breakfast, in his damp stained undershirt, anxious to get back to Sten's old cabin and change into clean clothes.

"When I said *we're* gonna have to do something about Marburg," Fran continued, "I meant you and me, Judd. I'd go after him on my own if I had to, but I know you'd want to come along, and anyway, you've got the makings of a better tracker than me any day."

Judd looked up at her. "I was figuring me and Homer would go after him," he said, mildly.

"No," said Fran. "Joe needs Homer to be here. Besides, I know this country pretty good, and I want to check a few places out. I've got a hunch Marburg's lying up not too far off."

"Oh?"

"The old Leggatt place is a likely start."

"The fruit farm?"

"Yes. I've been thinking you'll need to look over the place pretty soon anyway. We just haven't gotten around to it yet. Sten and me, we went down there coupla months ago to clear around some of the trees. The cabin's still in good repair. Funny, I was going to suggest Ike and Pedro used it but they seem happy where they are."

"Would Marburg know about it though?"

"He had maps, didn't he? He woulda studied the whole valley pretty close. Anyways, it's a thought I'm gonna follow up on."

Judd stood up. "Alright," he said, "I'll get back, get fixed up and join you here."

"One more thing," she said. "If we're going hunting we won't want to be too obvious. You'd be too easy to recognize on that buckskin. Take Sten's bay mare. She's fast and reliable, and she needs work. You can saddle up here and I'll ride along with you. We'll go on from there, come at the Leggatt place from the back."

Judd grinned at her. "You seem to have it all figured out."

She shook her head. "No," she said seriously, "Only up to the Leggatt place. After that I'm following you."

Fran was planning only a short ride, but Judd insisted they took food and wet weather gear with them. Clouds were building up and rain seemed likely, and there was no knowing how far they would have to go to find Marburg.

Judd saddled the bay mare and when they reached Sten's cabin he put on clean clothes, tied a blanket roll behind his saddle and slid his Winchester into his scabbard. They went on across the rock and shale on to the old Indian trail Judd had followed on his way back from Double Diamond. After a couple of miles Fran indicated a shallow, sandy draw heading off to the south. This they followed for about ten minutes, well out of sight of any chance watcher, and then Fran told him to wait while she rode slowly up the side until she could see out across the valley.

She motioned him to join her. About a half-mile away down the slope was the Settlement's eastern boundary fence. Looking to his right he saw they were just past the corner where it met the northern boundary. Fran indicated a small stand of firs just beyond it.

"The Leggatt place is just up behind those trees," she said. "We could leave the horses in there and go check the cabin on foot."

They had a long look around before coming up over the rim of the draw. There was no one about. They walked their horses slowly down and into the fir trees and tied them.

Judd took his carbine in one hand and they made their way through the trees until they could see the one-room cabin. From where they were, about fifty yards away, they had a view of the back and one side. All was quiet. There was no smoke from the chimney, no horses in the little corral. The ground this side of the cabin was overgrown with weeds and undisturbed. Standing just inside the trees they waited for several minutes, then Judd handed her the Winchester.

"I'll go see if anyone's to home," he said. "Keep me covered."

He ran quickly to the corner and eased along the back wall to the window. Bending low, he peeped over the sill into the room. It appeared to be empty. He waved to Fran to go to the corner, indicating that he would continue around to the front and she should go the other way.

They met at the door. It was open and Fran kept watch outside while Judd investigated.

Clearly, the room had been occupied lately. There were recent scuff marks on the dirt floor, and although there were no personal belongings lying around, the ashes in the fireplace were still warm to the touch.

Judd joined Fran at the door. She said, "The ground's pretty damp around the pump and there's fresh boot prints. Somebody's been here this morning."

Judd said, "Well, if you're right and it was Marburg, it looks like he moved on. There's nothing inside for him to come back to. Let's go check the corral."

The corral had obviously been used that day. Judd spent a few minutes checking around the exit searching for the latest hoof prints. Eventually he gave a satisfied grunt.

"Come here, Fran," he said. "Look, there's tracks of two horses, went off together from the look of it. See? Here, they set off at a trot, side by side."

"Two horses?" said Fran, puzzled. "Why would Marburg want two horses? A packhorse, mebbe? Or is there someone else with him?"

Judd examined the hoofmarks more closely. "I reckon there's two riders," he said. "But let's follow them up along to make sure."

The tracks led out and around the nearest block of overgrown apple trees, where they diverged by several yards for a distance as they headed on towards the end of the valley.

Judd said, "Yeah, that's no pack horse. There's two riders for sure."

He'd hunted down a good number of outlaws and bad men, either on his own or in a posse, and the idea of taking a woman with him on a hunt would have been unthinkable. But he no longer thought of Fran as "just a woman". She'd shown she was as capable of pulling her weight as any man. And as she herself had said, what she may lack in feminine charm, she made up for in other ways.

But he felt he ought to ask the question. "How d'you feel about tackling two of them?"

"There's two of us, ain't there?"

"Okay." Staring in the direction the riders had taken, he was puzzled. "They're headed back to where we came from. Why would they go that way?"

"Only one way to find out. If they started out at first light they won't be much more than a coupla hours ahead of us. Let's go get the horses and catch them up." She looked up at the dark clouds now fully overhead. "We better get going before the rain washes out the trail."

The tracks were easy to see and they put spurs to their horses until they came to the rock and shale they'd crossed less than half an hour before. It was much more difficult from here and Judd decided to take a chance and go on until they reached the old Indian trail. Then they could scout around for sign.

It was Fran who spotted the prints of their quarry only a short way along the trail.

She said, "This just about clinches it for me. Who in the world would want to come along this godforsaken trail unless they were looking for somewhere to hide out? It must be Marburg, and whoever's stringing along with him."

"Yeah," Judd agreed. "And I don't like to say it," he added,

"But I can't help thinking that could be Billy Bates."

They set off again at a good speed and soon came around the long finger of rock and up into the series of long corridor canyons Judd had passed through a month ago. All the while the sky had been steadily growing darker and they could hear thunder coming closer. Then, as they were coming out on to the high rocky area with the scattered crags and bluffs, the first heavy spots of rain fell.

They halted and put on their slickers.

Judd said, "It'll be hard enough to pick up their tracks on all this loose stuff without rain. I guess we better keep to the old trail and hope to pick up sign from time to time. What do you think?"

Fran said, "I've been trying to give a sense to why they'd be headed this way, specially. If they carry on along this trail they'll pass through Double Diamond range and I wouldn't think they'd risk being seen. But they could take the turn-off, up through some pretty rough territory and on to NHK or the Tomahawk. Beyond that they'd come out toward the mining country."

Judd thought about it for a moment, then nodded in agreement. "Yeah, that would tie in with the kind of people they are, wouldn't it? Sneak up and hit us one last time, then scuttle off on this little known trail right out of the country to just the sort of place their dirty tricks are made for."

As he spoke lightning flashed, followed almost immediately by a massive clap of thunder. The wind suddenly got up and rain slanted across the broken ground straight toward them in drenching sheets.

Fran pulled her hat down low and hunched her shoulders under her slicker.

"I guess this'll slow them down some!" She raised her

voice to be heard over the noise.

The rain pelted down on them, blotting out the landscape. It brought a chill with it, too; they were over eight thousand feet high up here.

"Might make them look for a place to lay up," Judd shouted back.

She moved her horse close alongside his. "Along here, a far piece ahead," she said, "There's cliffs with caves in. Over to the right, as I remember. Sten brought me here one time, showing me around when I first came to live with him. I don't know if I could find them again, but it came to my mind that mebbe they might know about them."

"Okay," said Judd. "Better keep a real sharp look out from here on, see if they turn off the trail. You take the right side. I'll look left."

They pushed on, feeling very exposed as lightning flashed from time to time and thunder crashed around them. The pelting rain poured down upon their heads and shoulders, the light was dim, the trail slippery and sometimes inches deep in water, but every so often they came across signs of the two horses they were following, and were reassured. After an hour they had covered perhaps eight or nine miles and then the rain began to ease off and visibility improved.

Fran pulled up. She said, "I think we can't be far from the caves." She pointed ahead and over to their right. "I seem to recollect that weird rock like a bent steeple, red streaks all down one side."

Beyond it in the distance there were higher crags and spurs with broken cliffsides.

They rode on more slowly, scouting the land toward the steeple rock, checking all patches of softer, sandy ground for hoof marks, and fairly soon Judd noted the partially washed out prints of one horse leaving the trail and leading in that direction.

They grinned at each other in satisfaction. Fran had guessed correctly, it seemed.

"We don't know how far ahead they may be," said Judd. "They could see us coming, so we better keep our eyes peeled up ahead. You follow this one, I'll go look for the tracks of the other, but we'll keep a watch of each other. Okay?"

Leaving her, he continued along the trail and a few hundred yards further on he found the other horse's tracks, also heading out to the right. It appeared that the two men were separately searching for somewhere to lay up.

Off the trail the ground was rough and difficult and the going was slow, but they pressed on steadily more or less parallel to each other until Judd saw Fran waving and pointing to her left and slightly ahead of him. Her man must have changed direction, as her progress started on a line converging with his. He soon came upon a disturbed area where the horse he was following had stood waiting for a while, and then he found the tracks of Fran's quarry as well.

He took out his field glasses and had a good look around, searching along the faces of the cliffs and crags ahead for whatever may have caused his man to stop. Over to his left about a mile away he saw what could be a cave and as he watched a thin curl of smoke drifted out of it.

As Fran to came up to him he nodded and passed her the glasses. "Found 'em!" he said, "Way over to the left. See the smoke of their fire?"

She checked for herself. "Yes, I see it," she said. "Can't see their horses, though. But it looks to be a big cave, big enough to have them inside with them." She handed the glasses back. "What now?"

The wind had eased and the rain began again, not so fierce

now but hazing the view.

"We're a mite exposed out here, even with this rain," said Judd. "They could see us coming if they were keeping a lookout, which I'd doubt or they wouldn't chance a fire."

"No, they'll be too darn pleased with themselves," said Fran. "No reason to think they'd be followed, specially not so soon."

"Right," said Judd. "Still, we'll get out of their line of sight. Let's pick our way over to the right of them, and come up on them from the side."

Half an hour later they'd eased along the cliff face to within two hundred yards of the cave. Stopping where a crack running at an angle up the cliff had left a wide overhang, they dismounted and tethered their horses to big rocks beneath it. Then they looked out to survey the ground around the front of the cave. Apart from some widely scattered large boulders there was little cover except for a few stunted trees growing from crevices in the rock.

It was still raining.

Judd said, "I'm going to work my way out to where I can get a good view into the cave." He indicated a great jumble of broken slabs of rock jutting out from the cliff about halfway between them and the cave. "Can you get down there and cover me with your rifle if need be?"

"Yes, sure."

"Okay." He took off his slicker and laid it across his horse. "I'll get wet but I'll move a mite easier," he said, shucking his Winchester. "Now, they're going to have the chance to give themselves up, Fran. I doubt they'll take it, but they don't know I handed in my badge and we'll take them in to stand trial if we can."

"You want to give them a chance?" She stared at him in

disbelief. "What chance did they give Sten? What chance did they give Joe and me?"

Judd said, "Maybe I've been a lawman too long, Fran, but I didn't hand in respect for the law along with my badge."

She glared at him, "Okay, just so long as it's clear, if I have to shoot I won't be aiming to miss!"

"Well, come to that, neither will I," he said, moving out into the rain.

"Good luck," she said, and started toward the heap of rocks.

Judd moved in a wide arc, scurrying from one bit of cover to another until he was directly in front of the cave. Then he crawled in very cautiously to lie flat behind a large boulder less than fifty yards from the entrance. He saw that Fran was in position, standing behind a great upright slab, rifle at the ready.

The men had built their fire not far from the front of the cave on the right hand side. Its dim light revealed the shape of one man lying full-length behind it. Then the other came into sight, reached forward with a stick and stirred the embers into flame. It was Bates. Judd lined up his Winchester and shot straight into those flames.

The result was rewarding.

Both men leaped up as burning ashes were sprayed all around them. Bates was beating frantically at his clothes.

Judd called, "Okay you two, come on out! Hands in the air!"

There was no reply. He called again. Still no reply. Then he shot once more into the fire.

The reply came immediately this time. They'd waited until they could locate him and a bullet ricocheted off the boulder an inch from his head, stinging his face with chips of rock. Almost instantly Fran opened up with her Henry rifle. She'd obviously seen where the shot had come from.

As echoes of the shots chased each other along the cliffs before losing themselves out on the plateau, Judd could just make out a figure crawling slowly away from the left hand side toward the back of the cave. He took careful aim and fired. The figure jerked violently, then lay still.

They waited. The rain was easing off but Judd was soaked through anyway.

He called out once more for the men to give themselves up, and after a short while he saw a white cloth being waved about, well back inside the center of the cave.

"Okay, come on out," he called.

Bates shuffled forward very slowly, holding a long stick with a white rag tied on it straight out in front of him. He stopped at the cave entrance, a pathetic-looking creature, unshaven and ragged, far from the dandy Judd had first seen in the Drovers.

Judd stood up beside his boulder. "Where's Marburg?"

"Dead. You got him."

"Come on, right out!" With his Winchester at hip height Judd signaled Bates to come forward.

"What for? You ain't got nothing on me."

"I'm taking you in for questioning about the murder of Sten Petersen."

"Yeah?"

As Judd started toward him, Bates waved the stick at him. Too late, Judd registered that he was holding it in his damaged left hand, and before he could bring his own gun up, Bates drew his six-gun right handed and fired.

From the shock of the bullet Judd knew he was hard hit. He squeezed the trigger of his Winchester and felt the carbine jump, but the recoil seemed to stagger him and he saw his bullet kick dust at Bates's feet. Then he was falling and Bates was standing over him with a sneering grin, pointing his gun at Judd's head.

"You Petersen's is easy meat!"

"Not all of us," said Fran from ten feet away, and as he turned she put a bullet through his belly, then worked the lever of her Henry rifle and shot into him again.

CHAPTER THIRTY-THREE

Judd opened his eyes into a dim light. Slowly he realized he was in a room somewhere, lying on his back in a soft bed and propped up by many pillows. Looking to one side, he saw that the light came from a curtained window. It was either late evening or very early morning. Everything was peaceful and still.

He tried to ease his body forward to look around the room, but a searing pain scared him and forced him to lie back. Then he remembered. Bates had fooled him, shot him in the chest before he'd been able to get his own gun in play. He recalled falling and seeing the muzzle of Bates's gun inches from his face, then there was nothing except a long period of time when he seemed to be half asleep on a horse, his face in its mane.

Where was he? And how did he get here? It puzzled him, and for a moment his muscles tensed, then slowly, very slowly they relaxed. He felt so tired. His eyes closed and he dreamed he was a child asleep on a stagecoach and his parents were taking him back to Kentucky to fetch Sten. From time to time the stage jolted, rolling him around inside it, and once he thought someone woke him to give him a hot drink.

Something made him open his eyes again. It was now much brighter in the room and there was the scent of lavender water, which seemed to have come with him from his dream. His mother had favored it, reckoned it was soothing.

He turned his head. A pleasant-looking, middle-aged woman in a dark blue dress was standing by the bed, regarding him with a serious expression, which slowly changed to a gentle smile.

"Hello," she said.

He had a sudden thought. "Fran! Where's Fran?"

"She had to go out," the woman said. "She'll be back soon." She placed a cool hand on his forehead. "How are you feeling?"

He thought about it. He had a throbbing headache, his chest hurt and felt very tight and his mouth was dry. But mainly he just felt very, very weak. He smiled his lopsided smile.

"I've felt better, but a drink of cool water would help."

She stepped across the room to where a pitcher and glasses stood on a small dresser by the window. She half filled a glass and brought it to him.

"Lie still," she said, pushing her arm behind his shoulders and easing him more upright. She placed the glass against his lips and he took a sip.

"Barley water," he said. "That's real good." He drank some more.

When the glass was empty she gently lowered him to his pillows

"Where am I?" he said. "And how did I get here?"

"You're at the Double Diamond ranch," she said. "As to how you got here, you'd best ask Fran. When you're feeling well enough."

"How is she? Is she alright?"

"Yes, she's fine. And she'll be glad to see you're awake at last."

"At last? How long did I sleep, then?"

"You weren't asleep, you've been unconscious. And I

think that's enough questions. You settle back now and rest." She crossed to the window and closed the drapes.

"No, wait," he said. "I want to see Fran. I want to know what happened."

She came back to his bedside and looked at him severely. "You are a very sick man, Mister Petersen. You are not strong enough yet for all these questions and answers. You need to rest." Then, seeing his expression, she added, "I'm Rosalie, and I'm here to nurse you."

"Nurse me? Am I hurt that bad?"

"Well, yes, you are," she said. "In fact, for the first two or three days they thought you wouldn't pull through."

"First two or three days! How long have I been here, then?"

"Nine days now."

"Nine days!"

"Like I said, you're a very sick man. Doctor Campbell told me when he brought me out here a week ago you might have a fifty-fifty chance if you lasted a week. Well, you've lasted the week, so now you just rest and we'll see if we can improve on those odds."

He closed his eyes, trying to get a hold on his situation. He knew he'd been shot and it must have been bad because he was too weak even to sit up without help, but he could not grasp the idea of being in bed for nine days, or of being at the DD ranch. It was too confusing, made him dizzy to think of it. The bossy woman was right. He needed to rest.

The next time he woke it was night. He felt better, just a dull headache, but he was very thirsty. He moved his head. The light from a dimmed lamp shone softly on the woman asleep in the armchair beside his bed. It was Fran and she looked at peace.

He'd not seen her wearing women's clothes before. Her dress was plain red with a tight-fitting bodice tapering low to her waist and buttoned up to a high collar. Around her shoulders was a shawl of darker color. She'd combed her yellow hair up and arranged it in a twist, fastened on top with a pretty red comb and a red ribbon bow. He studied her face. It was a lovely face. She'd said she might lack feminine charm, but it wasn't true. He withdrew his hand from beneath the covers, wanting to reach out and touch her, and at his movement her eyes opened.

"Oh, Judd, you're awake! No, don't move. Lie still." She stood up and took his hand.

He smiled at her. "Any chance of some more of that barley water?" His voice sounded hoarse.

"Yes. Yes, of course."

As the nurse had done, she put her arm behind his shoulders and supported him as she held the glass to his lips. He drank it all and she lowered him gently back on to the pillows.

"You okay?" he said. "You're sure looking good."

"I'm fine," she said, "And you're looking better than you have been. How are you feeling?"

"Oh, well, I'm feeling weak as a kitten, but it's good to see you. What happened? How come we're at the DD?"

"What do you remember?" She sat in the chair, took his free hand and held it.

"Being hit and looking up in the rain and seeing Bates's gun in my face. Funny, I knew I was going to die, but I didn't feel anything. I was just waiting. Then I woke up and saw that nurse woman."

"Rosalie, yes. She's been a real treasure. She saw you through the worst of it."

"She said I've been here nine days."

263

"Ten days now. You slept all day yesterday."

"Okay. So what happened, Fran?"

She looked away. "I got to Bates just in time and I shot him. I kicked his gun away and left him where he fell. I saw you were hit in the chest and the bullet must be still in there. I plugged the wound best I could, then I went for our horses. I got you up on the mare somehow and tied you on. Then it seemed best to come on here - it wasn't any further than going back to our place and I figured we'd get help. I didn't really think you'd make it, but you did." She looked back at him and smiled. "When we got here, Matt Watkins sent someone in to town for Doc Campbell. Then I left you with Cassie and went back with two of their hands and we fetched the bodies back on their horses. Doc was here when I got back and he took out the bullet. He said he'd do what he could but you'd lost too much blood."

She squeezed his hand and smiled at him shyly. "I told you to hang on in, 'cos we stood to lose too much for you to back out now. I guess you must have heard me."

Judd smiled, "Somebody must have. But what about Joe? Who's looking after him?"

"Joe's here, being spoiled by Cassie. Once I'd told Matt the whole story he took over. He told me to go and get Joe and bring him back here, and I was to take Ed Flynn and a couple of his hands with me and leave them there to help rebuild the house."

"Hey, that's real neighbourly of him," said Judd.

"And there's more good news," she said. "Ben Cowan came out with Doc, and he said George Pitt told him the bank put out a reward for Marburg and the recovery of the missing money. I went and got our share yesterday, seven hundred dollars. That'll give us some of the stake money we need."

Judd grinned at her. "So you started already by investing in a new dress."

"You noticed." She smiled back at him. "It was Cassie's idea. She told me I should buy some women's clothes, and I may say she was right. It's good to feel I look like a woman should look."

"Well, you sure look good," he said. "You and Cassie, you're getting on okay, then."

"Yes, we are. We're probably closer now than we've ever been. You must have said something that impressed her that time you came here, 'cos she's sure changed her tune toward Joe. Can't see enough of him."

There was a light tap on the door. Nurse Rosalie stood there in her dressing gown.

"I heard voices," she said. "Is everything alright?"

"Yes, thank you, Rosalie, everything's just fine," said Fran.

"Well, you remember that our patient must take it easy still. He's not out of the woods yet. I'll take over here if you want to get to bed."

"No thanks, I'll stay here."

"Alright, but remember what I said. Goodnight."

When Rosalie had left them, Judd said, "Where does she fit in?"

"Well, that's another piece of luck. You recall that after he handed in his star, Tom Kramer went down south to help an old friend's widow run a freight business in Raton? Well, when he got there they decided there was getting to be too much competition from the railroad, so they sold it and got married instead."

"Got married? Tom Kramer married?"

"Well, yes. Nothing terrible in that, is there?"

"Uh, no, I guess not."

"Okay. Well, Rosalie is Mrs. Tom Kramer. They'd come to

Twin Springs on their honeymoon because Rosalie wanted to see where Tom had been sheriff. They arrived the day Doc Campbell got back from stitching you back up, and soon as Tom heard the state you were in, Rosalie offered to come and look after you. She was a nurse all through the War Between the States, so she knows about gunshot wounds."

"Seems I owe her," said Judd. "Breaking into her honeymoon and all. And what about Tom, is here too?"

"He's over at the Tomahawk. It belongs to the Cattlemen's Association now and they asked him to manage it for them. He and Rosalie are going to settle there. He's called in here a couple of times to see you."

"It'd be good to see him," he said. "You know, I never pictured him as a settling man."

He lay quietly for a while, staring up at the ceiling. Then he said, "I never pictured myself that way, either, but I guess I'd never met anyone before that I'd want to settle with."

Fran looked over at him and smiled a little. "And now?" she asked gently.

"I guess I could picture it now," he said, still looking at the ceiling.

"That's good," she said, "Because Joe and me, we need a good man to settle with us."

He smiled. "Then I think I'll go to sleep now, Fran. Come and see me in the morning and bring Joe with you, will you?"

He closed his eyes, and in his mind he saw the clear waters of Tinkers Creek flowing through the gap in the great rock wall, and beyond it, a herd of fat cattle scattered over the thick grass of the upper valley.

Printed in Great Britain
by Amazon.co.uk, Ltd.,
Marston Gate.

8794570R00148